CARRIER

These are the stories of the Carrier Battle Group Fourteen—a force including a supercarrier, amphibious unit, guided missile cruiser, and destroyer. And these are the novels that capture the blistering reality of international combat. Exciting. Authentic. Explosive.

CARRIER . . . The smash debut thriller about the ultimate military nightmare: the takeover of a U.S. Intelligence ship.

VIPER STRIKE . . . A renegade Chinese fighter group penetrates Thai airspace—and launches a full-scale invasion.

ARMAGEDDON MODE . . . With India and Pakistan on the verge of nuclear destruction, the Carrier Battle Group Fourteen must prevent a final showdown.

FLAME-OUT . . . The Soviet Union is reborn in a military takeover—and their strike force shows no mercy.

MAELSTROM . . . The Soviet occupation of Scandanavia leads the Carrier Battle Group Fourteen into conventional weapons combat—and possibly all-out war.

COUNTDOWN . . . Carrier Battle Group Fourteen must prevent the deployment of Russian submarines. The problem is: They have nukes.

AFTERBURN . . . Carrier Battle Group Fourteen receives orders to enter the Black Sea—in the middle of a Russian civil war.

ALPHA STRIKE . . . When American and Chinese interests collide in the South China Sea, the superpowers risk waging a third World War.

ARCTIC FIRE . . . A Russian splinter group have occupied the Aleutian Islands off the coast of Alaska—in the ultimate invasion on U.S. soil.

ARSENAL . . . Magruder and his crew are trapped between Cuban revolutionaries . . . and a U.S. power play that's spun wildly out of control.

NUKE ZONE . . . When a nuclear missile is launched against the U.S. Sixth Fleet, Magruder must face a frightening question: In an age of computer warfare, how do you tell friends from enemies?

CHAIN OF COMMAND . . . Magruder enters the jungles of Vietnam, searching for his missing father, when Communists launch a missile at an American plane. It could be the beginning of a long and bloody war. . . .

Don't miss these CARRIER novels—available in paperback.

book thirteen

CARRIER

Brink of War

KEITH DOUGLASS

JOVE BOOKS, NEW YORK

CARRIER 13: BRINK OF WAR

A Jove Book / published by arrangement with
the author

PRINTING HISTORY
Jove edition / July 1999

All rights reserved.
Copyright © 1999 by Penguin Putnam Inc.
This book may not be reproduced in whole or in part,
by mimeograph or any other means, without permission.
For information address: The Berkley Publishing Group,
a division of Penguin Putnam Inc.,
375 Hudson Street, New York, New York 10014.

The Penguin Putnam Inc. World Wide Web site address is
http://www.penguinputnam.com

ISBN: 0-515-12470-2

A JOVE BOOK®
Jove Books are published by The Berkley Publishing Group,
a division of Penguin Putnam Inc.,
375 Hudson Street, New York, New York 10014.
JOVE and the "J" design
are trademarks belonging to Penguin Putnam Inc.

PRINTED IN THE UNITED STATES OF AMERICA

10 9 8 7 6 5 4 3 2 1

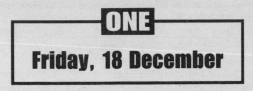

ONE

Friday, 18 December

0900 Local (+3 GMT)
USS Jefferson
Off the northern coast of Russia

Vice Admiral Tombstone Magruder:

I could feel the cold radiating in from the steel hatch that led from Flight Control to the flight deck. The air duct overhead was pumping out intermittent blasts of hot air, but couldn't keep pace with the arctic air separated from this compartment by only an inch of steel. The enlisted aviation specialists behind the service counter were bulky and sexless in layers of sweaters, foul-weather jackets, and long underwear. All of them wore gloves and black watch caps pulled down tight over ears and forehead. They crowded around one point located directly under the counter, surreptitiously elbowing and jostling. From the occasional bliss on their faces, I deduced that somebody had managed to smuggle in a highly illegal, completely unsafe, and critically necessary space heater. It was cached out of view of the officers who'd undoubtedly make them remove it from the space, citing the potential for electrical fires, shock hazard, and class alpha fires should the hot filaments make contact with one of the stacks of papers cluttering their work space behind the counter. A conscientious officer would confiscate it, preventing any one of those highly unlikely risks from escalating into a problem, leaving the enlisted men and women to combat the cold as best they could.

I studiously ignored it. *An early Christmas present, guys, and probably the best one you're likely to get this year until you get home.* "My bird ready?"

The chief in charge of the space nodded. Chief Jabrowski, a gnarled veteran of ships and flight decks with almost thirty years in the Navy, was only four months away from mandatory retirement. His eyes were ice blue, framed by a network of wrinkles and creases that marked the face of any man who spent so many years at sea. He had a small, dark mustache, flecked now with the same stray white strands that were scattered around his temples. His hair was clipped close to his head, almost a Marine Corps cut. Red, wind-burned skin, wrinkled down to a thin pair of lips curved up in a surprisingly congenial smile.

"Double nuts," he answered. "They're de-icing again now—can't be too careful in this weather."

I nodded, understanding the dangers of operating in this brutal environment. Even though the day outside was stunningly clear and bright, harsh sunlight spilling across the dark black of the nonskid on the flight deck, there was always the danger of icing as moisture from the air condensed on metal surfaces. I'd spent my share of time in cold weather ops. So had the chief.

Besides, the double nuts bird was worth taking care of. The zero-zero tail number designated it as the CAG's aircraft, and it was usually kept in top shape. Not that that's the only one he flew, but it meant something to the squadron that they'd assigned this bird to me.

And to me. Too many years ago, I'd been skipper of VF-95. I hadn't forgotten it—and neither had they.

"Any other last-minute problems?" I asked, knowing there weren't or the chief would have told me about them.

He shook his head. "Nary a one." The odd Arkansas twang seemed alien in this near-freezing compartment.

The handler, Lieutenant Commander Bernie Hanks, was now scurrying over to pay his respects. When I entered the compartment, he'd been deep in argument with a yellow-

shirted flight deck handler, gesticulating at the carrier's
flight deck mock-up behind him and tapping impatiently on
the wooden cutout form of an E-2 Hawkeye. I caught the
gist of the conversation in a few words, the eternal argument
about how and where to place too many aircraft in too little
space.

The technician wanted to move the Hawkeye down into
the hangar bay for maintenance work, and Bernie wasn't
buying it. Maybe after flight ops, yeah. But not right now.
No way, not a chance in hell. And if the helmeted and
goggled yellow shirt in front of him didn't like it, well then
he could just shit in one hand and—

A pointed, entirely unnecessary cough from the chief cut
the argument short before Bernie could complete the traditional Navy suggestion. No love lost between the chief and
Bernie, clearly. Otherwise, the chief would have been a little
bit smoother, a little bit faster with the cough and would
have saved Bernie the embarrassment of not noticing my
arrival.

I let my eyes rest on the chief for a moment, twitched the
corner of my mouth to let him know I was on to his game.
The bland, completely innocent look I got in return was all
the answer I needed.

"Admiral, I'm sorry . . . didn't notice you—" Bernie
began.

I cut him off with a gesture. "No need—Chief was just
filling me in. I take it we're good to go?"

Bernie nodded. "Green deck whenever you want."

I leaned forward and rested my elbows on the service
counter. "How bad is that E-2?"

Bernie scowled. "The green shirts think everything is an
emergency," he muttered. "You know how it is."

Every specialty on the flight deck is identified by a
different color jersey. Yellow, the handlers and flight deck
control people, the ones who owned deck space and
anything moving on it. White, safety and medics. The
grapes, the purple shirts, handled the fueling, and the ordies
who loaded weapons on the planes wore red ones. The green
shirts were mechanics and avionics technicians, anyone

working on the aircraft. Brown, the plane captains who owned the aircraft when the aviators weren't around.

"Pretty bad, Admiral," a much-maligned green shirt spoke up from behind the flight deck mock-up. "We're going to have to pull the engine."

I winced. Although *Jefferson* was no longer under my direct command—though it had been years ago—I took anything that affected her combat capabilities personally. Losing one of the four Hawkeyes—an electronic surveillance bird the equivalent of the Air Force AWACS—was more critical than turning a fighter into a hangar queen. The Hawkeyes were our eyes and ears in a battle and were capable of controlling multiple flights of U.S. fighters against adversary air. Additionally, although her capabilities were more limited than the AWACS, the Hawkeye could serve as electronic intercept aircraft and provide a whole host of intelligence information.

"What happened to it?" I asked.

"FOD, I think," the technician answered. "Chipped rotor blade. At any rate, we're gonna have to pull the engine. Can't fly the way it is."

Bernie broke in again, apparently not comfortable with letting the technician talk directly to me. A mistake, that—I'd garnered some of my most important information on how the ship was doing from talking directly to my enlisted men and women.

Batman's enlisted men and women, I should say. They were his now, had been since he'd relieved me as commander of Carrier Battle Group 14.

"Jones, take the admiral out to his bird," Bernie ordered.

"I can find it myself," I said gently.

"If you like, Admiral," Bernie answered, clearly a bit miffed this his courtesy had been rebuffed.

I hadn't meant to be rude. Sometimes the constant immediate deference to my presence and opinions, my every need and want, became entirely obnoxious. If truth be said, all I really wanted out of life in this Navy was what I'd wanted from the very beginning—to strap a Tomcat on my ass and go screaming through the air until I damn near grayed out from my own G forces.

But times change, and so do duties in the Navy. For me, every promotion meant less and less time in the cockpit, more time spent on administration or training, or any one of the other myriad duties a flag officer acquires along with the additional pay. Sometimes, you almost get nostalgic for somebody who'll tell you you're full of shit.

Just at that moment, two of the people who might be willing to do just that walked into the compartment. One I knew would for sure—the other would be willing to soon enough, albeit the words would be couched in the gentle euphemisms a junior used to a very senior officer.

The first man was Rear Admiral Everett "Batman" Wayne, now in command of Carrier Battle Group 14. I'd known Batman since my earliest days in the Navy. We'd gone to Basic together, selected Tomcats out of the pipeline, and started circling around each other about the time I was a lieutenant commander. Wherever I went, Batman was there. As we got more senior—he by some odd split of his promotion year group, one year junior to me—the Navy had taken to detailing Batman to relieve me wherever I went. It became something of a joke to us, first when he'd showed up as my replacement as commanding officer of USS *Jefferson*, then later more seriously when he'd relieved me as commander of Carrier Battle Group 14.

Batman was a little bit shorter than me, not by much, but enough to make a difference in a bar fight. He had my dark hair and dark eyes, but they were set in a face that was as mobile and cheerful as mine was impassive. Or at least that's what I've been told—I can't see the supposed great stone face that earned me the nickname Tombstone.

Over the past several years, Batman had fought an increasingly difficult battle against fat. Since his assignment to *Jefferson,* even though he spent countless hours on the Stairmaster, he was starting to thicken up around his waistline. Not enough yet to make him look ridiculous in a flight suit, although God knows he rarely got a chance to wear one of those, but enough to be noticeable to someone who'd known him for a long time.

Batman had in tow a junior aviator, one I knew well and had been expecting to meet me up here. Lieutenant Skeeter Harmon, a fellow Tomcat pilot. I'd been on two cruises with Skeeter now, and I liked what I saw. He'd gotten off to a rocky start in his first few minutes onboard the carrier after I'd rescued him from a TAD assignment on another ship, and gotten into a fight on the flight deck with a kid who was trying to keep him from getting chewed up inside an inbound disabled aircraft. But he'd more than made up for it by now. There weren't a whole lot of guys who were his equal in the air—me maybe, although that would have had to have been in my younger days. Now youth and reflexes sometimes won out over age and wisdom. That's the way it is in fighter air.

He was a tall kid, lean and lanky. Maybe three percent body fat, if that. Black, with his hair clipped close to his skull. If his attitude was any indication, he cut a wide swath through the available women when he was ashore. I'd never heard him bragging about it, but gossip travels fast on a ship.

"You out of here, Admiral?" Batman asked.

"Shortly. Now that you've got my wingman here, it's looking like a sure thing. I'm not sure I really believed it before that."

Batman's answering grin told me he understood all too well the difficulties of getting stick time for a flag officer. "I didn't want him getting held up by anything that could wait," he agreed, and gave Skeeter a gentle shove forward. "He's all yours, Admiral. Bring him back in one piece."

Skeeter spoke up. "It's the Russians you ought to worry about, sir." The cocky, easy grin on his face was his trademark. "Gonna kick some serious Russian ass, I am."

I almost smiled in spite of myself. The young pilot didn't even realize how sweet a deal this was. All he could think about was the flying.

Skeeter and I were headed to a small Russian air base located at Arkhangel'sk. Relationships between the United

States and the former master of the Soviet Union were allegedly a good deal warmer than the weather. It had started with Russian ships making port calls in the United States, a gesture we reciprocated. Cruisers, destroyers, even submarines, all carefully sanitized—cleared of classified material—and open to what had once been our bitterest enemies.

The Russians, unable to get their own primitive aircraft carriers under way due to engineering problems and lack of maintenance, had suggested this somewhat lopsided mission that we were on now—the *Jefferson* would visit the port of Arkhangel'sk, and in exchange, the Russians would host a professional conference aimed at both Russian and American fighter pilots. The conference was to be held at their version of Top Gun, a small, remote airfield located one hundred miles south of Arkhangel'sk. A few days of professional conferences, the usual looky-loo demonstrations, then the pièce de résistance—a display of aerial combat techniques using real MiG-29s and -31s versus Tomcats. The outcome would be decided by a panel of judges drawn from other countries, and the engagements monitored by United States Navy fighter training gear, called MILES gear. It's a network of low-power lasers and tiny receptors mounted on the skin of the opposing aircraft. That data, along with cockpit-mounted cameras, would supply a complete record of each engagement.

In addition to two Tomcats, we were taking along a C-2 Greyhound, commonly known as a COD—Carrier Onboard Delivery—with some maintenance technicians, radiomen and secure communications gear, and a small security force. Not that we expected to need the latter. Washington had already approved the details of the visit, which included using Russian forces to guard our aircraft. I guess the thinking was that since it was their idea to play, the last thing they'd do would be to foul up their chances of access to American markets by playing games with our aircraft. I wasn't happy about it. The in and outs of diplomacy can be frustrating, particularly when they have the potential to affect my safety in flight.

Well, we had a few surprises for them if they tried to renege on the agreement. Not many—but a few.

"Let's get going," I said. Outside the steel-cold hatch, freedom waited.

"There's a lot at stake this time, Tombstone." Batman's voice had an odd cautionary note in it that I didn't recognize.

"Sure, baseball, apple pie, and motherhood. C'mon, Batman. This ain't even the real thing." I tried to make my voice light, but something in his voice bothered me.

I stood watching him for a moment, suddenly aware of how much older we'd each gotten. Life at sea takes it out of you. Batman and I had had a few more advantages than the rugged chief behind the desk, but I could still see the effects of too many hours without sleep, too many missed meals, and the sheer, life-sapping stress that we operated under every day.

Batman was shaking his head now, something clearly on his mind. I took him by the elbow and drew him off to a far corner of the compartment. "Is there something I don't know?" I asked.

Batman shook his head again. "Of course not." But he wouldn't meet my eyes.

"There is, isn't there?" I pressed. I was out of line, even if I did have one more star on my collar than he did. Command of this CVBG was his, not mine. In all probability there were things that JCS wanted him to know, tactical considerations that would make no difference to me on the ground. Still, being out of the loop bothered me.

"What is it?" I demanded, my uneasiness overriding my sense of propriety.

Batman finally looked up at me. "Nothing you need to know."

Shit, I'd made him actually say it.

"If you're certain?" I let the question hang in the air for a moment, then clapped him once on the shoulder. "Fine, we're out of here. Keep our airfield in one piece—I don't want to get stranded in there."

Batman seemed unwilling to let me walk away. He

fidgeted for a moment, then asked, "How much longer, Stoney? What if there aren't any answers this time?"

I considered the question, as out of line in its own way as my earlier one had been to him. "There are answers, I think. Maybe not good ones—but answers nonetheless."

"He's probably dead." Batman's statement was brutal.

The anger I'd reined in over the last months swept over me now, harsh and demanding. If the Vietnamese and Russians had done what I thought they'd done, someone would pay. All those years of waiting, not knowing, then the final curt announcement by the U.S. that all the missing-in-action aviators that were presumed to be POWs would be reclassified as KIA—Killed In Action. The assurances from both Vietnam and Russia that none of the men were still alive. The stone wall even a senior military officer ran into, trying to find out the truth.

Someone was going to pay.

But not Batman. He was on my side if anyone was, trying to shield me from the pain of too much hope.

I put aside the anger and nodded. "Probably. But if there's a chance—"

It was Batman's turn to nod. He sighed, then said, "I know, I know. In your shoes, I'd be doing the same thing. Listen, either way—and on both counts—good luck. We'll be waiting for you when you're done."

Skeeter was fidgeting impatiently behind me when I turned back to him. "Let's go," I said.

"I send the RIOs on out ahead, sir," Skeeter answered. "You want to get any useful work out of them, you got to stay on them."

I laughed at that, hearing the classic arrogance of a pilot, letting it sweep away the last vestiges of my anger. A good RIO—Radar Intercept Officer—in the backseat had kept my ass from getting shot down more than once. You like to fly with the same one in combat all the time, because you get attuned to each other's moves. Skeeter was taking his usual partner, Lieutenant Commander Sheila Kennedy, along for the ride. Since it'd been years since I'd had a running mate, the skipper of VF-95 had loaned me his XO,

Commander Gator Cummings. Gator was a sharp fellow, one of the best. He'd jumped at the opportunity to go. As XO, he'd be fleeting up to skipper in a year or so, and then he'd be fighting for stick time like the rest of us.

I pushed open the hatch, stepped out into the freezing air, and shut everything else out of my mind as we preflighted the aircraft. You don't want to make mistakes when you're launching off a carrier, particularly not in weather like this. The sea that surrounded *Jefferson* was only a few degrees above freezing, and our survival time if anything went wrong would be counted in seconds rather than minutes. The Sea-Air Rescue—SAR—helo was launching while we finished up the preflight, a bit of bravado if I ever saw it. If anything went wrong, all SAR could do was recover the bodies.

Finally satisfied, I motioned my RIO over and we climbed up into the cockpit. Two enlisted technicians heavily bundled in foul-weather gear followed us up, made sure our ejection harnesses were securely fastened, then pulled out the cotter pins that disabled the ejection seats. After they withdrew, we buttoned up, and my RIO began reading through the pre-start checklist.

I went by the book, double-checking each step as we worked our way through the standard procedures. Finally, the comforting spooling sound of a Tomcat engine starting, the massive turbofan engines that were going to kick some serious MiG ass.

Off to my right, Skeeter finished up a few seconds after I did. I released the brake, taxied forward slowly in response to the yellow shirt's direction, and positioned the Tomcat on the catapult. Skeeter waited behind the JBDs—the Jet Blast Deflectors. The COD was queued up farther back waiting for the fighters to launch before she taxied forward for her cat shot.

I followed the hand signals from the yellow shirt, cycling the stick for a final check of control surfaces, sliding the throttles forward to full military power, and finally taking one last visual check of my wings. I gave the yellow shirt a thumbs-up—he responded with a sharp, precise salute, releasing control of the aircraft to me. I returned the salute, checked on my backseater, then braced my back and head against the seat.

The noise from the engines was deafening, far past mere sound, acoustic fury that flooded the cockpit, seeping in through flight suit and Nomex to penetrate my very bones. It was urgent, demanding, all-encompassing, binding my flesh to the airframe and melting us irrevocably into a single fighting force.

The acceleration began slowly as always, a thump, a small jar, then the sensation of sliding forward on the catapult. We picked up speed quickly, accelerating up to 134 knots in a matter of seconds. There was a final, shuddering jar as the steam piston reached the end of its run—and the end of the ship.

Tomcat double nuts staggered into the air, her wings grabbing for lift. There was, as always, that single sickening moment in which we were falling, plummeting ever closer to the sea black as ice while the sheer power of the Tomcat's engines fought to overcome the pull of gravity. A soft cat, one that had launched us off the end of the ship with insufficient airspeed to maintain airworthiness, was every Naval aviator's worst nightmare.

I felt it immediately, the slight pull upward as the Tomcat caught the air and fought for altitude, nose slightly up but concentrating on speed rather than altitude for the first couple of moments. Finally, that steadying sensation that told me we were going to stay airborne. As soon as it was safe, I eased back on the yoke and started gaining altitude.

I climbed to seven thousand feet and waited for Skeeter. I could see him below, climbing rapidly, then he circled and joined on me from behind and above, settling into a rock-steady position to my right.

I keyed the tactical circuit. "Good to go?"

"Roger."

I had a feeling Skeeter would have added something to that laconic comment if we hadn't been on tactical near the Russian coast and I hadn't been an admiral. I nodded approvingly—at least the brash young pilot was starting to show some good head work.

Jefferson was still clearly visible below us, a massive, floating fortress that represented the bulwark of America's military power. Even after spending so many years on carriers, launching off carriers, and recovering on them, I could still marvel in her impressive appearance. A floating office building, turned on side, her hull plunging down far below the surface like an iceberg.

Icebergs—involuntarily, I scanned the water around her. No, that wasn't a probable danger here, not in this part of the North Sea. However, the ice forming on the surface of the waters was.

The Russians were used to this. Ever since their earliest days as a blue-water Navy, they'd spent an enormous amount of time and money developing special ice-breaking ships to keep their seaways open. With most of their ports clobbered by deep layers of winter ice for up to four months out of the year, ice-breaking ships were essential to their being able to maintain a worldwide presence with their navy.

That was something that bothered me about this mission, had from the first moments it was described to me. Why couldn't a goodwill mission take place in the summer months? It would still be cold but not this bitterly brutal. The ice, always the ice—during the winter, we were completely dependent upon Russia's ice breakers as winter closed in on the port.

It wasn't solid yet, not as far as I could see. Nearer the coast, where the cold was already seeping into the deep heat sink of the ocean, ice was forming, barely indistinguishable from the frozen, snow-covered ground around it. It was thin, a sickly black-and-gray coating, one with no regular consistency to it. But another storm blowing through, the meteorologist had assured me, would soon turn the tide. Within three to four weeks at the very latest, Arkhangel'sk and all the other ports lining the Kola Peninsula would be iced in.

This whole fiasco—for that's how I'd started to think of

the mission from the very beginning—started with the institution of a new American national security strategy. The President called it "cooperative engagement." It meant that we were supposed to win the post–Cold War competition by cozying up to the former Communist nations, letting them get a taste of good old capitalism and converting them to our way of life by sheer attraction. A number of hoary adages were cited in support of this concept—that democracies don't start wars, that free trade decreases the need for conflict. We'd taken it to ridiculous lengths a couple of years ago by actually trying to buy up the world's supply of combat aircraft, starting with a gaggle of MiG-29s from Moldovia.

In my humble opinion, having fought too many wars in too many countries, the strategy ignored another important principle: Good fences make good neighbors.

However, no one ever asked my opinion, and this current mission was a prime example of cooperative engagement. We were going to Russia as part of a friendship visit— friendship spiced up with a little healthy competition. I guess it's too cold to play football up here, so our leaders came up with the next best thing.

Since we'd had a couple of years to play around with a MiG as well as some damned good intelligence on the MiG-31, I was pretty certain my team could take on any group of Russian pilots easy. Sure, they knew a fair amount about the Tomcat as well, but there's really not much in the Russian training syllabus that prepares them for going one-on-one with a smart, aggressive American fighter pilot. The difference is initiative—an American fighter pilot has it. A Russian one doesn't. He's trained to listen to the ground intercept controller, the scope dope on the deck who tells him which targets to engage, how to attack them, and everything from when to refuel to when it's time to wipe his butt.

There was the difference in aircraft type to consider as well. The Russians had been cagey about exactly which aircraft they wanted to fly against us, the MiG-29 or the MiG-31. Both of them posed the same challenge for the

Tomcat, with the difference being that the -31 had a bit better avionics and targeting suite and a smidgen more power. Both MiGs, though, had one thing in common. They were angles fighters, smaller airframes that relied on speed and maneuverability to win engagements. In level flight, they could cut inside a Tomcat's turn radius, curling in around behind the heavier, more powerful American fighter to slam a missile up your ass before you could even think about it. In a fair fight, one-on-one at a constant altitude, the Tomcat doesn't stand a chance.

That's why we don't fight fair. There's no glory in it, not if it means giving up tactical advantage to some Commie bastard who's listening to his GCI.

The advantage a Tomcat has is that it's a massive, powerful airframe, eight thousand pounds of metal and armament strapped onto two screaming turbofans. The F-14 can climb faster, harder, and farther than a MiG ever dreamed possible.

Great, so you grab altitude—there's no inherent virtue in that, except for one little odd law of aerodynamics. Altitude and speed are interchangeable—you can trade one for the other in whatever direction you're headed.

See, the Tomcat starts climbing, turning away from the MiG. The MiG has to follow—if he doesn't, the Tomcat simply turns and comes in on his ass from behind. So the MiG starts climbing, trying to figure out exactly how far up to follow the Tomcat, making his own break for the deck just before the Tomcat can use that superior altitude to build up speed and cut back in behind him. The climbing game and trading altitudes isn't his preferred fight—he'll try to start his break back into level flight in time to catch the Tomcat at the same altitude and force the Tomcat back into the angles fight, not letting him use his superior power and speed against the MiG.

The Tomcat driver, on the other hand, *wants* to be yo-yoing up and down in the sky like an idiot, forcing the MiG to bleed off airspeed and sacrifice maneuverability. Get the MiG going slowly enough and it's either an easy target or the MiG has to forget about trying to shoot you down while he concentrates on pulling some airspeed out of his ass in order to stay airborne.

The bottom line was that we knew what kind of fight we were in for, regardless of which MiG showed up on the ramp. Skeeter had had his share of experience with the -29 and I'd seen both versions in action, including an advanced prototype that the Chinese had built based on Russian designs.

The Russians had made a fairly interesting pitch for this whole contest, and I still hadn't exactly figured out what was behind it. They'd proposed four separate contests, and left the possibilities for additional training opportunities open. "As available," the message had said. Made me nervous—flexibility in the Russian mind always indicates something devious afoot.

The first contest would pit a young American pilot and backseater—that would be Skeeter and Sheila—against a young Russian pilot.

The second would pit two more experienced aviators against each other—veterans of the Cold War, Russia had insisted. The Navy picked me for that one, since I've probably got more stick time against Russians than any other pilot in the Fleet. Gator was a good choice as well, since he'd cut his eyeteeth fighting MiGs with Bird Dog driving.

The third would be a bombing run, probably by the younger opponents. The final contest would be two-on-two, and of all the engagements, that was the one I was certain we would wax their asses in. American fighters are trained to fight in pairs, in a loose deuce formation. One aircraft high, keeping the big picture—and let's not forget that altitude that he can trade instantly for speed—and the other forward and below, sniffing out the threat and engaging first with the longer-range weapons such as Phoenix. We train in pairs, think in pairs, and win in pairs. The Russian equivalent, pairing a pilot with a GCI operator, didn't stand a chance.

There was one more contest going on, one that only a few other people knew about. It didn't involve aircraft, flying, or even airborne weapons. It was a hell of a lot more personal—and, of all the four missions, the least likely to succeed.

A couple of years ago, during one of the innumerable conflicts that seem to spring up around the world, I learned something that shook me to my very core. A Cuban radical told me that there was a very good chance that my father had not died on a bombing run over Vietnam. Before he left, he hinted that my father had been captured alive but seriously injured and taken to Russia for further interrogation.

Russia. The very thought of it made my blood run cold, and the careful compartmentalization I try to maintain in the cockpit started to crumble. This wasn't the time to start thinking about my father and Russia, not if I expected to be able to put on a diplomatic show of goodwill when I landed. If I found proof that he'd survived the ejection, that he'd been taken to Russia as I expected, then I'd . . . I'd . . .

I'd what?

Batman had hit it on the head when he'd asked what I'd do if nothing came of this. The short answer: I didn't know.

I have a few memories of my dad—nothing very specific, just fragments of memories, more like quick snapshots than specific sequences of events. I remember a pair of cowboy boots, my first attempts to hit a foam softball with a plastic bat, a birthday party here and there. He was gone so much during the early years, deployed with his squadron and doing what he knew was important to do for the country—fighting the war that no one was very sure we were winning.

For thirty years plus, I've believed he died over that godforsaken land. Even though he was officially listed as MIA—Missing In Action—we knew he was gone. When the word finally came changing his status to KIA—Killed In Action—it was more a confirmation of something we'd tacitly accepted for years rather than any real change. It wasn't until I married Tomboy that I realized how very much I missed him.

My uncle, Dad's brother, did what he could. A damned

fine job, most of the time, filling in for his younger brother as the father figure in his only nephew's life. Mom seemed to appreciate it. We did, too, but not to the extent that I do now.

Uncle Thomas thought I was getting suckered on this. He believed with all his heart that his younger brother died over that bridge. He tried to talk me out of this mission, but in the end, when all else had failed, he came through with the goods.

Not that it was that tough. When you're chief of naval operations and a front-line candidate for the chairman of the Joint Chiefs of Staff, you draw a lot of water. If once in a while you use it to do something for your family, how wrong can that be? Especially when you're making up for something the U.S. screwed up over the years.

So I'd wangled my way over to Vietnam on *Jefferson* and spent some time on the ground tracing my father's steps—or at least what I thought were his steps. There'd been one clue, a scrawled saying in the cinder block wall of one prison camp: *Go west.*

Russia. The rumors had been floating around for years that Russian military advisors had taken American POWs back to the Soviet Union for further interrogation. The moment I saw that phrase scribbled over my father's signature, I knew that was what had happened.

West—and into the Soviet Union, in those days the most brutal regime in the world. What the Viet Cong came up with paled in comparison to the GRU and Stalin. If my father had gone into Russia, odds were he'd been brutally interrogated until they'd leeched every last bit of information they thought they could get out of him—then shot.

Were records even kept back then? Not likely—Stalin had executed millions simply because he could, and a full accounting of any American POWs was not only unlikely but probably impossible as well. Hell, the Russians weren't even admitting they'd ever taken any out of Vietnam—now, in the post-glasnost era of peristroika, what incentive did they have to admit to that particular war crime?

None. None at all.

It might have ended there, but there was another piece of evidence. Two cruises ago, a Ukrainian officer admitted to me that he knew my father in Russia. That meant there might be records—or, at a minimum, someone who might remember him.

Not officially, of course. The party line was that none of it had ever happened. But there were more avenues of information than government agencies and press releases. I'd found some of them. In at least one instance, they'd found me, and the possibility that my own government, the one I'd faithfully served for so long in uniform, might have lied to me about my father cut deep. I didn't want to believe it of my own country.

Tracking down the truth about POWs is like being on a ship. You want the real scoop on what's going down, the latest in information and data, you don't watch the skipper's announcement on closed-circuit TV. You might— just *might,* mind you, if you can get access—head for the deepest, darkest compartments in the intelligence spaces, the ones that they call SCIF—Specially Compartmented Information. This is the stuff you always hear called "burn before reading," so sensitive that the average fighter jock never even knows the capabilities exist. But even with all its esoteric magic, SCIF isn't the place for the real truth.

No, every sailor knows where to get the gouge—MDI. Mess Deck Intelligence. Somehow the cooks and the galley slaves and the mess cooks knew the real truth about what's going on far before anyone else on the ship. MDI is the tightest, fastest, and most righteous information collection and dissemination network in existence. Don't ask me how it works—no one knows—but it does.

Within the family-of-POWs network, there's something similar. It doesn't have a physical location like MDI does, but it's damned near as effective. The outer layer is all for show—the Internet web pages, the public posters and pamphlets and the letter writing campaigns, the copper bracelets we wear in remembrance of those that aren't coming back. That's just the tip of the network, just like the skipper's daily pep talk on the closed-circuit TV. Underneath that are the E-mails, the hand-delivered copies of documents and resources passed from family to family when electronic means are deemed too sensitive, the volumes and volumes of in-country contacts that these survivors have amassed over the decades since Vietnam.

Discolored photos, shards of personal belongings, snatches of transcripts blurred by being photocopied and handled so many times, evidence—of what? Of men that were alive and weren't brought home, just like my father.

I'd had some help on the first part of my search for my father in the form of in-country contacts. Now that the trail pointed to Russia, information was significantly harder to get, more ambiguous, and, in some cases, downright wrong. But it was there, flowing from the other survivors, the Navy Department, even from immigrants.

During the Vietnam War, the air bases just outside Arkhangel'sk had attracted the Central Intelligence Agency's attention. The activity around the base was inconsistent—aircraft parked on aprons, a cover story that claimed the base was an advance training facility, but a notable lack of routine takeoffs and landings. You expect a sort of cyclical activity at a training facility as classes graduate and new students arrive: a spate of simple orientation and formation flights as student pilots become accustomed to new aircraft, followed by increasingly difficult training missions including ACM and bombing runs; then, a period of quiet, the time after a class graduates and the next one starts; then the whole cycle repeated over and over again.

That didn't happen at Arkhangel'sk. In fact, it had more transit flights—aircraft originating from somewhere outside our satellite coverage and vectoring in to the isolated base—than it did training flights. That worried the CIA enough to give this one particular base code-word sensitivity and scrutiny.

They called it Hidden Archer, the name itself peculiarly appropriate for the facility. Over the next five years of painstaking observation and critical analysis, the CIA arrived at the conclusion that Hidden Archer had one primary function—to serve as a debriefing facility for captured aviators.

In the early days of the Vietnam War, satellite technology wasn't what it is today. But by late 1970s, even after the war was officially over, we had satellite and surveillance capabilities that would have seemed like Buck Rogers science fiction to military men of just a few decades earlier. We could read license plates on cars from space, discern a man's face as he walked between buildings. In response to these technological developments, training for aircrews changed, and the SERE—Survival, Evasion, Rescue, Escape—schools emphasized continually looking up at the sky, every chance you got. There was no telling when a satellite or high-flying reconnaissance aircraft might be overhead, and exposing your face to the sky maximized your chances of being identified.

At the time he was flying, my father knew something of how fast technology was coming along. He was an engineer by training, and from all accounts a pretty damned smart man. My uncle says I remind him of my father, his brother. I usually take it as a compliment, but there's something in me that protests at that. I've been shot down a couple of times, but I always made it out somehow. Out of the cockpit, out of the fire zone. That's the one difference I'm sure of between me and my father.

But what my father knew about satellites added credibility to the odd, ragged photo that had turned up carefully sandwiched between two pieces of cardboard. It had come to my house, not the office, in a nondescript brown padded envelope. Address in neat, printed letters, no return address. Correct postage, and a postmark showing it was mailed from Washington, D.C.

Not much to go on. I suppose I could have reported it to the FBI, had them dust it for fingerprints or DNA or some such, but I didn't. I looked at the grainy photo and saw my own face staring back at me. It was blurred, either a high-resolution camera shot enlarged past its tolerance or a shot taken while moving. But the similarity was unmistakable. Even with some of the features blurred, I could see the line of my jaw in it, the set of my head on my own shoulders. It wasn't me, but it was someone who looked a hell of a lot like an *older* me, a Tombstone that the forces of gravity and time had warped and wrinkled.

I debated over it for a couple of days, then showed it to my mother. She recognized my father instantly.

So, given that someone—or something—had taken a picture of my father much older than he'd been at the time he'd disappeared over the bridge, what were the odds that he was still alive? Minimal—both my mother and I knew that.

The second bit of the puzzle was the one that bothered me the most. A clipping taken from what appeared to be a small, cheaply printed newspaper. The same man, noticeably older than he'd been in the first photo, smiling and waving at the camera.

The date—seven months ago.

This time, I did go the official route. Having three stars on my collar, plus the four that my uncle sports, gives us a fair amount of horsepower. Within a couple of hours, the intelligence organization at the Pentagon was able to identify the paper and produce a complete page, the one this clipping had been torn from, along with a translation of the article.

The man in the picture was celebrating his recent marriage. His first, according to the Russian writer.

Not according to my mother. Over the years, she'd found ways to live with losing Dad. On the surface, she sounded like she was convinced he'd died. She and Batman were alike in that way, although I think Batman's conviction went to his core. With Mom, it was just a way to survive. But I could tell from her involvement in the POW/MIA groups that she'd never really given up hope.

The paper covered a small area around Nikolayev, another military air base to the south. While not as important as Hidden Archer and the Kola Peninsula during the Vietnam War, Nikolayev had had its own share of notoriety as a weapons test facility.

I was going there. I wasn't certain how or when, but

sometime during the next two weeks I was going to Nikolayev.

"Lead, two." Skeeter's calm, professional voice broke into my thoughts. I'd been flying the aircraft by reflex, caught up in the anger and the possibility of hope, blinded by my emotions. Skeeter, in an unusually tactful maneuver for him, had simply brought my attention back to the present.

"Lead," I acknowledged. "Starting pre-landing checklist."

"Roger—we are, too."

I could hear my RIO fumbling through his checklist. I flipped open the right section and began reading aloud.

We made a beautiful, precision formation approach, with Skeeter slipping in to land just five seconds after I did. He maintained the precisely correct formation distance throughout the approach, touchdown, and taxi, one of the smoothest bits of formation flying I'd seen in a while. You don't do a lot of formation landings on an aircraft carrier, and maintaining proficiency is tough.

A yellow follow-me truck met us at the end of the landing strip. I used my nose-wheel steering gear to fall in behind him. The turbofans were spooled down to a gentle thunder now, oddly reassuring in the notion that I could turn, power up, and be airborne again within moments if I wanted to.

There was something surreal about taxiing down a Russian airfield. For those of us raised in the Cold War, the idea that someday we would be voluntarily landing some of our most advanced fighter aircraft inside Soviet territory would have been unthinkable just five years before. Five years—just a small portion of the time I'd spent in uniform, but longer than Skeeter's entire career to date. He'd joined the Navy *after* the Berlin Wall fell, *after* Desert Storm and Desert Shield, at a time when the most formative politicians of my career were just old bogeymen.

No matter that Russia—and China, as well—continued to foment disorder and conflict in this brave new world we fought in. The official party line was that it was over. We'd won, and were now entitled to a well-deserved peace dividend.

Then why did I end up with MiGs shooting at me and my aircrews so often?

I glanced back at Skeeter, who was now closing the distance between us. How would it be, to have grown up in his times? How much difference did it make in the way we saw the world—the Russians, in particular? I resolved to have a quiet word with him again about the need for a little respectable paranoia while we were on the ground in Arkhangel'sk.

It probably wasn't necessary. Commander "Lab Rat" Busby, the senior intelligence officer onboard *Jefferson,* had briefed us extensively on our visit. In particular, he'd pointed out that it was important for us to watch everything we could, make note of anything that seemed new or different from what we already knew about Russian aviation. He gave us two solid capabilities briefings, complete with quizzes, getting us up to speed on the very latest U.S. information on Russian systems and technologies so that we'd know what to look for.

Like most nasty games, intelligence collection works both ways. The birds we were flying into Russia were specially configured, stripped of some of the very latest toys and technologies we didn't think they knew about yet. Most of the avionics were useless without the Zip drive cassette plugged into the instrument panel in front of me—Lab Rat made sure we understood that. We were to take our Zip cassettes with us everywhere we went, keeping them on our persons at all times. Without them, the Russians could learn nothing of use from the bare carcass of our airframes. And there were other telltales as well. The most sensitive avionics compartments were wired with small devices intended to keep anything but a charred black box from falling into their hands. Lab Rat assured me that the fires were too localized to do any permanent damage to the airframe, and that even if one were triggered, we'd be able to safely fly the aircraft out. I was not reassured.

"What happens if we lose one of these super-secret Zip

drives? Or damage it?" Skeeter had asked. An eminently sensible question, I'd thought.

"Your Tomcats will still fly without them, if that's what you mean," Lab Rat had answered. "You'll lose most of your advanced decision aids as well as some resolution on your targeting packages, but that's about it. The techs on the COD will take some diagnostic software with them, a few replacement parts, but not replacement disks."

"Can they make anything out of them without the Tomcat's gut?" I'd followed up.

Lab Rat looked thoughtful. "Honestly, I don't know. The guys at NSA—National Security Agency—don't think so, but I wouldn't want to bet on it. It's supposed to require the same crypto load that's in your communications circuitry, but you know how that is. With computers they've pirated from the West, they might be able to get something out of the tapes. That's why there won't be any duplicates on the COD."

"Sounds risky, putting us in over there," Skeeter said.

Lab Rat nodded. "I think so, too. But evidently this is important to somebody with a hell of a lot more firepower than I have. So we do what we can to minimize the risks. Really, though, I don't think there'll be any problems. Not if you're careful with the Zips. The Russians need us for friends right now a lot more than we need them."

And that was the truth. With a resurgent China prowling Russia's borders, massing and moving divisions of armored troops every couple of weeks for supposed routine exercises, Russia had good reason to want to be on good terms with the United States. We'd faced China down before, in the Spratly Islands and in other hot spots around the globe, something Russia couldn't do on her own right now.

Finally, we reached the end of the apron and a yellow-shirted handler stepped out from the crowd to replace the follow-me truck. Confidently and with stunning precision, the yellow shirt began flashing the standard hand and arm signals used on the flight deck of a carrier to signal to us.

"You believe this fellow?" Skeeter said, his amusement

clear over our private coordination circuit. "Man, they been practicing or *what*?"

"Get that out of your system before we shut down," I ordered. "They've put some effort into it and the last thing we need to do is start off by pissing them off laughing at their personnel."

"Yes, sir, Admiral. I kind of figured that out, sir, and there ain't a trace of a smile showing on this young black man's face." Skeeter sometimes fell back into a sort of uneducated slang whenever I made the very dangerous mistake of underestimating him. This time, I figured I deserved it.

"I'm talking to myself as much as you, Lieutenant. We're all on new ground here—you see something that looks like an opportunity to step on our dicks, I hope you'll be pointing it out real quick. Got that?" I said.

"Yes, Admiral." This time, Skeeter's voice was back to normal. "You hear that, Gib? No dick stepping."

"Kind of you to worry," Sheila answered angrily.

I laughed in spite of myself. If the KGB or GRU or whatever weird collection of initials that was Russia's current intelligence agency was listening in, they were going to have fun figuring that one out. Skeeter's RIO was markedly short of the required equipment.

The Russians have always done ceremonies well. Massive, forbidding shows of force imbued with the ancient dignity of a grim warrior society. Ahead of us, at the edge of the airfield, Army troops were massed in formation, almost a brigade's worth I estimated. Twenty tanks flanked the formation, each with its barrel elevated only slightly above the arc that would put a missile directly on our assigned parking spot. Officers and dignitaries were festooned in the drab olive-green-accented-with-red Army uniforms, the darker, more traditional blue-black of the Navy, and a few uniforms I couldn't recognize right off. No doubt they'd changed some since the days of the Soviet Union's break-up—at least in name.

Many brass, as befitted the historic nature of this occasion. For just a moment, I wondered whether or not we'd made an error in not following suit and ferrying in an aircraft load of dignitaries of our own. Just for balance, if nothing else. How did the Russians see that lack? As a sign of disrespect, an American insult in the refusal to take these games seriously? Or would they take it as a sign of weakness, this deploying of two advanced fighter aircraft to Russia's own soil without the appropriate formalities and dignitaries?

It all seemed too trivial, given what my real mission was. For a moment I felt the fury again, but I was no longer certain whether it was directed at the Russians for taking my father or at my own country for letting it happen. Two betrayals—my father's trust that the U.S. would come and get him, and my own for believing what I'd been told for so many years.

I taxied in, stopping neatly on the spot indicated by the technician. Skeeter pulled in behind, slightly aft and to my right just as he was in flight. I twisted around, trying to catch a glimpse of the COD, but it was still too far out.

We ran through the postflight and preshutdown checklists quickly, not wanting to keep our hosts waiting. Finally, our engines spooled down, and I popped my canopy. I could see the COD now, barely visible on the horizon.

The rush of air was bitterly cold, condensing immediately into clouds as I breathed out. It bit hard into my exposed skin, and I jammed the fingers of my gloves down a bit more securely. The icy air found a thin exposed strip of skin between the glove and the sleeve of my flight suit, burrowed into it, and tried to race up my arm.

"Let's get the hell out of here, Boss," Gator said. "Colder than a—"

I cut him off with a gesture. "Remember, we're in Russia now. Anything you say can and will be used against you. And not in a court of law either, buddy. Quiet, now—here they come."

A rickety ladder was pushed forward to our Tomcat. I motioned it away after I noted that the edges were not coated with any padding to prevent it from scraping the fuselage. The technicians paused, uncertain, and I beat them to the punch by popping out the footholds on the Tomcat, the boarding ladder, and clambering down myself. I jumped lightly off the last step, flexed my knees as I hit, and felt the shock of the cold concrete start to seep into my boots. My RIO hit the deck a few seconds after me.

There were three officers approaching me, flanked by what looked to be a translator. I recognized the two in front from the intelligence briefings: Field Marshal Gorklov and Admiral Ilanovich. I snapped up a formal, correct salute, holding it until they'd returned it. Then I held out my hand. "Vice Admiral Magruder, General. An impressive reception—thank you."

I saw that both Gorklov and Ilanovich understood, but they waited until the translator finished. Then Gorklov held out his hand and said, "Welcome," in heavily accented English. "Field Marshal Gorklov. And this," he continued, gesturing to his right, "is Admiral of the Fleet Gregorio Ilanovich."

I tendered another salute, then a handshake to the admiral. In the scheme of things, he technically outranked me, but I was certain that a three-star admiral in the United States Navy had far more firepower under his control than Admiral Ilanovich did. Still, he had home court advantage—one rarely gets in trouble for being too courteous.

Ilanovich's appearance puzzled me for a moment, and it took me a couple of seconds to dredge up the information from Lab Rat's briefing. The Russian admiral was clearly not a pure-blooded Russian. His eyes were narrowed and dark, and the high cheekbones and coloring hinted of an exotic mixture of Cossack and Asiatic blood. Probably some Ukrainian as well, since that country is noted for producing the very finest naval officers. Enough Ukrainian, at least, to compensate for the general prejudice against the Far Eastern blood.

Ilanovich himself was part of the Russians' attempt to demonstrate their similarity to American culture. My team had two white men, one black man, and one white woman on it. The admiral was Russia's attempt to cover all bases in one body.

Well, almost all.

I made the introductions of the rest of my team quickly, first my RIO, then Skeeter and Lieutenant Commander Kennedy. We'd been through this drill a thousand times, and each one followed my lead, a salute followed by a handshake.

"It is very cold out here," the admiral said finally. He gestured toward the hangar. "We will tow your aircraft inside, and if you will come with us—a brief reception, nothing formal. No need to change, you will be meeting with fellow aviators." He shot me a sidelong glance, rich with sly amusement. "They, like yourselves, dislike undue formality." ·

I smiled politely, realizing that it was probably true. Aviators the world over are renowned for their lack of the traditional military courtesies and ceremonies that mark every important event. Given a chance, about 99 percent of us would rather be in a flight suit and airborne.

Admiral Ilanovich fell into step beside me. "I think I know much more about you than you know about me," he began. He looked at me, as though waiting for a response.

"I'm sure you're correct," I said neutrally. It was an amateurish sort of foray into the world of intelligence, a quick attempt to find out just exactly what I knew about him. And what I didn't. "I hope we will have the chance to remedy that over the next several weeks."

Admiral Ilanovich regarded me with quiet amusement. "Oh, I am sure we will. Especially in the air."

"I look forward to it."

"They told you, did they not?" he continued without missing a beat. "That I will be flying the MiG-31 against your Tomcat." He gestured back in the direction of the hangar, vaguely indicating my aircraft. "The Hornet—now, that would have presented a real challenge. I would like to do that someday," he continued. "Go one-on-one with one of your Hornets. Much more maneuverable than the Tomcat, wouldn't you agree?"

"In all except one instance," I agreed amiably. "They can't pass a tanker without wanting a drink."

Ilanovich laughed. "Of, of course. That is the problem with all of the smaller aircraft, is it not? Fuel consumption—why, until we developed an in-flight refueling capability for the MiG-31, that very thing imposed serious limitations on our combat readiness. No, I was speaking of course about the weight-to-thrust factor."

"Of course," I answered, feeling a slight twinge of uneasiness. Just what was this admiral driving at? Everyone knew about the performance characteristics and differences between a MiG and a Tomcat—no news there. Nor any opportunity for any intelligence gathering—anything I could tell him about that he would have already read in *Aviation Weekly*.

"And your young Navy lieutenant, his name was . . . Kyrrul?" I asked, changing the subject. "He will also be flying?"

"Yes, he is the one." Gregorio Ilanovich looked faintly amused. "A fine flyer—with perhaps not as many kills as your young Skeeter, but very capable nonetheless."

Another small bit of intelligence—while it was no great state secret, Ilanovich had made a point of telling me that he knew my young lieutenant's call sign. And my own, most likely.

"Tell me, Admiral," I said casually, "in naval aviation, do your aviators adopt call signs such as ours? I'm certain that you've heard mine—Tombstone." I wondered how many hours of Russian intelligence it had taken to fight over the exact meaning of that one. Did it mean that I was a gunfighter, one who consistently reduced my opponents to graveyards? Or were they perhaps misled, as some were, by thinking it had to do with a gunfight at the O.K. Corral in Tombstone, Arizona? The actual answer was far less interesting—some of my early squadron mates had simply thought that my face was as expressionless as a tombsone. They said I looked stern all the time, and hinted that I lacked a sense of humor. While nothing could be further from the truth, I didn't mind having most people believe that. It keeps them off guard.

"Something similar, and perhaps a good deal racier. We

are not bound by considerations of political correctness."
The admiral walked on for a few steps longer, his boots
tapping out a staccato rhythm on the pavement. "My own
call sign, for instance—it has changed several times, but the
latest one I have had for fifteen years. Translated loosely
from the Russian proverb from which it is taken, it comes
out as 'Watch Your Ass.'"

I laughed out loud, despite my resolution to maintain a
somber and professional demeanor. "Watch Your Ass? Hell
of a call sign, Admiral. I like it."

The admiral clapped me on the shoulder, obviously
amused at my reaction. "We will see if you like it over the
next several weeks. I think you will not be laughing then as
much."

"Well, I guess we'll see. When is the first engagement
scheduled?" I asked.

"This afternoon." The admiral noted my look of surprise
with sardonic amusement. "Unless, of course, that is too
soon? Perhaps you have maintenance problems with your
aircraft, or need to rest up after your grueling journey?" The
sarcasm was in the words, not in the tone—it had been
merely a forty-five-minute flight from *Jefferson*'s wind-
swept deck to this airfield.

"Not at all," I said immediately. "I'm ready to fly right
now."

"We thought perhaps the younger men would begin." He
motioned behind him, pointing out the young officer carrying on a conversation in broken English with Skeeter, a
translator hovering behind them. "Ah, their endurance, their
stamina—it makes one wistful, does it not?"

I wasn't sure how to take this statement. Did he mean that
the reflexes and stamina of our young pilots outweighed the
experience that he and I undoubtedly possessed in equal
measure? I wasn't certain, so I settled for an expression of
vague neutrality. "No vodka at the reception, then," I said.
"Not if we're flying." I raised my voice slightly to make
sure that Skeeter heard me, and turned my head to see him
nod in agreement.

"Well, then. A little refreshment, then back in the air."
Admiral Ilanovich smiled.

I followed him into the crowded hangar and saw the large
buffet tables covered with food, a cluster of aviators already
well into the vodka by their appearance. Not for the first
time, I wondered just what we'd gotten ourselves into.

Another flash of anger at the sight of so much food and
drink. If my father had been brought here, odds were that he
hadn't had quite such a sumptuous feast spread out in front
of him, that the faces weren't smiling, slightly flushed with
vodka and good cheer. For just a moment, I felt my father's
presence so close and near to me that I could almost see
him. I tried to make out his expression, but the details were
too fuzzy.

I'll find out what happened, I swore as I stared at the
welcoming Russian forces. *I'll find out—and I'll make them
pay.*

TWO

Friday, 18 December

1000 Local (+3 GMT)
USS Jefferson
Off the northern coast of Russia

Commander Lab Rat Busby:

CVIC—pronounced "civic"—is the Carrier Intelligence Center. It is located on the 0-3 level of *Jefferson,* just down the flag passageway from the admiral's quarters and battle stations. From the passageway, it looks like just another compartment, albeit a highly secure one with a window opening up onto a guard desk and a heavy steel cipher-locked door separating it from the rest of the world. Admiral Wayne makes jokes about the locks being designed to keep me and my herd of intelligence specialists in rather than the general public out, and I don't always disagree with that. The enlisted technicians and intelligence officers that work for me in this nerve center of the carrier battle group can be a slightly odd bunch.

Odd—but very, very good at what they do. Like now.

One of the electronic warfare technicians had buzzed me in my office and asked me to step into the signal evaluation center. It was just two doors down from my administrative spaces, and I didn't waste time asking him why he thought it was important. The EWs—earthworms as they are familiarly called—know when it's important to jump the chain of command and get right to the decision maker. I give them a lot of leeway on this.

Now I was standing in front of the tall rack of Navy gray equipment boxes, some of them covered with patch cords going in and out, others with LED displays. The earthworm, a bright, smart young kid from Omaha, Nebraska, with that corn-fed, scrubbed-face, blue-eyed look that you associate with Midwesterners, was pointing at the high-frequency end of the spectrum. "There—it did it again. You see it?" he asked excitedly.

I frowned, trying to turn the chatter of electronic signals into something that made sense to my eyes. It had been years since I'd stood watch in front of these very consoles, and developed an eye for what was normal and what wasn't in the electromagnetic spectrum. I was pretty good at it back then, but time and other responsibilities had kept me away from the equipment for a long time. Maybe too long, according to the look on the technician's face.

I glanced down at the hard copy chattering out from the printer, hoping that if I could see the same noise held still it would make more sense. I breathed a sigh of relief when I saw it—it did, indeed, make a lot of sense.

"Communications burst," I hazarded, then glanced over at him to see if I was right.

He nodded, obviously pleased. "Of course it is—and not just once. There—it's going again."

I nodded again, feeling my competence come back. "Classification?" I asked.

The technician looked thoughtful. "It sounds like—feels like—a routine communications data burst. But the frequency—it could be ours, it could be theirs. It's probably theirs, in these waters. The intelligence summary says we don't have anything in the area." He left unspoken the possibility that our own intelligence sources weren't telling us everything they knew about the disposition of U.S. forces in the area. When you've worked in the intelligence field for as long as both of us had, that was a given.

"But you do think it's a submarine?" I pressed.

He nodded. "We can get pretty accurate on the location

now," he said, blithely assuming that I didn't know the critical equipment parameters of the gear now in front of me. "That spot it's aimed at—empty ocean. At least according to the radar. Now if we had an S-3 or something overhead, we might know for certain."

"Anything from the undersea warfare commander?" I said, referring to the destroyer squadron, or DESRON, that occupied the 0-8 level of the aircraft carrier's tower. The recent changes in battle group organization had not left any of the traditional warfare commanders untouched. The DESRON, for decades called the Antisubmarine Warfare (ASW) commander, was now referred to as the Undersea Warfare (USW) Commander. He had charge of all the USW assets in the area, ranging from P-3s deployed from shore stations in support of the battle group, to the S-3 submarine-hunter killers that flew off our own flight deck, to the host of other national assets, including our own submarines.

This deployment, he didn't have that much to work with. Unlike most battle groups, we were traveling without a submarine. Given the sensitive nature of our deployment into Russia's northern waters, that seemed a politically sound decision. Additionally, we were out of range of most P-3 maritime patrol aircraft, which left us only with the organic helos and S-3s on the flight deck above me.

"Nothing from the DESRON," Petty Officer Martin confirmed.

I studied the signal for a while longer. A few more brief repetitions at the same frequency, each one of which made Martin tense up and lean forward in his chair. The printer continued its chattering, spitting out hard copy of all the data. It had two options for printing, either a graphic representation of peaks and valleys of signal strength or a numeric display with rows and columns of dense, closely spaced numbers. A guy in practice, like Martin, usually preferred the numbers. Older and less trained eyes like the graphic representation.

"I'll wander up and see the DESRON," I said finally. "Keep an eye on it—call me up there immediately if there's any change. Anything significant, anyway."

Martin nodded. "Go wake 'em up, just in case they're napping, sir."

I smiled despite myself. EWs are convinced there's no rating on the ship that works as hard, or as smart, as they do. Sure, they admit that there's a certain glamour in flying aircraft off the ship, and working on the flight deck, and even in maintaining the USW pictures as the DESRON is supposed to do. However, they have a lingering distrust that everyone else isn't doing his job quite as well as the EWs are.

Part of it is based on fact. There are very few ratings onboard the aircraft carrier that have as many sailors that are as smart as EWs. Just to get in the program, they have to be in the top 2 percent of the Navy in intelligence, and in terms of sheer raw brainpower, many of the EWs are damned near brilliant. Most of them are a good deal smarter than the college graduate pilots and RIOs they brief and debrief every day. Maintaining the properly respectful and military attitude toward their seniors is often quite difficult for them. In their minds, the facts are simply indisputable—EWs are smarter, so the more senior people ought to pay attention to what they say.

Pilots, especially the very young or inexperienced, don't always see it that way. They are all too impressed with the insignia on their collars and the sheer fact that they are naval aviators. Sometimes they don't listen as well as they ought to. The EWs know that, and I've got them pretty well trained to come running to me when they have a collar count discrepancy problem. I let them rant and rave, wait until they calm down, and then either take care of the problem or placate them.

In this case, I knew what Martin was thinking. There might have been a little sniff of a submarine somewhere, something that an Aviation Antisubmarine Warfare Technician—or AW for short—hadn't taken a good look at. The other fellow might have dismissed it as noise, or maybe—and I think this is what Martin privately suspected—he was too busy shooting the shit with his buddy to do his job. When Martin had called up, he'd probably gotten an offhand, quick answer—"No, buddy, no submarines in this area. If there were, we'd know about it." Something in the tone hadn't convinced Martin, and I could tell he was glad I was going up to take a look myself.

I clapped him on the shoulder and said, "I'll look at the data myself, Martin. Good catch on the signal."

Martin snorted. "Wasn't much to catch, sir. If it were a snake, it would have bit me on the ass."

I left him watching the scope and hustled up the six ladders leading to the 0–8 level, the home of the DESRON. They were located in the forward part of the tower, just behind the admiral's bridge. The admiral's bridge was normally vacant unless there was a reason for the admiral to have his own navigator and staff keeping a careful eye on the carrier commanding officer.

I stood for a second outside the DESRON spaces, catching my breath from the quick trip up the six ladders. It's a lot if you do it fast, even if you are in shape. I spend an hour a day on the Stairmaster, and I still manage to get winded when I'm in a hurry.

Finally, I stepped into the small compartment. In the back part of it, a paper-plotting table took up most of one corner, standing just barely out from the bulkhead so that sailors could move all around it. In the forward half of the compartment, a watch officer sat in a chair and stared at the status boards lining the bulkheads. Against one wall was a JOTS—Joint Operation Terminal Set—that displayed most of the data inputs from the other ships in the area, including commercial traffic. Some people claim that JOTS stands for Jeremy O. Tuttle, the renowned father of naval electronics who rammed through its implementation in the fleet by the force of his own personality.

"Good morning, Commander." The lieutenant who was the watch officer stood, took his hands out of his flight jacket, and gestured toward the pilot. "Anything we can do for you today? It's pretty slow out here—no contacts of any sort."

"Thanks, just up checking things out," I said neutrally. "I imagine it's pretty slow for you guys up here?"

The lieutenant nodded. "Wish we had somebody to play with," he said, his tone almost wistful. "The S-3s are biting bullets to at least get some stick time, but you know how the politics of it are." He shrugged and made a vague gesture toward the ocean around us. "Don't want to piss anybody off by doing our job."

I nodded, understanding what he meant. The Kola Peninsula was home to some of Russia's most advanced submarine bases. The Kola Peninsula is home to the northern fleet, Russia's largest and most powerful seagoing organization. The largest complex of bases is on the Kola Inlet, a swath of thirty-two miles stretching from the Barents Sea to the north to the junction of the Tuloma and Kola Rivers to the south. Severomorsk, the northern fleet headquarters, the commercial port of Murmansk, along with Arkhangel'sk and Polyarnyy, were just a few of the areas of strategic military interest.

One of the most fascinating bases in the area was near Bolshaya Litsa, only about thirty-five miles from the Norwegian border. A variety of submarine piers, maintenance facilities, and normal Navy activities ring the area, but the southeast facility is the most interesting. Several large, underground tunnels for ballistic missile submarines are cut into the mountains. According to Norwegian intelligence estimates, the tunnels are large enough so that any North Fleet missile submarine, up to and including the massive Typhoon, can pull into these tunnels and re-arm during time of conflict. The masses of rock provide protection from all but the most concentrated nuclear attack.

For the DESRON commander, and the young lieutenant who was his watch stander, being this near to such a massive concentration of Russian submarine activity was a godsend.

Except for the fact that they weren't allowed to play. As I said, these were sensitive areas for the Russians, and I'd wondered from the start why they agreed to allow a U.S. battle group—albeit a smaller one than normal—to come so close to their most strategic assets.

One of the conditions had been that the U.S. had to promise to conduct no undersea warfare activities or intelligence gathering during our visit. Admiral Wayne had argued strenuously that that meant only that we would not prosecute—i.e., pepper with sonobuoys and run to the ground—any Russian submarines we happened to find.

The Pentagon said otherwise. Not only were we not allowed to track submarines we did find, we were strictly prohibited from doing anything to find those submarines in the first place, up to and including discouraging pilots from making reports of visual contacts on submarines. No sonobuoys in the water, no active or passive sonars activated—except for safety of navigation in constrained waters; Admiral Wayne won that one concession from them—and no submarine hunter killer aircraft. No magnetic anomaly detectors, no passive acoustic tails in the water from the destroyers, and no satellite intelligence. Indeed, at the moment that she inchopped the Northern Sea, the USS *Jefferson* had been removed from several routing intelligence reports that located foreign submarines.

"Was the commodore tempted to just shut down shop?" I asked, referring to Captain Stephens. The commander of a destroyer squadron is, by tradition, referred to as Commodore. While at one time commodore was an actual rank, equivalent to the one-star rear admiral now, modernly it was used as a term for the senior officer in charge of a like number of units. That is, the senior captain in charge of a number of destroyers is called Commodore, the senior captain in charge of all S-3 squadrons is referred to as Commodore, etc., etc.

"Commodore Stephens isn't that kind of man," the lieutenant said glumly. "I know what he means, though. If the shit hits the fan, we need to be maintaining tactical awareness."

I refrained from pointing out that there was nothing to maintain awareness of, not without any sensors. "How about the USW module down in CDC?" I asked, referring to the small compartment off the carrier's combat direction center that also housed a USW staff, ship's company rather than DESRON.

"They've closed up," the lieutenant said flatly. "No need

for them to be up, really. Unless they're controlling some helos, they're just duplicating what we're doing."

"So you really don't have any way of knowing if there are any submarines in the area, do you?" I asked. I pointed at the blank displays, the silent radio circuits that normally would have been filled with reports from maritime patrol aircraft. "Not unless you get a lookout report."

The lieutenant nodded. "The theory is, the Russians are supposed to steer clear of us to avoid an incident at sea. INCOS, you know." He snorted. "Like that's going to be excuse for the captain if anything happens. We run over one of their submarines, we're still dead meat."

INCOS was the agreement struck between the former Soviet Union and the United States to prevent tragic incidents at sea. After years of Russian spy ships and combatants playing chicken with U.S. forces on training missions, both sides had hammered out an agreement to supplement the normal prudent seamanship rules of the road in international waters. The two nations specifically agreed not to hazard their vessels, not to come too close to each other. In civilian terms that meant no playing chicken. They also agreed not to train their fire control radars on one another, not to interfere with vessels that were refueling or conducting flight operations, and to generally take every measure possible to avoid any risk of collision at sea.

But I knew what the lieutenant was saying as well. Under INCOS, since the Russians knew that we were not maintaining our normal underwater lookout, the Russian submarines in the area would have a duty to stay well clear of us. But if we ran over one, our ass would still be grass. No wonder the commodore wanted a watch maintained up here.

And no wonder Petty Officer Martin had gotten such short shrift from the DESRON's watch team. It wasn't that they knew the area was clear of submarines—it was that they simply had no information at all about it. When pressed by one eager EW, the AWs had no doubt become truculent and unresponsive. Martin was right in this case.

"One of our fellows saw something a little bit odd," I began.

The lieutenant nodded. "Called up here and talked to Scruggins a few hours ago," the lieutenant said, and pointed at an AW lounging in the corner with a green plastic mug of coffee resting on the edge of the plot. "Wanted to know what submarines were in the area. Of course, I told him we didn't know."

I doubt you told him that, I thought. *Martin's got a very, very good memory, and that's not what he heard you say. Your fellow said there were no contacts in the area, not that your gear was down.*

"In other words, you can neither confirm nor dispute Petty Officer Martin's contact report," I said quietly. "Let's not get in some pissing contest, here, Lieutenant. Right now, I'm the only source of USW information that you've got."

The lieutenant looked like he was going to start to huff and puff, then he quickly subsided as he realized that what I was saying was true. "Sorry if we conveyed that impression, sir," he said finally. "Of course, we appreciate the information. And we'll keep a good lookout in that area— that is if we're ever allowed to bring any assets online."

For the second time that hour, I had to soothe an ego. "Just some crossed wires, Lieutenant," I said in a reassuring tone of voice. "If you want, how about I take one of your AWs down with me? Let him look at the data that Petty Officer Martin's got—he may be able to give us a clue as to the classification of the boat."

The AW slouched in the corner scowled slightly. "I'm not sure I'd be much help, sir," he said pointedly. "Your guy sounded like he knew what he was talking about."

"No, I think that's a fine idea," the lieutenant said, cheering up markedly. Evidently the possibility of transferring his problem child to someone else's care and control for a few hours sounded enticing. "Go ahead, Scruggins—the commander will take you down to CVIC and get you set up."

I eyed the lieutenant, suddenly convinced that I was able to read his mind. "Of course, a lot of our data is highly classified," I continued. "Can't talk about it on the sound-powered phone lines or the ship's telephone system. And it would seem kind of silly to use a special encrypted circuit just to communicate between my people on the 0–3 level and yours on the 0–8."

The lieutenant nodded vigorously. "Couldn't agree with you more, sir." He turned back to his slightly disgruntled sailor. "Scruggins, how about you run up position reports and debriefs as needed, then? Shouldn't be more than two or three times every hour." The lieutenant patted his own flat, trim stomach with satisfaction. "That's how I stay in shape, running back and forth between my stateroom and here. It'll be good for you, Scruggins."

The AW groaned audibly now. He stood, his hand jostling the coffee cup that stood on the paper overlay for this area of the ocean. "But, sir, I—"

"Off with you now, Scruggins," the lieutenant said briskly. "Winder can keep the plot up—such as it is."

"No need to worry about the coffee, Scruggins," I continued brightly, now convinced that I'd made a new friend in the lieutenant. Sure, he was a lot junior to me, but it never hurt to have a friend on every staff. "We don't allow coffee around the equipment in CVIC. A shame, too—we have to keep it so cold down there. That damned equipment, you know."

A subdued and disgruntled Scruggins followed me down the five ladders to CVIC. From the little he said, he struck me as an OK fellow, although with a marked lazy streak. Aviation ratings are like that, just like their officers. If it doesn't involve being up in an airplane or flying, they don't have much use of it.

Scruggins had to be a bright fellow, his attitude aside. The AWs, as a rule, were almost as smart as the EWs. Almost.

I introduced the two petty officers, and left them in Martin's compartment, circling warily around each other like dogs about to stick their noses up each other's butts. They'd thrash out their pecking order, Scruggins would get interested despite himself, and the two would end up coming up with an answer to the intermittent electromagnetic signal we were picking up.

All in all, a good solution. And that was what leadership was all about.

Scruggins would finally come clean with Martin, and end up blaming the powers that be for his lack of data. In some way or another, he'd end up apologizing to Martin for the lousy answer he'd given him before. In the end, the two petty officers would end up honor bound to protect the carrier battle group against the horrible decisions made by their superior officers, taking on the challenge with the gusto that can match any two other underdogs in the world.

It would take more than a little commander-level leadership to solve the bigger problem, though. While I may be able to get two technicians talking to each other and forming up into a team, that didn't solve my real problem—what to do about a submarine in the area. I headed down the passageway to find the admiral's N2 and brief him on the detection. In all probability, he'd want me to go see the admiral.

Intelligence—you run into more no-win situations in this game than in any other warfare area. There are rarely certainties—only probabilities, indications, and warnings, and the vast database of what the enemy has done in the past. When you're wrong, everybody remembers it. When you're right, sometimes they never even know it.

Another odd Catch-22 to the intel game: The very best intelligence that peeks right into the enemy's knickers is often stuff you can't use. It comes from national assets, the buzzword for satellite or other top secret airborne detection systems, or from a spy on the ground somewhere. Or from a native source—in this case, maybe a Russian dockworker who's making a little bit of extra money telling his buddies when submarines come and go in port. Whatever the case may be, the intelligence itself can be so highly classified that to give any hint at all about it would be to blow your sources completely or disclose some intelligence gathering capability that you would really rather the enemy didn't know about.

The classic example of this was the case of Coventry during World War II. The British had already broken the

Enigma code, the cipher used to encrypt Nazi Germany's most sensitive communications. They were reading the German's mail, and knew that a massive air raid was planned against the small village of Coventry.

They knew it—and could do nothing. If the British had attempted to evacuate the thousands of innocent civilians in Coventry, they would have exposed their own intelligence gathering capabilities to the Germans. The Germans would have abandoned Enigma, and moved on to another system that might have taken months—even years—to break. The British commanders were forced into one of the most gut-wrenching decisions an officer can ever make.

They made the right one, but at a cost that must have haunted them until the end of their days. They did nothing to warn Coventry of the inbound Nazi raid, took none but the most routine air defense precautions. As a result, a flood of Nazi bombers crossed the Channel and smashed the small village into rubble, killing thousands. The lower levels of the British war-fighting organization knew nothing about the Enigma code, and responded in their normal fashion with a deployment of antiair barrages and Spitfires. But it was too little, and too late, for the people of Coventry.

That's where the modern saying came from, of being sent to Coventry as an expression for being ostracized. In earlier times, to have been in Coventry was truly to have been left out permanently.

I briefed the admiral's N2, a senior intelligence captain by the name of Carl Smith. At first glance, Carl Smith was a nondescript, colorless man. He was even shorter than I was, and twenty pounds lighter. He'd never met a uniform that fit him well, and was constantly fighting to keep his shirt tucked in, his belt buckle centered, and his pants pulled up. Looking at him, you'd probably dismiss him immediately.

That would be a grave mistake. Carl Smith's thin, plain face fronts one of the finest brains in the intelligence community today. He'd been deep selected for every rank since lieutenant commander, and was one of the most brilliant theorists on the capabilities and intentions of the cluster of post–Soviet Union countries that were making trouble around the world. In addition to his education as an intelligence officer, Captain Smith was a student of history. He could recall every major and minor battle that I'd ever heard of, and had all that data stored in some fashion that made it instantly accessible to him. He was capable of the most amazing feats of military and tactical reasoning, drawing on examples and knowledge that were way beyond that of most officers.

On top of that, he was funny as hell. Carl had a saying: *Nothing is too cruel if it's funny.* He was one of the biggest practical jokers onboard the aircraft carrier, although most officers were reluctant to believe it. It seemed incomprehensible to the swaggering jet jockeys that prowled the corridors of our carrier that this small, wimpy looking 0–6 could have engineered any one of the evil yet hilarious stunts that they'd been victims of. Moreover, he was too senior for easy retaliation, although I suspect occasionally that Carl would have welcomed the attempt.

At any rate, he listened carefully to what I had to say about the electromagnetic signals, nodded knowingly as I described the interaction between DESRON and CVIC. Finally, he spoke. "Good move, that," he said, referring to my adopting Scruggins into the CVIC community. "Seen that before—you take a guy like that, he's not all bad. He's just bored, doesn't have anything to do. All that tension gets turned to evil purposes, sort of like Lex Luther and Superman. Bet he turns into a model sailor now that you've given him a purpose in life."

"Let's hope so. At the very least, it'll keep Martin happy. The guy likes to have a mission; he's sort of a crusader. I'm willing to bet that both he and Scruggins can learn something from each other."

"In the meantime, what do we do about the submarine problem?" Captain Smith asked. He eyed me quizzically, waiting for my suggestions. That was just like Carl—he'd probably already decided how to proceed, but wanted to give me the benefit of the doubt. Like I said—a nice guy.

I shrugged, somewhat at a loss. "I don't know there's much that we can do at this point," I said. "No sensors, no prosecution—hell, we're so close to Polyarnyy that we'll be lucky if we don't run over a couple dozen of them in the next two weeks. Taking into account the political considerations, I don't see that we have any options at all."

Carl nodded again. "About the way I figure it," he agreed. Then Carl shook his head, as though clearing away a particular train of thought. "*Your* admiral's not making this any easier, you know." He said it quietly, with very little hint of emotion.

I froze. The whole point of the statement was to let me know that he, Captain Carl Smith, intelligence officer for the entire battle group, knew several things that he wasn't supposed to. First, he knew that Admiral Tombstone Magruder and I were on close terms. No big surprise there—I'd been the ship's N2 intelligence officer when Admiral Tombstone was in command of the carrier battle group not so long ago. My tour normally would have been up a year ago, but I'd opted to extend it for a year.

Second, he knew about Tombstone's father and what the admiral was doing in Russia right now. Now, that was more of a surprise.

Most of the ship knew that during our last cruise Admiral Magruder had found indications that his father had survived his ejection so many decades ago over Vietnam. While they might not have the specifics, they did know one thing: At some point the admiral's father had been alive and in country.

What they didn't know was the rest of the story. How Admiral Magruder had tracked his father's trail across country in the company of a dissident militant group, had survived an all-out air strike on the area that had obliterated the physical evidence of his father's existence.

Even more importantly, most of the ship—I thought all of the ship—was ignorant of what had happened next. Of Admiral Magruder's growing involvement with the MIA-POW groups, of the photographs he'd received in the mail from them. Admiral Magruder had come to me with the second event, and I eventually wormed the rest of the story out of him. He seemed relieved to have someone he could talk to, an intelligence officer who understood the clandestine and uncertain murky waters of the world he was entering. I tried to provide some perspective to him, cautioned that it might still yet all turn out to be a fabrication. He knew that, and on some level wanted to discuss it, but a part of him clung stubbornly to the possibility that his father might still be alive.

During our last briefing, just before he and the other members of his team had flown off the carrier, I'd come back to revisit the topic one more time. "You're going to be in country, Admiral," I said, using the term "in country" deliberately. In most circles, that refers to being on the ground in Vietnam, but using it to refer to Russia would, I hoped, carry a double meaning for Admiral Magruder.

He nodded, signifying he caught my drift. "I know that. We'll be on the lookout for anything of use."

Again, a hidden meaning. "No active collection, though," I cautioned. "Despite all this love and brotherhood, Russia's not our closest ally."

Tombstone smiled, a brief, wintry stretching of his lips that did not reach his eyes. "The essence of all warfare is seizing opportunities that present themselves," he said obliquely. "Just like intelligence. The best stuff comes not from your own efforts, but when someone else screws up."

I glanced at the other three officers sitting at the table. "Would you excuse us for a moment?" I glanced back at the admiral for permission. "The admiral and I need to go over a couple of other measures."

Tombstone waved one hand. "I'll meet you in the handler's office," he said to Skeeter. A few moments of scuffling feet and chairs scraping, then we were alone in the small briefing room. "Admiral, with all due respect—have you got something planned?" I asked, trying to tone down the worry and concern in my voice.

Tombstone regarded me gravely for a long moment. I was suddenly extremely conscious of the gap between our ranks, his three stars against my silver oak leaves. I knew he was letting the silence drag on deliberately, to put me in my place. Nevertheless, I persisted. "Admiral, again, with all due respect, sir—I have the utmost regard for you, you should know that by now. But I'm deeply concerned that you have some . . . personal agenda in this visit. Sir, I know of no way to put this politely. But as intelligence officer for this ship, I feel I must ask—are you going to continue the search for your father during this mission?"

There was no immediate answer from Tombstone, just a slight change in his posture. It was barely perceptible, more an air of increased caution and wariness than anything else. He kept his eyes glued on me, his face revealing nothing. Finally, he spoke. "I understand your position, Commander Busby," he said, his voice cold and formal. "Be advised I'm well aware of my duties and responsibilities as a flag officer during this historic visit to Russia."

I nodded and waited for him to continue. But Tombstone had evidently said all he was going to say and had made it very clear that he did not wish for this conversation to continue.

"Hypothetically speaking," I tried again, "if you were to happen across any intelligence gathering opportunities while you were there, it might be helpful if I were standing by to assist you. Just hypothetically speaking, you understand. I wonder if you would be adverse to allowing me to suggest a series of simple code words that would, still hypothetically, enable me to be prepared to assist you. That is, should the occasion arise."

Tombstone appeared to consider this, and then inclined his head just a fraction of an inch, granting permission for me to continue.

"Just a few words: *West,* if you find any evidence of your father's presence in Russia." I abandoned the hypothetical scenario I'd tried to play out, since none of it would do me any good if it came to a court-martial. It was clear that the admiral did not wish to place me in a compromising situation and was trying to shield me from whatever he had planned. Nonetheless, I had no doubts that Tombstone had a plan. He always did.

"If I hear the word *west* mentioned in casual context in your narrative, I will know that you have found something.

Westward will indicate physical evidence. *To the west* will indicate HUMINT—human intelligence. Somebody who remembers something, an old-timer telling stories. I don't have to tell you how unreliable HUMINT can be."

"Go on," Tombstone said almost disinterestedly.

"If for some reason you are in physical danger, or feel that you may be compromised in any way, mention something about your backache. You can phrase it in any way you wish, whether it has to do with the lumbar supports in the Tomcat or a workout you had, just something about your back. I'll know then that we may have to be prepared for some sort of extraction."

"I hardly think that will be necessary," Tombstone said, a thread of impatience in his voice now. "And this is all hypothetical, is it not?" He shot me a hard, penetrating look. "And just what are you going to tell Admiral Wayne about all this?"

It was my turn to fall silent and consider my position. There was a strong bond between me and Tombstone, one that went back several cruises. I had the utmost respect for him, both as an admiral and an aviator, and I'd seen him pull this battle group's ass out of the fire too many times not to trust him implicitly. Yet my current assignment was as Admiral Wayne's intelligence officer, not Admiral Magruder's. Admiral Wayne, Tombstone's oldest friend in the Navy, had first claim on my loyalties.

"I think you know what the answer has to be, Admiral," I said finally. "If it affects the battle group in any way, I will have to tell Admiral Wayne. Other than that, I see no need to keep him briefed. What you tell him is up to you."

Tombstone nodded. "Your concern is appreciated, Lab Rat," he said, his voice losing the earlier formality. "I don't have to tell you—hell, you're the one who knows most of the story. Maybe more of it, from what I hear about you intelligence people. You probably know exactly where my old man was and are holding out on me, aren't you?"

"I wish I did, Admiral," I said quietly. "I would tell you if I did—and if I've got anything in this office that you need, you know you've got it." We worked out a few more details on the codes we'd use. Tombstone would be sending back daily situation reports, using the radiomen and the secure communications gear in the COD, receiving updates from the carrier the same way. Finally, we had something we figured would cover most possibilities.

"Admiral, about Admiral Wayne—" I said finally.

"We don't tell him. Not unless he's got something tactical on the front burner." I wondered a little at the tone of Tombstone's voice, but simply nodded my agreement. Their friendship ran long and deep, but evidently there was a difference of opinion on this particular mission. I wondered what it was.

Tombstone sighed. "There are officers that you work with every day, ones that you fight with and go on cruise with, and learn to trust in any tactical situation. They get fewer and fewer as you move up in rank, until at my level they're far and few between. There's that kind of people—and there are friends." His voice had taken on a reflective note, almost wistful in its tone. "Right now, I need the second kind of friend. I'll tell you this, Lab Rat. This is the worst thing I've ever had to do in my life. I'm not even sure I want the answers. What if he was alive? What happened to him here in Russia? Did they break him? Was there a chance for him to return to the United States—to me and my mother—that he turned down? I don't know which is worse, contemplating torture or brainwashing." For the first time in many years, I heard a trace in his voice of the anguish he must be experiencing.

"Tombstone, if there's anything—" He cut off my comment with a hard gesture. All traces of the emotion that had swept over his face earlier were gone. "If there's nothing else, Commander—I've got a hop to make." He stood, concluding the conversation.

I held out my hand. "Remember, I'm here if you need me."

Tombstone nodded and took my hand, holding it hard as he shook it. "I'll remember that. And if I get my ass in trouble, you make sure my old buddy Batman sends in the

cavalry, you hear? Don't let him leave me rotting in some
Russian hellhole because he's after my stars."

A joke. As feeble as it was, the fact that Tombstone had
made one stunned me. "I'll do that, sir."

I walked with him to the massive steel door that makes up
the entrance to CVIC, and as he stepped over the sill and
knee knocker, I said, "Good hunting, Admiral." He didn't
even turn around to look, but made a small wave of
acknowledgment as he strode away toward the handler's
office.

Now, sitting across the table from Captain Smith, staring
into those preternaturally bright gray eyes, I had the feeling
that he was seeing the whole scene replaying in my brain.

"Admiral Magruder understands his situation," I said
carefully, hoping Carl would not ask me direct questions
that I could not answer without either violating the admiral's
confidence or lying. "You know how these sea stores are."

Captain Smith nodded slowly, his eyes fixed on mine,
probing and brilliant with intelligence. "Intelligence officers
hear a lot in their careers," he said quietly. "Sometimes I
think we ought to be granted the same privileges and
immunities as a clergyman. It might be appropriate, don't
you think?"

What could I say? In his delicate, surgical way, Carl was
letting me know that he suspected something was up. He
was also paying me the ultimate compliment, by not forcing
me to divulge what I knew or forcing me into a lie. By not
asking any other questions, he was implicitly saying that he
trusted my judgment, that he was relying on me to come to
him if there was anything that he needed to know about
Admiral Magruder and the Russians.

"Admirals aren't required to tell us everything, Commander. Sometimes they even lie."

"I wouldn't put it that way, sir."

"I would. And I'm not talking just about Admiral
Magruder. We all have *our* admirals, the one's we'll go to
the wall for. Tombstone just happens to be yours. You
follow what I'm saying?"

I thought I did. It was advice—and a warning. Captain

Smith and Batman, me and Tombstone. As long as I didn't intrude on the former relationship—and didn't pry—Captain Smith wouldn't press me on what I knew about Tombstone. In that moment, I felt more afraid of my senior intelligence officer than either of the admirals.

"It sounds like an interesting idea, but it couldn't be an absolute privilege," I said warily. "After all, our first duty is to the Navy."

He nodded, evidently satisfied with my answer. "Speaking of the Navy—I think you and I need to go fill in Admiral Wayne on this submarine. As we've agreed, there's damn little we can do about it, not without violating most of the restrictions we're operating under. Still, we'd better let him know ahead of time, get him prepped up for the fight in case it comes to that."

I followed Captain Smith across the passageway to the chief of staff's office. Captain Smith knocked lightly on the door, then stuck his head inside. "Admiral in?"

The chief of staff grunted, and motioned toward the admiral's cabin. "He's trying to crank out some paperwork—he'd probably welcome the distraction."

We crossed the rest of the admiral's mess, the large combination sitting area and dining room that serves the twenty or so officers attached to Admiral Wayne's warfighting staff. Captain Smith rapped lightly on the door, then pushed it open as the brass placard on the door instructed. "Good morning, sir. Got a moment for some intel?"

"Come on in, Captain," Batman's voice boomed. "God, I'd give anything for a reason to quit reading this crap. Anything interesting?"

Captain Smith waved me on in behind him. Batman's beady brown eyes lit up when he saw me. "Well, to what do we owe this honor? Come on, Lab Rat, pull up a chair. Don't see too much of you these days. How've you been doing?"

In marked contrast to Tombstone, Admiral Batman Wayne was a gregarious, jovial fellow. A hair shorter than Tombstone, with a figure that ran to roundness and a booming voice and quick wit, he was a people person in a way that

Admiral Magruder would never be. That joviality did little to mask his sharp sense of tactics and operations, however, both on a tactical and political level. Batman had spent several tours in Washington, D.C. Back there, he'd learned to kill with position papers and formal briefings instead of Sidewinders and AMRAAMs, making him as deadly an adversary in budget fights as he was in the air. He was a good man to work for, and I'd jumped at the opportunity to stay assigned to *Jefferson* while he was in command.

"Commander Busby has been filling me in on some anomalous detections," Captain Smith began, then summarized in a few sentences our tactical position, our lack of assets, and the detections we'd had over the last twenty-four hours. "Bottom line is, there are submarines around, although I can't give you a classification without assigning some more surveillance assets to it. But I wanted you to be current on the situation, in case you have to take this battle to a higher level."

Batman looked thoughtful. "Anything threatening in what you've observed?" he asked quietly.

I shook my head. "It's a communications burst, not a video downlink transmission." Translation: not targeting data, but maybe position reports.

Most Russian submarines are capable of entering into a data link with orbiting Russian aircraft or satellites, instantaneously transmitting and receiving targeting and weaponeering information. Had there been a Russian Bear in the vicinity armed with antiship missiles transmitting data to a submarine, it would have been an entirely different scenario.

"It's a satellite transmission, I'm pretty sure," I said. "Not from a Bear."

Batman nodded gravely. "So, maybe they read the weekly familygram, baseball scores, that sort of thing?" he mused. "Our submarines get 'em—why not theirs?" We both knew the answer to that one. The Russians were not nearly as concerned about the health and well-being of their submarine crews as the Americans were. Hell, even the lead shielding around their reactors was inadequate to prevent widespread sterility among Russian submarine sailors.

"But you know, I'm thinking that these subs—if they are subs, mind you—pose a serious hazard to navigation." I could tell by his self-satisfied expression that he'd had this very possibility in mind when he'd wrung that concession out of his seniors. "Let's put some S-3s in the air, make sure there are no uncharted wrecks up ahead of us. Or astern of us, for that matter. And I'll move a couple more S-3s up to an alert-thirty status. Maybe some helos, too." He glanced up at us to see if we had any suggestions.

"I guess that's all we can do," I answered. "Frustrating, though."

Batman nodded his agreement. "Who else have you told about this?" he asked, his voice now sounding markedly nonchalant. "Just the two of you?"

Carl and I glanced at each other, uncertain what the admiral was getting at. "My EW knows," I said. "And probably one AW. A couple of DESRON watchstanders, but their lieutenant can keep them quiet."

Batman nodded, a small trace of relief on his face. "That's all, though? Just you four?"

"Yes, Admiral," I answered, now letting my puzzlement show in my voice. "I think so?"

"We can make sure, though," Carl said quickly.

Now, that surprised me. What was Carl doing, trying to suck up a little bit to his admiral? Completely out of character from what I knew of him. But why did this whole thing matter? The entire field of electromagnetic signals, the detection, analysis, and classification of them, was among the most highly classified of anything onboard the carrier. Only those with a need to know—a real need to know— would have been routinely informed about the detections.

"If that's what the admiral wants?" Captain Smith asked. He waited for an answer.

Batman looked annoyed. "This isn't a tough question, gentlemen. I simply want to know how many people know about this submarine detection. That's all."

An uneasy silence filled the admiral's cabin. I had the

sudden conviction that there was something we weren't being told, something that Batman knew and we didn't. Modifications on his rules of engagement? Some intelligence source received back-channel during his Pentagon briefings prior to deployment. I shook my head, not liking being on the other end of a closely held secret. Spooks keep secrets from other people—it's not supposed to work in the opposite direction. "I don't think anyone else knows, not unless Martin has talked to them," I said. "He came straight to me with the data, not through the watch officer."

"Good. For the time being, let's keep it that way. You two, your two technicians, and me. I'll talk to the DESRON myself. No further dissemination. Got it?"

I nodded, still uncertain what the admiral was getting at. "It may reoccur, Admiral." I waited to see if he had any suggestions. "If it does, more people may know about it."

Batman considered that for a moment, then said, "I have a feeling about this," he continued, clearly making up this story as he went along. "Russians tend to do things in patterns—if this is some sort of routine communications, it'll probably occur tomorrow at the same time. Or exactly twelve hours off of this, if that's the sort of schedule they're on. For the time being, make sure your two guys—Martin and Scruggins was it?—have the watch for two-hour time periods surrounding this detection time and the time exactly twelve hours off. That ought to minimize the number of people that know about it."

Carl and I glanced at each other again. I could see that he reached the same conclusion that I did, almost at the same instant. Whatever game the admiral was playing, we weren't going to call him on it. He had no duty to explain his reasoning to us, and we had no right to demand it. What was clear now was that the admiral wanted dissemination of this information limited to the people that already knew about it, and he wanted USW assets in the air conducting what he claimed were safety-of-navigation operations.

Captain Smith stood and I followed his lead. "I understand, Admiral. That's what we'll do, sir. Should there be any further detections, we'll make sure you're briefed immediately."

Batman stood now, too, rocking back and forth on the balls of his feet and his heels. "Good, good. That's what I like about intelligence officers—you don't have to explain everything to them. They understand . . . well . . . that sometimes there are nuances to situations. Other things that have to be considered, that sort of thing. Keep me posted," he concluded abruptly, apparently suddenly aware that he sounded like he was rambling. "That's all."

After we left the admiral's cabin, Carl and I went back down to my office spaces to talk to Martin and Scruggins. We found them seated in front of the high-frequency spectrum analyzer, with Martin pointing out to Scruggins the critical features of the communications burst he detected. "It looks just like a lofargram," Scruggins said, referring to a low-frequency analyzing recording graph generated by sonar equipment.

"Same general principles," Martin agreed. "Now, you see here—" His voice cut off abruptly as he saw me standing in the doorway.

I strode into the room, followed by Captain Smith. "Martin, and you, too, Scruggins—I need some help here," I began. That's often a good way to start with sailors, because needing help is something they understand. Moreover, it was God's honest truth, and I knew they would appreciate that as well. "I don't know why, I don't know any of the details, but the admiral wants this kept real quiet. This communications burst you are detecting," I elaborated.

The puzzlement I saw on Martin's and Scruggins's faces mirrored that of my own, I was certain. "Don't ask me why—I'd tell you if I knew, but God's honest truth, I don't." I briefly outlined the admiral's plan for keeping the two of them on watch during the period of signal vulnerability, and they nodded appreciatively. Both were clearly intrigued by the unexpected secrecy and sensitivity of their data, and were eager to continue maintaining ownership of the problem. Finally, I asked, "Any suggestions?" including in the question whether or not I'd told them everything they needed to now. I hoped so—it was all I knew.

"No, sir," Martin said thoughtfully. He glanced back at Captain Smith, then over at Scruggins. "I think we can manage."

"That's good, real good," Captain Smith said.

I hoped he was telling the truth this time.

THREE
Friday, 18 December

1300 Local (+3 GMT)
Arkhangel'sk, Russia

Lieutenant Skeeter Harmon:

The little Commie bastard tripped me on the way to the hangar. Oh, if you asked him I'm sure he'd say that I slipped on a piece of pavement, or didn't notice a recessed pad eye inset in the concrete, but that's not the truth. It was just as Admiral Magruder was looking back at me to make sure I knew that I'd be flying that afternoon—like that would be a problem for me or something—and I was trying to let him know that I'd heard him, that I was paying attention, and that no, I wouldn't go swilling down pints and pints of vodka and then climb back in the Tomcat to kick this cocky little bastard's ass, when it happened. One second I was proceeding along, trying to listen to the Russian guy practice his broken English on me, letting Tombstone know I was a-OK, good to go, and ready to take on the world, when my right foot hit something. I didn't fall, caught myself pretty quick—after all, I am a fighter pilot, aren't I? Excellent reflexes, good sense of balance, top marks in spatial orientation, right?

And I think maybe he didn't exactly realize I saw him, you know? I mean, he waited until he thought I was distracted before he edged over a little and just stuck out his foot in front of me.

But he's got a lot to learn about Americans. Me, in particular. For one thing, unlike the guys he's been used to fighting against, I can do more than one thing at once without some GCI on the ground telling me when to take a leak. For another thing, I have excellent peripheral vision. I mean, truly excellent.

So when I say the little bastard tripped me, I think that's pretty much the truth. Now, as to why—that's an entirely different question. Maybe he wanted me to see him, get some sort of first shot in on me. Or maybe he thought he'd shake my confidence a little, make me think I was more tired than I really was.

So I didn't let him know. Made some little remark about it and let it go at that, but I'd seen him. And that put me in the firing position, asshole.

The rest of the reception went pretty much as planned. I had my backseater, Lieutenant Commander Kennedy, under close control. I guess she had orders from Tombstone to keep an eye on me, make sure I didn't act like a jerk to the Russians. But if truth be known, I ended up keeping an eye on her as much as she did on me. The Russians aren't big on having either blacks or women fly their aircraft, so Sheila and I stood out like—well, like a black male and a white female. They gathered around us, not saying a whole lot, like they wanted to reach out and touch us to see if we were for real.

Sheila didn't back down, not a bit. She wouldn't—not her. You've got to fly with somebody to really know them, and Sheila and I had logged enough hours together in work-ups to have a pretty good idea of where each other stood. No, we didn't necessarily like each other much—but hell, that's not a requirement for a pilot and a RIO. As long as you trust the other guy to do his job and keep some asshole from shooting your aircraft out from under you, that ought to be enough. It was for us.

I thought the Russians were pretty well snowed by Sheila. It's easy to do—I made that mistake with her from the first. A little short blond-haired, blue-eyed cutie pie, something you might find on your local cheerleading squad if you were real, real lucky. You might ask her out a couple of times, even think about making it serious—until you found out she had a mean streak about a mile wide and a temper not a whole lot longer than Bird Dog Robinson's. Now that would have been a pair, teaming up those two. They would have killed either a lot of Commies or each other within the first thirty minutes.

And Sheila's not only her real name, it's her call sign as well. Somebody who thought Australian was the hottest liberty around decided that, since "sheila" down under is slang for female.

Anyway, Sheila and I found that flying together was pretty much all right by us, so the skipper left us teamed up for this exhibition. I suppose we might have been offended, like they were trying to see us as some equal opportunity poster children, but the truth was that we were just so very, very good. The captain knew it—and we knew it. The way I figure it, there wasn't a single logical choice in the squadron except for the two of us for this mission.

I drew Sheila aside as soon as a hole broke in the Russians around her and said, "You hear what the admiral said? We fly the first mission this afternoon."

Sheila nodded, a slow, strange smile spreading across her face. I'd seen her knocking back the caviar, so I was hoping it wasn't due to indigestion, but she just said, "We're ready."

I nodded. "Bothers me not having a guard on our birds, though."

Sheila finished licking the last bit of fish eggs off one of those crackers, swallowed it in one gulp, then said, "So we preflight—and we check the telltales." She shot a glance at one of the Russians standing nearby, as though wondering whether he understood the slang.

After we'd done our shutdown, Sheila and I had set up a number of carefully prearranged little traps for anyone who wanted to mess with our bird. Nothing fancy, just a piece of tape here, a little scuff and some oil there—enough so we'd know if somebody was tinkering with anything on the aircraft. Besides, maintenance had fitted some special locks on both the compartments and the engine intake covers. If somebody tired to bypass the key system, there would be a larger splotch of red ink on the inside panel. Not enough to let our guests know that they'd been busted, but enough to alert us to double-check for problems.

An hour and a half later we were both back out on the flight line, checking out our bird. I reminded Sheila to wear her gloves, since the metal had already cooled so much that we'd lose skin if we came in contact with the bare metal. Even in early afternoon, the sun was low in the sky, reminding me of how far north we were. I was almost surprised we had any daylight at all.

Not that it mattered much, not with the Tomcat. I wasn't so sure about the MiG.

We double-checked the Tomcat for any problems. All of our telltales were just where we left them, and I didn't even see anything that gave me a hinky feeling. Finally, satisfied that nobody had been tinkering with her, we climbed back up in. The enlisted technicians double-checked us as efficiently as Americans would have, making me wonder who the hell they'd been practicing on. As far as I know, the MiGs and other fighters in the Russian inventory don't have exactly the same setup for the four-point ejection harness and the ejection-seat safeties.

I kept my distance from the MiG. I like formation flying, especially when it's with somebody who's pretty damned good.

Like Admiral Magruder. There was nothing about the admiral in the air that gave me any reason to worry about him. Oh, his reflexes might be a little bit slower—even he'd admit that. But he still had what it took. Surprising, at his age. I had to figure he was nearly forty-five.

I watched the MiG's roll-out carefully, staying behind and to the right of him, and pulled my own Tomcat off the tarmac exactly where he had. I caught up with him soon enough, slid back into a locked wing position to his right for just long enough to let him know I was hot, then went for altitude.

We'd rebriefed the ground rules in preflight, both in English and in Russian, with both of our admirals listening in gravely. Both of them made the point of saying that this was simply a test of airmanship, not combat; that there was no reason to risk life or equipment, that safety remained a paramount consideration. I wondered how they managed to make the same bullshit sound so much alike in both Russian and English.

I looked over at Kyrrul and saw he wasn't buying it any more than I was. He bore watching, and not just because he was supposed to be some hotshot fighter-jet jock. No, he was a sneaky little bastard. He'd tripped me.

We meandered up to thirteen thousand feet, and I switched buttons to the tactical frequency we'd agreed on. The air traffic controller was switching rapidly between Russian and English, directing us into our starting positions thirty miles apart. On the controller's signal, I put my radar in standby mode, hoping Kyrrul was doing the same thing. That was the deal—neither of us knew where the other was, and we were both starting from that point with no initial intelligence. The floor was seven thousand feet, the ceiling twenty-nine. I wondered about that number for a moment, whether it said anything about the MiG or not. No matter— I'd remember to tell the intelligence weenies when we got back to the ship.

I knew Admiral Magruder was up in the tower, keeping an eye on the tactical picture. He didn't speak much Russian, just a few phrases, but a radarscope looks the same in any language. He'd assured me he'd keep them honest, and that I would fulfill the same role when he was in the air.

Finally, the signal came. I heard the admiral's voice come out of the circuit—"Good luck, Skeeter, Sheila"—and then we were off. I flipped the AWG-9 radar back into search mode. It took a microsecond to warm up, then it kicked in and started acquiring crap in the sky. A nasty picture for a few moments then, suddenly, clarity. That was one of the advantages of holding this little experiment in Russian airspace. They had no compunctions at all about clearing out the whole area of commercial and private traffic just for their own war games. A pretty big deal from what I could see of the industrial area down below us.

We picked up contact on the MiG almost immediately. You hear all sorts of things about advanced radar systems, but in my mind, there is nothing that can beat the AWG-9 radar as a fighter weapons control system. Even in the older models, it could track up to twenty-four targets and guide missiles to six of them simultaneously. Everything feeds into it, I mean everything—although it was developed particularly for the Phoenix air-to-air missile, it also takes care of your Sparrow, Sidewinder, AMRAAM missiles, as well as the gun—though later upgrades have replaced almost all the old components with miniaturized digital packages. With the AWG-9, you get good detection capability out to a hundred and fifteen nautical miles, across a front of more than a hundred and fifty nautical miles. The latest versions track targets as low as fifty feet off the ground and up to eighty thousand feet, a vast improvement over the earlier look-down limitations of the original system.

I caught the MiG in general search mode and immediately switched over to single-target track mode. My RIO did, actually, although the way Sheila and I worked together it was like we were one mind.

"He's acquired us," Sheila warned. Like I needed her to tell me that—I could hear the insistent *beep beep beep* of her ESM gear going off.

The MiG knew we had him, too. He turned away from us, probably in preparation for enticing me into an angles fight at this altitude. I wasn't buying it. I put the Tomcat into a steep climb, grabbing for altitude. We were closing each other at well over Mach Two, and I was hoping to force him into an altitude game early on. Not that I thought the very first maneuver would win—they would have put their best guy up, and I was certain he wouldn't fall for a rolling yo-yo immediately. However, I couldn't let him get me on the defensive, make me start reacting to his maneuvers at altitude.

The basic game plan wasn't complicated. Standard tactics against a MiG, something the admiral wanted to see in operation for himself. We knew it generally worked—hell, we kicked their asses every time we'd come up against them—but in this encounter we had full telemetry of both the Tomcat and MiG, something our science guys would drool over later back at VX-1.

Not that gathering scientific data was my primary purpose in life. Mostly, I just wanted to kick his ass.

I rolled up through twenty-five thousand feet, with Sheila feeding me information continuously on what the MiG driver was doing. He milled about uncertainly at altitude, then reluctantly gave chase. He couldn't catch me, I knew, so I was sure he was counting on calculating the exact moment of my climb, when I'd tip my nose over and start back down. He'd cut out of the pattern at that point and wait to catch me on the downswing, slipping in behind me for a tail shot. Or what would have been a tail shot, if we had actual missiles. Both of us sported blue-painted dummy loads rather than the real thing.

It's slightly inaccurate to call them dummy loads, because they're much more than just dead weight on your wings. Each one of these missiles, although it has no warhead and no propulsion system, is a simulator in its own right. It stores tracking data from the AWG-9, records your firing orders and targeting information, all of which can be downloaded later for study. Additionally, each one of these has the MILES gear mounted on it, the laser simulators for the actual missile.

I pulled out of my climb at twenty-nine thousand feet, letting the Tomcat nose over gently to give me a good look at the MiG. He was still climbing, but rolled out of it as soon as he saw me stop my ascent. He peeled off to the north, in level flight away from me before the Tomcat had even nosed over.

I felt the G forces push me back in my seat as we started our descent. "Not too far, Skeeter," Sheila warned.

Right—like I need a RIO to tell me how to fight an air battle. I clicked my mike once in acknowledgment. As we descended past twenty-four thousand feet, the MiG was already starting his turn back in toward us. I knew what his plan was: use his maneuverability against my speed, catch me when my inertia was too great to let me turn away from him. He was closing quickly now, descending slightly to maintain an excellent firing position on my tailpipes. Sheila's ESM gear increased its frantic beeping, indicating that he'd shifted to targeting mode.

At the third frantic beep, I hauled back on the yoke and pulled us out of the descent, simultaneously rolling to my right to bleed off additional airspeed. It's always a trade-off, this altitude versus airspeed game, and I was betting that I knew my Tomcat performance characteristics a hell of a lot better than he did. When I finished the roll, I was at seventeen thousand feet, accelerating and ascending into nose-on battle with the little bastard.

Thirty seconds later, we screamed past him so close that I heard Sheila gasp. Yeah, a little bit too close—more so than had been briefed, that was for sure. The rules of engagement said that we were to maintain a one-thousand-foot altitude separation at all times. But as much as they run on about the damn MiG's maneuverability, I figured it was at least more his hit than mine. Besides, we hadn't been that close—but RIOs are like that, always getting excited about stuff.

"Maintain your separation," I heard a voice say over tactical. I groaned, recognizing it immediately. Not the Russian GCI, or the air traffic controller. No, this was somebody I had to listen to—the admiral.

"Aye, aye, Admiral," I responded immediately. "He got me a bit on that one."

A moment of silence on the net, then, "Right." Even over the circuit, I could hear the admiral's tone of voice well enough to know that he wasn't buying it.

"Let's just try that again, shall we," I said out loud.

"You heard the admiral," Sheila answered.

"I'm not talking about that," I snapped. "The rolling scissors—you know that's what is going to get him in the end."

She sighed. I let it pass.

We pulled back into a steep descent, and this time I kicked in the afterburners to give us an extra boost of power.

The MiG overshot us, and had to turn back into our plane of attack. By the time he was back in position, following me up, I was passing twenty-four thousand feet again.

"He's got you," Sheila snapped. "Jesus, can't you let me get in position for just a second to get off a missile?"

"Always so eager," I murmured. "Just wait for it, baby." I could get away with that kind of comment in the air, although not on the ground. I might even have to pay for this one later, but I was enjoying myself just too much to care.

I waited for twenty-nine thousand feet again, then edged over into another descent. This time, I rolled it, and in afterburner that generated some significant G forces for my backseater. She yelped in protest at the lack of warning, then shut up and started her M1, the forced breathing exercises that keep you from graying out. Harassing her about panting in the backseat is always good for a few laughs. At least on my part. Too bad she's so quick with the elbows-to-the-ribs routine—my last bruise was just starting to fade.

Again we descended, this time passing much closer to the MiG, who had not rolled out quickly enough. I waved as we went by, straining to move my hand under the mounting G forces. Just as we passed, I saw him roll out of his climb and stay inverted to keep an eye on me as I descended. Then he pitched nose-down into a descent himself, almost immediately in firing position on my tail. Again, the sharp warning of the ALR-67 threat receiver was my cue. I banked back out of the descent, swinging out in a tight arc to drop in behind the MiG.

"Nice, nice," Sheila said. "I've got him   got a lock!"

"Sidewinder," I agreed, toggling the weapon selection switch on my stick to the appropriate location. We were close, almost close enough to go for the gun. For just a moment I was tempted.

"Get it off now," Sheila said. "Quick, so I can take a second shot if we need to. Hurry before he—"

The MiG shuddered, twitching a little as though the pilot were going to pull out of his descent. He held it for a couple seconds longer than I thought he would, but I didn't mind. I pickled off one Sidewinder, then another, letting the heat-seeking missiles get a good look at the hot exhaust flaring out of his tailpipes. At this range, it was a nobrainer.

"Skeeter, you have to—"

The MiG broke off suddenly, pulling up sharply and almost stalling, then accelerating away in level flight. I swore, jerked back on the yoke, and rolled out as well. But sixty thousand pounds of Tomcat, even with five hundred and sixty-five square feet of wing area, is not near as maneuverable as a MiG-31. He had time to cut a hole in the sky and come back around to be directly overhead before I saw level flight.

"The little bastard—let's see if he can keep up with this!" I swung the Tomcat around and went back into a steep, bone-rattling climb.

"No point in it now," Sheila said, disgust heavy in her voice. "Do you realize what you just did? Skeeter, you idiot—why don't you ever listen to me?"

"What the hell do you mean?"

Admiral Magruder's voice over tactical answered the question for me. "Tomcat 101, RTB."

"Return to base? What the hell for?" I asked, tactfully keeping my finger off the Transmit button.

Sheila answered immediately, "Don't you listen to the briefs? We had a seven thousand altitude restriction, you idiot. He suckered you, big time. And you followed him right down, right to the edge of the envelope. He had time to pull out before he broke seven thousand feet—you didn't. Six thousand nine hundred and forty-five feet—you lose."

"No fair!" I said. "We got off two Sidewinders before we reached—"

"You broke the altitude restriction—you were dead before the missiles left your wing," Sheila said wearily. "Quit arguing and answer the admiral, Skeeter."

I paused a second, collecting my thoughts. The admiral's voice came over tactical again. "Tomcat 101—acknowledge last transmission. RTB—now!"

Finally, I toggled the mike. "RTB—roger, wilco." I

didn't bother to ask why. The admiral knew—and now, so did I.

We were only twenty minutes out from the base, but it seemed to take forever to get back there. The air was cold and clear, perfect flying weather, but somehow I was enjoying it a hell of a lot less than normal. It was the same Tomcat curled around me, a metal shell that felt like my second home. The reassuring thrum of the turbofan engines, the familiar heads-up display that almost felt like a part of me—none of that had changed. It was still the most powerful fighter ever built, a hell of a lot better than the MiG-31.

The aircraft hadn't failed—I had.

There was no use trying to blame it on Sheila, or bemoaning the fact that the MiG pilot had a guy on the ground feeding him information and keeping him from breaking through the artificial barriers set up for our engagement. The GCI concept is wrong, way wrong. Fighter pilots have to be free to operate in wolf packs, choosing their own targets and defining their own engagements. The time lag between aircraft and the guy on the ground is just too great to make for effective combat.

Then how come I'd lost this engagement?

It wasn't real. If it had been real, that MiG would have been dead.

But real didn't matter—not now. We'd set out to prove a particular point and I'd screwed it up by not paying attention to my altitude. Sure, Sheila might have been a little bit louder in warning me, or even the admiral could have spoken up—no, no use trying to find somewhere else to fit the blame. Flying the aircraft was my responsibility, and mine alone. Sheila had her hands full with the radar and targeting at that point, and even though she'd started to warn me about the altitude, it wasn't her fault.

Out to the north, I could see a thin, oddly colored line on the horizon. At this altitude, I had an excellent view of the coastline, the array of military bases and commercial points along it. The supertankers, massive and imposing close up, were smaller than matchsticks.

And there was the *Jefferson,* way off, barely visible to the naked eye although we were holding her position solid in the link. I let my hands rest easily on the control and steered out toward her. The sea round her was a dark, angry gray, forbidding and menacing. Ice was already fouling the water around the shoreline, creeping out gradually as the calm seas did nothing to prevent its formation. In closer to land than *Jefferson* I could see two other surface ships, probably the icebreakers we'd been briefed on earlier. It would be their job to insure that *Jefferson* had clean water around her and didn't get mired in the ice. An aircraft carrier is tough, but the hull simply isn't built to withstand the massive pressure that an ice float can bring to bear on man-made metal.

The dark line on the horizon was growing thicker now, and I saw an odd shot of white spark through it. I toggled my ICS. "You see that? Looks like we've got some weather blowing in."

"Yeah, looks like." Sheila's voice was calm and noncommittal. "I guess they know it on the ground."

I shook my head. "They should, if they've got the same weather prediction capabilities that the United States has. Do they?"

"How should I know?"

"Well, I better let them know when we get back down during debrief. We're supposed to be flying every day for the next couple of weeks, but if that shit rolls in there's not a chance in hell of us getting up tomorrow. Too bad."

"Well, maybe they'll take us on a sight-seeing tour."

"Wonderful. Just what I joined the Navy for." I couldn't keep up the light banter, pretending that nothing had happened back there. "Sheila—I blew it. Sorry, buddy."

There was a vague note of amusement in her voice when she answered. "What, Skeeter apologizing? You practicing up for what you're going to say to the admiral? Because if you are, let me tell you that I don't think that's going to cut it."

"I'm not apologizing, I just— Hell, I guess I am. I should have been watching the altitude more closely."

Just then, the air traffic controller's voice came on, directing me to a new vector for approach on the base. I lined up on the radial he indicated and glanced down at my altimeter. "Funny, they're starting our approach out this high."

"Tomcat 101, request you maintain angels seven on inbound radial. Currently show you at angels eight."

"Angels eight?" I said out loud. I glanced back down at the altimeter. We were at eight thousand five hundred feet according to my altimeter. What the—?

"Altitude—Skeeter, check your altimeter settings. Now!" Sheila said.

I clicked on the mike. "Request revised altimeter setting for Arkhangel'sk," I said.

The altimeter is one of those funny little instruments onboard an aircraft that will get you killed as fast as a missile. One of the first things you do on approach to a new airfield is reset the altimeter according to your charts. If you leave the altimeter set on, say, San Diego—basically at sea level—and you try to land at an airfield significantly above sea level, you'll discover the ground far sooner than you expect to.

I'd reset the altimeter according to our charts during our approach on Arkhangel'sk. The numbers came back to my mind—twenty-nine forty-nine. I glanced down at the setting. It read twenty-nine sixty.

I started swearing, while I flipped the numbers back to the right setting for Arkhangel'sk. "Damn it, somebody's been in here—Sheila, they tampered with our altimeter!"

"That explains it," she said, her dawning comprehension clear in her voice. "Skeeter, I didn't want to say anything. Your ego's big enough as it is, but I've never known you to keep up that lousy of an instrument scan. It's not your fault you were below altitude—somebody tampered with the altimeter. It was reading well above seven thousand feet when you were actually below seven thousand feet."

"I should have checked it," I said.

"We both should have."

"That sneaky bastard," I muttered. "Not enough that he tries to trip me, but playing with a man's altimeter can get somebody killed." Summaries that I'd read of too many aircraft mishaps flashed through my mind. Altimeter mistakes and lousy weather were responsible for too many pilots auguring into the side of a mountain. That I'd failed to catch that error pissed me off. "Wait till the admiral hears about this."

"Are you really going to tell him?" Sheila asked quietly. "You put yourself on report for that."

I shook my head, realizing that I was in a no-win situation. If I kicked up a stink about the altered altimeter, Admiral Magruder would know I'd screwed up on my preflight. Additionally, it would sound like I was whining. I couldn't prove that the Russians had tinkered with it, and I'd just look like a sore loser.

"What do you think?" I asked finally.

"We keep quiet and eat this one," Sheila said promptly. "But now that we know, we double-check it next time. The altimeter, and everything else, including the fuel. Real, real, carefully. And then we kick some Russian ass."

"I'd like that," I said when she'd finished, rather gratified at her vengeful tone of voice. "I'd really, really like that."

"Skeeter, level flight—no maneuvering!" Sheila said suddenly. "Don't twitch a muscle."

"Why?" I asked, although I obeyed her command immediately.

"It's that little bastard MiG. Looks like he wants to play some games." Her voice was grim.

I craned my neck back around to see. I saw him immediately, the MiG-31, barreling down out of the sky toward me in a steep dive. He pulled up in front of me, maybe half a mile ahead, waggled his wings from side to side for a moment, then executed a series of flawless barrel rolls. He pulled out of that smoothly, gracefully, dived under me then reappeared on the other side, looping around and around me like some sort of insane porpoise.

I swore quietly. "He wants to see aerobatics, does he? Well, let me just show him—"

"Not a twitch, Skeeter," Sheila warned again. "You don't know what he's doing. Two aircraft pulling unbriefed maneuvers in the same airspace is a guarantee that something's going to get fucked."

I kept on swearing, knowing she was right. Bad enough that the little MiG bastard was rubbing it in, but if I started pulling the same shit to show him what a Tomcat could really do, our chances of a mishap increased dramatically. So for now it was straight and level, vectoring back into the air base with my new altimeter setting and planning my revenge.

From inside a Tomcat, a Russian airfield feels pretty much like an American one. Easier to land on than an aircraft carrier, and international standardization of airfield markings and directions indicators makes getting around fairly straightforward. A white truck with follow-me lights was waiting to direct us to our assigned spot. Sheila and I ran the shutdown checklist quickly, but by the time we were finished, the admiral was already waiting for me just off the flight line.

I popped out a sharp salute and waited for the blast that was sure to come. To my surprise, Tombstone just stared levelly at me. "Admiral, about what happened up there . . . ," I began, and then let my voice trail off as I realized he wasn't looking for answers. I had the uneasy feeling this was going to be a one-way conversation. Just then, Sheila stepped forward. She saluted, then touched Gator lightly on the elbow and drew him off to the side for some RIO to RIO talk, leaving me alone with the admiral.

"Good move, Skeeter," the admiral said finally. "I liked the way you suckered him into revealing more about his performance capabilities. I don't think we've ever seen a MiG pull that dramatic of a maneuver before."

"What? You mean you think I—"

The admiral cut me off before I had a chance to dig myself even deeper. "Exactly the sort of intelligence we're here to gather," he murmured, motioning me to follow him back to the air control terminal. "Good work." I followed him, too stunned by his comments to start explaining. Was it possible that the admiral thought I'd really planned that maneuver just for that purpose? Or was he just offering me up a face-saving excuse?

And what did Sheila have to talk to the other RIO about that was so urgent? The altimeter, probably. While she might not want me making excuses to the admiral for my mistakes—hell, it wasn't excuse, it was reason!—she'd probably want to make sure that the admiral's own RIO double-checked their own altimeter before their first flight. Fool us once, shame on us; fool us twice—I let the thought go, oddly reassured by the admiral's explanation.

Even if it weren't true.

The Russians' version of a bachelor officers quarters were no great shakes. It was more spartan than anything I'd run into in the United States Navy. Damn near as uninhabitable as my own compartment onboard *Jefferson*. Before the modifications we'd made, I mean. Over a period of months onboard a carrier, you get around to customizing your compartment so it's not quite as bleak. My roommates and I had come up with a TV, a VCR, and a bitchin' stereo system that routinely drove the people next to us batty.

The Russian BOQ room was more like a cell. It held a narrow, uncomfortable cot and a chair. That was it. The head facilities were down the hall. Two showers, and I didn't hold out much for a good supply of hot water, judging from how grimy they looked. There were windows to the outside, no curtains or blinds, and I could already feel the cold radiating in through the thin, single-paned window. The shower curtains in the head looked slightly mildewed, and the toilet bowl was rimmed with rust stains inside.

I changed, sponged off the sweat as best I could, and got ready for the evening meal. The admiral had said it would be a formal affair, and I wasn't looking forward to it.

At the prearranged time, an escort picked us up to go to the banquet in the Russian officers club. Sheila, I was surprised to see, was tricked out in her skirt and heels. I was in my dress blues, the two stripes on my dress blue sleeves outnumbered by her two and a half.

We slipped into the overcrowded, stuffy room like we owned it. It was packed with Russians, all in what I figured were probably their best dress uniforms. There were aguillettes, medals dangling, and more brass than I'd ever seen in one place before. After the debacle of earlier that day, I felt like everyone was staring at me. Not only was I the most junior of just about anybody around, I was the one who'd screwed the pooch.

Or at least I was supposed to think I was. For now, Sheila and I were going to let them think that they had us fooled.

"I know something," I heard a female voice slightly behind me say. I turned to find a woman, a civilian by her dress, standing just behind me looking up at me. She was noticeably shorter than I was, her head barely reaching my shoulder level. Long auburn hair flamed in a crown on her head, spilling down her back in luxurious curls. Her eyes were brown, large and doe-like, and she stared at me with a look that was somewhere between lust and amusement. "About the flight today, I mean." She spoke English well, with only a slight trace of an accent.

I smiled at her. "A lot of people know a lot about today," I said. "We haven't had the pleasure. Lieutenant Skeeter Harmon." I extended my hand.

"Anna Doysta," she answered, slipping her small, cool hand into mine. Despite her slight size, she gripped my hand with surprising strength. "Of course, I know who you are. We all do. I was hoping for an opportunity to meet with you tonight." Her smile broadened, as though to leave no doubt about what she meant.

I laughed despite myself. "My pleasure, Anna," I said agreeably. "I suspect you'll be the high point of my evening, as well." I waved my hand at the assembled gaggle of officers and civilians. "And just where do you fit in to this operation?"

I was already sure I knew. She was charming, and certainly beautiful, and within the space of a few seconds had managed to stroke my ego in a way that few American women did. Certainly not Sheila Kennedy, my all too capable RIO and running mate.

But how foolish did the Russians think I was? I knew who Anna worked for, even if she would never admit it. This was the very sort of thing we'd been cautioned against by Lab Rat, an approach by an attractive member of the opposite sex while we were in Russia.

"But you must know what I do," she said, her tone of voice playful and amused, as though letting me in on a big secret. "They've talked to you, yes? I am a spy, of course." She gave a gentle, lilting laugh, as though to belie the seriousness of her answer. "At least, I am employed as one. Although there are very little opportunities for spying these days, at least in the last five years. I had hoped for a more glamorous career, but unfortunately my area of expertise is primarily agricultural. You know, finding out deep, dark secrets about Ukrainian wheat production, the Turkish soybean crop." She waved her hand in a small, dismissing motion. "Not what I expected when I joined the KGB."

"You're very up front about it," I stammered, trying to get my balance. I knew it, she knew it—but to admit it just like that? Glasnost and peristroika had gone a whole hell of a lot further than I ever imagined.

"Tonight, I am off duty," she said, her voice firm. "No spying—and I do not know enough about aircraft or airplanes to do a very good job of it, anyway. So shall we enjoy the evening? How are you finding your time in Russia?"

"Not what I had planned so far," I admitted. There was something completely and entirely disarming about her, a spy who admitted she was one. Especially a spy that looked like she did. "I didn't do so hot today."

She nodded. "I heard." She took a step closer and laid one hand on the crook of my arm. "You must be very, very careful," she said, speaking quietly. "I'm a very good spy—at least, in my area. I hear the others talk. When you go back to your aircraft, please check carefully this equipment called an altimeter." She stumbled slightly over the word, as though she'd never used it in conversation before. "You went too low, but I do not think it was entirely your fault." She glanced over at an assembled gaggle of Russian pilots. I could tell they were pilots from this distance, watching the arm movements as they reenacted the day's engagement for each other. "They do not like to lose—not for any reason. It was not your fault you were outside of the envelope." Again, her words sounded slightly awkward, as though she were unused to talking aviation or using the terminology of the trade. That, more than her self-proclaimed declaration that she was an agricultural spy, reassured me.

"What makes you say that?" I asked. I glanced over to see where Sheila was, wondering if I ought to get her in on this. But she was preoccupied with an American attaché officer. The diplomatic corps had turned out en masse for this function. They'll do anything for free booze.

I tried to get some more details out of Anna, but she turned my questions away deftly but pleasantly. She'd said all she was going to. Maybe if I'd had a chance to talk it over with Sheila, I might have figured out a way to get her to open up.

Anna's presence livened up the otherwise deadly dull proceedings of a formal dinner. She claimed the seat next to mine at one of the tables, and Sheila sat across the table from us with her tame attaché in tow. I caught her shooting hostile glances at Anna several times, but ignored it. RIOs, particularly female ones, tend to have a rather proprietary attitude about their pilots.

But there was nothing going on, nothing at all between Anna and me. There couldn't be. First off, I knew she was a spy, and getting involved personally with her to any degree would have resulted in a lot more paperwork than I even wanted to think about. Second, Admiral Magruder had already taken a look at us, shot me a warning glance that would have scorched the skin off a turtle, and was still keeping us under observation.

We talked about everything in the world except flying, ate, and I even allowed myself one shot glass of vodka. One, no more, not if I had to fly the next day.

At one point, after the dinner broke up and we were on the way out, I had a chance to introduce her to Admiral Magruder. Anna seemed quite taken with him, even stepped up close to whisper in his ear. Whatever she said to him made him go pale, but he merely nodded politely to her. Altimeters, maybe? Or something else?

Finally, the evening ended. I was tired by then, drained from the culture shock and disappointment of the day's flying, but determined that tomorrow would be different.

The BOQ was quiet and cold when I got back. I stopped in the head long enough to contemplate the probability of hot water, then gave it up as a lost cause after I'd let it run for about thirty minutes with no appreciable change in the temperature. I cleaned up the best I could and hit the rack.

Tomorrow would be another day—and one the Russians might not like nearly as much as I liked Anna.

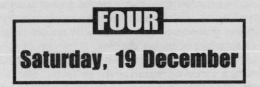

FOUR

Saturday, 19 December

0800 Local (+3 GMT)
Arkhangel'sk, Russia

Vice Admiral Tombstone Magruder:

The transition from life at sea to life ashore is always a bit awkward for me. It's odd to realize that more than half of my adult life has been spent living on aircraft carriers, in accommodations ranging from the cramped rabbit warrens of junior officer berthing to the more luxurious accommodations afforded a flag officer. Ashore, before my marriage to Tomboy, I'd lived in a series of increasingly comfortable and spacious apartments and town homes, occasionally buying one for a couple of years during a shore tour, only to revert to renter status with my next deployment. Being surrounded by the gray bulkheads of a Navy ship has more the sense of home to me than the plasterboard walls and brick of an apartment or house ashore.

Thus, when I awoke the first morning on Russian soil, the sense of disorientation didn't unduly alarm me. The first few days ashore were always like that.

It set in deeper, however, as I realized where I was. My compartment in the senior officers quarters at Arkhangel'sk base were almost comparable to those I would have been afforded in a U.S. Navy facility. They were spacious, consisting of two large rooms comprising a suite. Both the bedroom and the sitting room were furnished in an ornate, ponderous decor replete with gilt and heavy brocade. The entire effect was one of leftover Czarist regalia rather than bleak Communist accommodations.

At one end of the sitting room was a small, efficiency-style kitchen. I availed myself of the coffeepot, after sniffing suspiciously at the slightly stale brown grounds that were labeled "coffee" in Russian. I don't speak much Russian, just what I remember from a year of it at the Academy, but I knew the alphabet well enough to translate most of the more common words. While the coffee was brewing, I hunted down my bathroom and then conducted a more detailed examination of my quarters.

I'd had one-bedroom apartments ashore that contained less total square footage than these two rooms and the private head. The bathroom in particular was a study in contradictions, with a heavy archaic claw-footed tub side-by-side with a modern glassed-in shower cubicle. I tried the tap experimentally, and found that there was hot water, although it was a bit rusty at the start.

I heard the burbling hiss of the coffeepot in the sitting room cease, and wandered back in for my first cup of the day. I settled into a richly tapestried chair pulled up to a heavy wooden table/work area. Then looked around for a coaster or a saucer, something to prevent making any stain on the beautifully inlaid wood.

I was willing to bet my counterpart in the Russian Navy didn't live quite so well. Reports had surfaced for months that the officers had not been paid for almost six months, and I wondered at the tenacity and devotion to duty that kept them serving even without that. I supposed supporting their families and maintaining living quarters was a different matter under the Communist state, but still—I tried to imagine Tomboy's reaction should my paychecks suddenly cease, and shuddered.

There was a polite tap on the door, followed by scuffling of feet. I downed the rest of my coffee, then, still clad in my bathrobe, went to the door. I opened it a crack and peered out.

Admiral Ilanovich's aide was standing at attention a respectful distance from my doorjamb.

"With compliments from the admiral," he began, his voice stiff and correct. "If the admiral so pleases, would you care to join the admiral for breakfast?"

"Sure. Give me a couple of minutes to get cleaned up and get some clothes on." I opened the door a bit wider. "Come on in, have a seat while you wait. Want some coffee?"

The young Navy officer's face paled. Whatever he expected from the devil American capitalist admiral, it wasn't this. "May it please the admiral," he began, then fell silent as the need for tact exceeded his language abilities. I could see on his face that he was trying to puzzle it out, how to politely and respectfully refuse my invitation without offending this important American visitor.

I sighed. If I insisted, he would come in. Even have a cup of coffee. But the entire event would no doubt be followed by a series of increasingly aggressive interviews by the KGB, GRU, Border Patrol, or whatever else passed for internal security in the Russian society today. I wouldn't force that on him.

"I'll be right out," I said, and shut the door firmly behind me. I thought I heard a sigh of relief as I did so.

I hurried through my morning routine, not skimping but not overdoing it either. This was a breakfast between equals, not a command performance on my part. I would go, I would talk politely with the admiral, but I would not be intimidated. Not even after yesterday.

I paused while shaving, and reviewed the results of Skeeter's first engagement the day before. He'd been a fool, a damned fool to violate the imaginary floor set for the engagement. I'd been ready to scalp him alive, until I realized how that would look to our Russian hosts. I was glad I resisted that first murderous impulse when my RIO took me aside and quietly explained what had actually happened.

The altimeter—well, we'd make doubly certain we checked mine today, along with everything else that I had learned could go wrong in over twenty years of flying

Tomcats. I doubted that the Russians wanted to kill us—or to seriously sabotage our aircraft in any way. But if there were ways to subtly make us look inferior, to insure Russian superiority in each flying engagement, I wouldn't put tricks like the altimeter past them.

I had more to worry about than altimeters, though. Skeeter's little friend had made that clear. In a few quickly whispered phrases, she'd indicated that she knew why I was here. And, moreover, that she was going to help me.

It was her last sentence that worried me the most. Worried me, and at the same time sent a thrill of joy skittering down through my guts. *He's alive.*

How could she know? *What* could she know?

I finished shaving, then stared at the small array of clothes I'd brought with me, deciding what to wear. Finally, I settled on my favorite—a worn, well-washed flight suit, its fabric softened to the texture of chamois cloth by repeated trips to the mangling machinery of the ship's laundry. Maybe too informal, but it's what I would have worn every morning given a choice.

I reconsidered at the last moment. The khakis, perhaps. Ribbons, my wings—yes, the khakis. I slid the flight suit back into my closet with a small sigh of regret and slipped into the khakis.

The young guard was still standing at attention outside my doorway when I finally emerged ten minutes later. He stiffened, clicked his feet together audibly, and rendered another sharp salute. I returned it casually and said, "Lead on, son."

"At once, Admiral." He hesitated, as though waiting for me to precede him, until I pointed out, "I'm not sure I know the way. Would you please go first?"

He nodded, and led the way down a passage to the front door of the quarters. The reception area was furnished in the same style as my quarters, improbably elaborate for a bastion of Communist virtue. A Zil sedan was waiting outside for us, a driver standing at attention next to the backseat passenger's door. The engine was running and gouts of steam spewed from the tailpipe in the frosty air.

I slid into the backseat, grateful for those perquisites of rank that allow one to insist on a preheated car in the morning. Nice in Washington, D.C., almost critical here in northern Russia.

The sky was still brilliant and blue, the air cold and thick. Perfect flying weather if there were no danger of icing. Aircraft love cold air, since it's more dense and provides more lift.

Ten minutes later, we pulled up in front of Admiral Ilanovich's residence. Before I could even start to get out, the young Navy officer had popped out of the front seat and rushed to open my door. He saluted again as I emerged, and again I acknowledged the courtesy. The driver stayed with the car. I wondered if he would keep the engine running until breakfast was over.

Admiral Ilanovich was waiting for me, in a small, bright room at the back of the house. As I walked into the room, he gestured to a cook, who disappeared from the room, and returned shortly with steaming covered platters and fresh coffee.

We exchanged morning pleasantries, comments about the weather, and I expressed appreciation for his invitation and remarked on the luxury of my accommodations. Admiral Ilanovich gestured expansively. "We are honored at your visit. It is the least we can do, to show our appreciation for your participation in this opportunity to strengthen ties between our two services."

Tactfully put, I thought. I sipped the cup of coffee his steward had placed in front of me, noting it was a better quality than that stocked in my room. Evidently the lack of normal paychecks was not having a serious effect on the admiral's own lifestyle, though I wondered about that of his subordinates.

"So, we fly today, yes?" the admiral said pleasantly. "I am quite looking forward to it."

"So am I," I said, reaching out to take another biscuit from the warm, cloth-covered bowl. "It must be the same for you as for me—entirely not enough time flying, is there?"

Ilanovich chuckled. "Our duties ashore take up far too much time, do they not? I wonder, my friend—I may call you that, I hope—if you've ever considered whether it might be possible to decline a promotion? Have you ever been so tempted, as I have been?" He leaned back in his chair and patted his stomach appreciatively at the breakfast. "After all, we joined our services to fly, not to sign our name to what must be every piece of paper required to run our great fleets."

I had to laugh at that. "Of course, I've considered that. But it was no more a possibility, not really, for me than for you. Rank has its responsibilities, does it not?"

"And its privileges." Admiral Ilanovich leaned across the table to stare at me. "For instance, I was allowed to nominate myself for this particular goodwill mission. As a result, I was able to justify much more time flying this last month than I normally would have had. After all, it would not do for me to be out of practice when meeting so formidable an adversary as the famous Tombstone Magruder."

"I'm afraid my reputation is overestimated," I said slowly, not sure where the conversation was headed at this point. What point was he trying to make, that he'd researched my career and knew a bit about my flying? That was no surprise—I would hardly have expected less.

Similarly, our own U.S. intelligence agencies had provided me with a wealth of professional data on Admiral Ilanovich. I knew he'd spent extensive time flying in Afghanistan, had cut his teeth on ground attack aircraft against those deadly, unpredictable air defenses. He'd risen quickly through the ranks, survived numerous changes in the political climate, and fared even better under Gorbachev. He was one of the few naval officers to survive the dissolution of the Soviet Union and emerge even stronger, in both a political and military sense, afterward. Clearly, whatever his skills in the air, he was just as potent a politician as he was an aviator.

"We will have to make certain that none of our subordinates understand just how much enjoyment we get from flying," I said finally. "And I think you'll find our MILES gear provides a stunningly accurate methodology for reconstructing the engagements."

"Ah yes—the engagements." He smiled blandly, his eyes shuttered and closed. "The original plan was for the best three out of four encounters, both between our younger aviators and between you and me. Is that still satisfactory?"

I nodded. "Entirely so. Unless you had a change of mind?" Now, that would make me uneasy, a change of plans at this late a date.

"No, no—not I." He gestured at the double-paned windows behind us, at the clear sky and brilliant morning sunlight. "But it may be that the weather has other plans for us. There are reports of an approaching storm system that may delay our schedule for several days. All of today should be fine, but later in the week we may have weather problems. I, for one, am not inclined to risk either men or equipment in inclement weather."

"Of course. Never during peacetime." I smiled.

"Peacetime. Yes, it is odd, isn't it?" He glanced out the window, as though reassuring himself that the weather had not changed during the last few seconds. "There are no time limits on our engagement today, my new friend. Given that it has been so long since I've been in combat, perhaps you'll allow a few warm-up maneuvers? It's so rare that I have this chance."

I heard the wistful note in his voice and recognized it immediately. He wouldn't ask outright, not in so many words. But Admiral Ilanovich had just suggested that we dog it for a while in the air, take our time warming up and playing around before we got down to the business at hand. I liked him for that, and agreed immediately.

We finished breakfast on a pleasant note, each assuring the other of our undying friendship and professional respect.

My driver was waiting, with the car engine running. We went through the usual litany of salutes, and I was chauffeured back to my quarters.

Once there, I shed the khakis and slipped into my flight suit. Our first brief was scheduled for a little over two hours from now, so I thought I might head out to the airfield ahead of time and have a look at my bird.

I stuck my head out the door and saw my assigned Russian aide/gopher still standing at attention in the passageway. He looked surprised to see me. "Sir?"

"Let's go out the airfield," I said firmly. The startled look on his face told me all I needed to know—that my escort was not overjoyed at the fact of one Admiral Tombstone Magruder departing from his schedule of activities. But he made no protest, simply allowed me to step in front of him and lead the way out to the front of the building.

My car was waiting there, albeit without the engine running this time. I waited inside at the officer's insistence while he hunted down the driver, had him warm up the car, then bring it up close to the front door to minimize my exposure to the frigid air. I had on my leather flight jacket over my flight suit, as well as my heavy gloves, but the cold still bit into me with all the viciousness of arctic air.

Ilanovich had mentioned an approaching storm, but I saw no trace of it right now. Still, I could imagine how quickly it might develop. How utterly impassable the roads would become with an additional five to six feet of snow dumped on them.

We approached the hangar, and the driver spoke briefly into a portable radio lying on the seat next to him. The heavy doors rolled out of the way, and we pulled to a stop inside the hangar itself.

The two Tomcats were carefully spotted some distance apart from each other, and there was no indication of any untoward activity taking place around either one. The driver had pulled up in front of my own bird, the double nuts one.

This time, I let myself out of the backseat before the officer could scurry around to open it for me. I walked up to my Tomcat, and ran a hand over the smooth, sleek skin. It was freshly painted, lustrous and unmarred by overwork.

"Does the admiral require assistance?" my officer escort asked, now clearly nervous. I shook my head and waved a hand in dismissal. Enough of playing the games—I wanted some time alone to look at my aircraft.

The officer took up station a short distance away, again falling into a stiff parade rest position. The driver remained with the car, evidently at a loss. I started around the aircraft, first checking the nose wheel gear and the struts. I looked for evidence of any leaks, of any working or fraying on the joints, or anything out of the ordinary. There was nothing—indeed it looked as though someone might have wiped it down with a soft rag to remove any traces of dust or grime.

I moved on to the avionics bays, checking to make sure each door was still securely locked. I produced the ring of keys from a side pocket of my flight suit and opened each door carefully, checking for any evidence of tampering. Not that our locks would have kept any really determined spy out, but at least I could hope there might be some evidence of tampering.

There was nothing. I rapped experimentally on one wing—yes, the bird had been fueled, but that appeared to be it.

"Good morning, Admiral." I recognized the voice of my RIO, even from a distance. "You're up early, sir."

"Just wanted to get a look at her, Gator." I patted the double nuts bird lightly on the fuselage. "You're pretty early, yourself."

My RIO shook his head. "Got bored so I thought I'd come on down here and take a look at her." I read the unspoken suspicion in his face. We went over the Tomcat thoroughly for about an hour, lapsing into the easy companionship a pilot-RIO team should have. We talked tactics, emergency procedures, and we both had one factor clearly in mind during that. There would be no ejection over water, not if there were any way to avoid it. Our chances of survival would be so close to zero as to preclude any discussion of the matter.

Our adversaries showed up about an hour later, along with the umpire selected for the engagement. Of course, the MILES gear was the ultimate arbitrator of win-loss. We reviewed again the ground rules for the engagements, reemphasizing the altitude limitations. Off to my right I saw Skeeter wince slightly at that, but there was no help for it.

Grueling and brutal honesty is the only way to keep pilots from repeating each other's mistakes.

Neither Admiral Ilanovich nor I made any mention of our discussion over breakfast. But the understanding hung in the air, a clear gentleman's agreement between us. We'd both adhere to it, I knew, as long as we were certain the other fellow was, but national pride would demand that that all change in a heartbeat if it looked like the other guy was cheating.

Cheating—an oddly mild word to use about aerial combat. But then, these were odd circumstances.

Finally, interminable safety discussions later, our aircraft were towed out of the hangar by the ubiquitous yellow gear that dots every airfield, and positioned on their assigned spots. Gator and I ran one final preflight around the outside, double-checking the smell and consistency of the fuel. We agreed that everything looked all right, and Gator stepped back to let me precede him into the aircraft. I could feel the cold seeping in through my flight boots, even though I'd worn two pairs of socks. It gnawed away at my leather gloves through the steps up the side of the Tomcat, and if any part of my skin had been exposed, I know it would have frozen to the metal immediately.

I slid into my seat, wincing slightly as the cold plastic of it seeped in through my butt. My nuts drew up close to my body, frantic to escape the icy temperatures. The Russian technician who followed me in was thoroughly professional, checking the ejection harness and removing the safety cotter pins from the ejection seat. I kept my hands carefully clear of the ejection handle—surviving an inadvertent ejection while on the ground was only slightly more probable than living through an ejection over the frigid Northern Sea.

Off to my right, I saw Admiral Ilanovich undergoing a similar procedure in his aircraft. He ran through his checklist, and I heard the metallic grumble of his engines start up before we were ready. Gator and I paced through the required items on our NATOPS thoroughly, following the book letter by letter. Finally, we, too, were ready. The air inside the cockpit was starting to warm up from our combined body heat, and a huffer was standing by in case we needed its auxiliary compressed air to get a clean start on the engine.

At the signal from the yellow shirt, I engaged the engines, letting them idle and warm up for a few minutes before applying any additional power. Start-up had to be done carefully in these climates, since uneven heating as the engine turned could warp the micromillimeter clearances in our powerful engines. There was a little roughness in the beginning, nothing out of ordinary, and then the turbofans settled into their voracious, all-encompassing roar. I double-checked our radio circuits, got clearance from the tower, and then commenced the taxi. I let the admiral precede us into the air, waited until the turbulence he'd started up on the strip had dissipated, then eased the Tomcat forward.

We picked up speed quickly, and I luxuriated in the expanse of runway before me. Ever since I cleared the training pipeline, most of my takeoffs in a Tomcat had been off an aircraft carrier. Now there was no catapult to worry about, no jam-packed acceleration and quick leap into the air. I eased the Tomcat up off the runway, rotated smartly, and started climbing.

Following directions from the air traffic controller, radar still in a standby mode, I proceeded to our assigned patch of air to orbit and wait for the signal to commence. It came quickly, and I could hear Skeeter in the background in the control tower monitoring everything that went on.

Gator flipped the radar into search mode, and the picture sprang to life in my heads-up display. A few seconds of noise, which quickly dissipated into normal clutter and one solid, sharply outlined target.

"Tally-ho," I said. Gator clicked his mike once in acknowledgment. I put the Tomcat in a turn to the right, vectoring in on the admiral's position. I slammed the throttles forward, edging into afterburner zone, but refrained from kicking it in just yet. While Admiral Ilanovich was right about having made some excuses for extra stick time during the last month, I knew that I was still not at my best.

I'd been better, during the days that I was flying every day, launching in all sorts of weather and seeking out the elusive three wire under the worst imaginable conditions. Better to let it come back slow, get back in the saddle, and to squeeze every bit of enjoyment I could out of this hop. I hoped the admiral in the other aircraft was doing the same.

As though by telepathy, we settled in for a gentle game of angles, maintaining altitude and whipping our aircraft around in increasingly tight turns without varying altitude. I let the admiral sneak in behind me, gave him two seconds to set up for a shot, then cut hard away. He stayed on my tail easily, dropping back a bit so he could cut inside my turning radius if he wanted to. He didn't, but the way he handled his aircraft let me know that he could if he wanted to.

Good, so far he was abiding by the rules. The private ones we'd set up between ourselves, not the ones for public consumption.

I heard Gator scratching some notes in the back, recording his impressions of the MiG's maneuverability while I did the flying.

Admiral Ilanovich broke away suddenly, putting the MiG into a steep climb. I gave him a head start, then tipped the Tomcat's nose up and kicked in the afterburners. In the backseat, Gator grunted, performing what we call the M1 maneuver. It's a series of tensing gut muscles and exhaling and grunting, intended to force blood to keep circulating in the brain during high G operations.

The Tomcat quickly overtook the MiG, easily catching her and passing her in a matter of seconds. Under normal combat circumstances, I would have eased off, slid in behind him, and gone for the killing shot up the tailpipe. As I passed him, the admiral waggled his wings, indicating by our private code that he would have initiated chafe and flares at that point to distract the Sidewinder. Even odds in my mind as to whether or not the decoys would have worked.

"Watch the sun," Gator warned.

"I've got it, I've got it," I said. And indeed I did— keeping an eye on the sun was an essential part of fighter tactics, particularly when you like to use a Sidewinder or IR seeking missile. The dumber shots get decoyed by the heat source and can sail off toward outer space, trying to home in on the sun.

But there was little way I could miss it now, since it was glaring through the windscreen at me, bouncing hard and brilliant off every metal surface around me. The heads-up display looked slightly washed out, and I turned the Tomcat slightly to clear up the image.

We were leading the MiG now, still widening the gap between us and demonstrating the superior weight-to-power factor inherent in the Tomcat's design. I stayed well inside the edge of our envelope, not wanting to give away any more tactical information than I had to. Undoubtedly the Russian admiral knew a whole lot about Tomcats—but there was no point in confirming anything that might still be theoretical at this point.

We fell into a series of gentle yo-yos, the same maneuver that had trapped Skeeter the day earlier. Admiral Ilanovich repeatedly cut out of the pattern and rolled back in on my tail, while I hope I surprised him a couple of times by pulling up well short of where he thought I was going to be and circling in behind him. This wasn't a dogfight—it was more like two cats playing with a mouse. Each stalking and pouncing at the other without really intending to kill.

The sheet joy of flying carried me up on a wave of euphoria, giving me a feeling of sheer exhilaration and joy. This is what I had joined the Navy for, this all-encompassing and engrossing business of bonding with a piece of metal and putting it through its paces in the air. Who would have thought twenty years ago that I would be soaring out under the frigid northern sun, twisting and maneuvering in the air against a Russian MiG without one of us dying?

In the last fifteen minutes of the engagement, as we'd agreed upon, we both got down to business. We were still in a rolling scissors, when Admiral Ilanovich cut sharply in behind me, turning the formerly gentle banks and turns into a hard, braking reversal. Before I knew it, he'd come around and was climbing up my ass. Gator's ALR-67 gear spouted off a quick series of beeps, indicating that he had us targeted.

I activated countermeasures, spewing out flares and chafes over the frozen ground below. Just as they departed the fuselage, I jammed the Tomcat's nose down, increasing the altitude separation between us to almost two hundred feet. He may have been dogging it on his turn characteristics, but I had a trick up my sleeve as well. It was one that he'd no doubt read about, had probably even studied, but I hoped he was as lulled into the rhythm of our aerial maneuverings as I had been. We drew ahead of the MiG, and the tempo of the beeping increased. Just as I was sure Ilanovich was about to launch, I popped the wings out of their swept-back design, overriding the automatic configuration control. I also popped the speed brakes.

The effect was like stomping on the brake of a moving car. The Tomcat lost speed dramatically, immediately, quickly slowing to almost stall speed. Within a second, the MiG overshot us, and I jammed the throttles back forward to full afterburner and restored the swept-wing configuration of the aircraft. Now we were on his tail, our radar in targeting mode and IR seeking missiles at the ready.

"Fox two, fox two," I said over tactical, indicating that I'd launched a heat seeker at the MiG. I rolled out of the pursuit, rolled away from his line of travel, pitched the nose of the Tomcat up, and started gaining altitude as fast as I could. Ilanovich saw me, pulled off one of those amazingly tight turns that I now knew he was capable of, and started following me into the air. There was no way he could catch me, but as soon as he steadied up on a course behind me, I cut to the right and broke out of the turn, circling back around to go head-on-head with him. "Fox three," I called, claiming a Sparrow launch.

Even as the words left my mouth, I saw the MiG jink violently, curving around underneath me and coming up behind in an attempt to break the missile lock. I heard the seeker head warble, then die out, indicating we'd lost lock. Before Ilanovich could settle in for the killing shot, I tipped the Tomcat over and was heading for the deck. Mindful of the seven-thousand-feet altitude limitation, I pulled up well ahead of the boundary, giving myself a margin of safety. Ilanovich appeared to have lost me briefly, but quickly reacquired. He came down after me, staying slightly above me and attempting to prevent another wild race for the sky. I was trapped between the MiG and the imaginary earth. I needed airspeed and distance.

Back in the afterburners, jinking and rolling and trying to prevent a missile lock. I turned at every opportunity, trying to avoid presenting that all too attractive engine exhaust to his heat seekers. Finally, I twisted away from him and headed for the open sky again.

Instead of the beautiful textbook example of a vertical rolling scissors, this was true dogfighting. I broke off my ascent suddenly, striving for minimum turn radius, wheeling and darting about in the sky as the MiG kept up with me. He could cut inside my turn radius at every opportunity, if he knew which way I was going. I feinted once, then curved back around to climb up his ass again. "Fox three!"

"Time is up, admirals," the air controller announced. "Please return to base, at your convenience." The message was repeated in Russian, although we knew Ilanovich's English was good enough that he'd understood it the first time.

"Well, what do you think?" I asked Gator, as I put the Tomcat in a gentle bank back toward the airfield. "We win that one?"

"I think so, Tombstone," Gator said thoughtfully. "That first Sidewinder shot—he wouldn't have had a chance after that. The one after you guys got serious, I mean."

"Yeah, I think so. But then again, he was within guns range for a bit there. We could have sustained some damage and not even known about it. If it had been for real." I let his reference to our initial easy pace go unchallenged.

I landed first, with Admiral Ilanovich not far behind. Being back on deck brought me down off the high I'd been experiencing in the air, and I felt almost disgruntled as I ran through the preshutdown checklist.

Admiral Ilanovich met us on the tarmac, midway between the two aircraft. I offered a salute as he approached, but he surprised me by simply walking up and throwing his arms around me for a quick, hard hug.

"It was good, so very good," he said enthusiastically. His pale face had taken on a new ruddiness, and his eyes were shining with the sheer pleasure of the flying we'd gotten in.

"It was, wasn't it?" I punched him lightly in the shoulder. "Damn you, for that last turn." He knew which one I meant, the one that would have surely sent a heat seeker up my butt if it had been for real.

"Ah, but your altitude—may I compliment you, Admiral, on your airmanship? It was truly a pleasure to fly with you." There was no denying the sincerity in his voice.

"And you as well. Perhaps we should call this one a draw, do you think?" I asked. I gestured up to the tower. "There may be points scored and decisions made, but between you and me, it was very, very close."

"Agreed—it was a draw." He rubbed his face with one hand, leaving a bright, ruddy mark on his skin. "I do have some influence with the judges, you know."

"I don't doubt it. Again tomorrow?"

"If the weather permits," he agreed.

We were back at the hangar by then, still buoyed up by the feeling of companionable competition. Skeeter and his counterpart were walking out to meet us, and the atmosphere between them was clearly not one of good fellowship. I nudged Ilanovich in the ribs, and he laughed. "I hope they don't realize how much fun we've been having," I said.

"I will not tell them if you do not."

We left it at that and went over to talk to our respective team members. I heard the younger Russian aviator's voice. Hard, almost sharp, but maintaining the line between courtesy and inquisition. Skeeter was just barely more tactful with me.

"Admiral Magruder!" I turned to see a man walking across the tarmac toward me, a pleasant expression on his face. "Congratulations on the fine flight, sir." His English was clear and unaccented. I frowned, trying to remember his name from the banquet the night before.

"I have some information for you," he said, when we were clear of earshot of everyone else. "I am to tell you — go west." With those words, he passed a small packet over to me, shielding his movements from view with his body. I took the packet immediately, and tucked it into my flight suit, careful to keep anyone, even Skeeter, from noticing.

Lab Rat had told me we might meet men such as this, contacts from the other agencies that had interests around the world. With those two words *go west* this man had irretrievably engaged my interest. I knew instinctively, with a sudden, deep surety, that within the package I would find the next step on the trail to finding my father.

He hadn't mentioned the woman I'd met the previous night, though. What was her name — Anna something? Were they working together? Anna was undoubtedly Russian, and Skeeter had filled me in on her occupation as an agricultural spy. Just what did her duties include? I'd made it a point to remind Skeeter to keep his little head under control, warning him I'd have the Cossacks castrate him if he slept with her. He'd assured me of his pure and innocent intentions, although from the look that Sheila sent him, I had some doubts. But I thought if anybody could keep him under control, she could.

So what now? Wait for Anna's people to contact me again? Or break off on my own, follow whatever instructions were included in the package that'd just been passed to me?

Or — last and least satisfying — do nothing. Look through whatever the man had slipped me and wait for one of them to approach me again.

I decided to do just that. After all, I'd been waiting for thirty years already. A few more days wouldn't hurt.

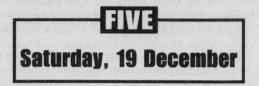

FIVE

Saturday, 19 December

1300 Local (+3 GMT)
Arkhangel'sk, Russia

Lieutenant Skeeter Harmon:

Lunch was pretty decent, probably better than decent by Russian standards. There was something that looked like beef stroganoff in one dish on a hot serving-line buffet and I filled up on that. I saw Sheila watching me and grinned evilly at her. We had a deal—no more burritos before flying—but I figured that the Russian version of beef stroganoff wasn't included in that agreement. Last time I'd splurged on Mexican before flying, she said she was either going to start carrying a gas mask or get a new pilot.

I was surprised at the crowd. There were a lot of the same faces as the night before, all evidently wanting another look at the tame Americans. I shot my sleeves a couple of times, showing off my fake Rolex. I figured they wouldn't know the difference.

Anna was there again, too, and promptly attached herself to my side. It was good to see her, and my reaction to her was even stronger this time. Even when your mind knows somebody is probably a Russian spy out to pick your brain for everything you ever knew about the national defense strategy, it's still nice to see a good-looking chick sitting next to you at lunch. Sheila's tame American attaché turned

up as well, all big white teeth and crinkling blue eyes of
him. He was maybe an inch taller than me and looked like
he worked out a lot. Still, I figured I could take him if I
had to.

"So, you are flying again this afternoon?" Anna asked.
She pulled a dish of fresh rolls toward me, nudging me
slightly. "Homemade—the very best bread in Russia," she
said proudly.

"Yeah, another flight this afternoon." I reached for one of
the rolls, felt the thin, butter-glazed surface crack under my
light pressure. Man, these fellows knew how to cook!

"You like flying?" she asked. "That's a good thing, yes?"

I started to answer, but my mouth was still full. I
swallowed hastily, then said, "A very good thing. There's
nothing better in the world than flying, and the Tomcat's the
best aircraft to do it in."

Sheila's American attaché spoke up now, putting in his
two cents' worth on the value of naval aviation. Like any of
us really cared what he thought.

"You know, the Russians have made some big strides in
developing their own version of carrier aviation," he said.
He turned to smile charmingly at Sheila. "But everything
they fly is a single seater. A big mistake, in my estimation."
His smile left no doubt that he was talking about her as a
RIO in particular.

I stifled the irritation I felt crowding the back of my
throat. Man, she wasn't falling for his line, was she? How
obvious could you get—he was damned near trying to look
down the front of her uniform.

But much to my surprise, my normally savvy RIO was
buying it. Big time, from the fawning look she gave him. It
really makes me sick, the way that some women are.

"That's so nice of you to say, Brent," she cooed. "Really,
I'd have to agree with you on that."

I heard a slight, muffled giggle to my right. I looked over
at Anna. She was shaking her head slightly in disbelief.

I grinned. It was as though she could read my mind, and
was agreeing with me about the sheer idiocy of Brent's run
on Sheila.

"You know, Brent," I said loudly, cutting off the love fest that was starting across the table from me, "you'll probably be interested in this afternoon's engagement as well. It's a bombing run, you know? Like when you come in fast and hard on a target and try to pop your load off right on one spot."

Sheila's head shot up and she fixed me with a glare. "All you have to do is drive," she said, reminding me of our respective roles in life. "The timing is up to me. And I can handle my end of things just fine, thank you."

Brent shot a puzzled glance back between the two of us, then shrugged. "I understand there won't be much to see, though," he said.

Sheila shook her head. "No, you won't be close enough to see ordinance on target, not unless you're in the observation plane. And I don't think you can wangle that."

Brent smiled. "Well, I guess I'll just have to rely on you to tell me all about it when you get back down."

Oh brother. He was really laying it on.

"That's not true, is it?" Anna said mildly. "Skeeter says he has a lot to do with whether ordinance gets on target. Don't you?" She turned those big, doe-like eyes up at me, smiling slightly.

"That's right," I affirmed. "Back in the old days, most of the ground attack aircraft were single seaters. One man can do it all," I said, letting my voice emphasize the word *man* slightly.

"One man still can," a new voice chimed in. I looked up to see Illya Kyrrul standing over me, smiling broadly. Geez, what was this? Everybody in the world seemed to be having a hell of a time around me, all taking potshots at my Tomcat. Well, I didn't have to put up with this.

"We'll see what the best way to do it is this afternoon," I said, pushing myself away from the table. I turned to Anna. "You were going to show me those historic etchings out in the front passageway, weren't you?" Her puzzled eyes met mine for a moment, then her face cleared and she nodded enthusiastically.

"Of course—the etchings."

As we paced off toward the door, I turned to shoot a victorious smirk at Sheila. I guess that proved where she stood in the pecking order of things. I had a real life Russian spy after me, whereas all she could muster up was a stupid old American civil servant. Once we left the banquet hall, Anna could no longer contain her amusement. Her light, silvery laughter seemed to tinkle against the walls inside the cavernous entrance. "These etchings—I have heard about that!" she said, as though delighted to find a quaint American expression in actual use. "It is a joke, yes?"

"A joke of sorts," I agreed. "But I was interested in these pictures." I pointed to the massive gilt frames lining the walkway down to the banquet hall. "Tell me about them."

"All heroes of the Mother Land," she said briskly. "Afghanistan, of course. Even World War I and World War II. The Great War, we call it, the first one." She began to walk me down the hallway, telling me the little she knew about the men in the pictures. At the end of the hall, she turned back to me and laid one hand on my chest. "I must thank you—you are helping my reputation as a spy immensely," she said mischievously. "My superiors will be convinced that I am so clever in getting secrets from you, meeting alone with you like this. But of course, there is nothing to it, yes?" She shrugged helplessly, as though acknowledging the absurdity of our positions. "We managed to fool my superiors—and your girlfriend."

"She's not my girlfriend—she's just my RIO," I said.

She paused to consider this. "Then why do you care if she act foolish over the other American?"

"Just because she's looking stupid," I said. "That guy—hell, he's nothing. She could do a lot better than that if she wanted."

"Perhaps I could scare up a Russian spy for her." Anna twinkled, then laughed again at the horrified expression on my face. "Oh, don't be so silly. It is hard enough these days to justify one's job. I am grateful that you have made it that much easier for me. Now, these other pictures . . ."

I couldn't figure it out. Maybe what she said was true, that everyone was so desperate to look like they had a job in this new Soviet economy that simply being alone with an American aviator was sufficient to secure her reputation as a devious Mata Hari in this new pecking order. But she hadn't asked me anything about flying, anything about tactics or my squadron, or anything at all that might possibly relate to military intelligence. Sure, she'd mentioned the bombing run, but it was evident from her questions and her comments that she really didn't know anything about military matters. Maybe she was just what she said she was—an agricultural spy, like industrial espionage or something.

Anyway, I was glad to be away from Sheila and Brent. We'd have some words when we got alone in the cockpit. She could be sure of that.

All too soon it was time to make our way back to the airfield and go through our very thorough preflight. Even though she'd been acting like an ass over lunch, I knew Sheila was as determined as I was not to get caught with another stupid trick like the altimeter. We preflighted everything, even the things that weren't on the checklist. Like the altimeter. Like the clock. After a while, I felt pretty stupid staring at the digital face and comparing it with the sweep of the second hand on my fake Rolex.

Finally, we were both satisfied. We motioned to the ground technicians that we were ready to strap in.

This time, we'd be judged not on ACM—Aerial Combat Maneuvering—but on our performance at both the MiG and the Tomcat's secondary mission—bombing. The pods slung on our wings were also capable of recording all the relevant data for a bombcat, as our aircraft was formally called when in this configuration.

In addition to the simulator pods on our wings, our bombing runs would be monitored by an observation team airborne over the IP—the Impact Point. The MiG and the Tomcat each had one real five-hundred-pound bomb slung under the wings, and this time Illya was going to see just how badly outclassed he was. I'd scored first in every bombing practice run on the range since I left the training pipeline, and I wasn't about to let some Commie bastard show me up this time. Not after the cheap tricks he'd pulled on me so far, for I was convinced that he was behind the altimeter reset as well.

The Tomcat is even better on bombing runs than a MiG. It's like comparing a Hornet with a Tomcat. The sheer power and massiveness of the Tomcat, which makes it less maneuverable in the air than either of those, makes it the preferred platform for carrying ground ordinance. The Hornets and the MiGs simply don't have the power to carry much, and that's the real reason that Hornets will never replace Tomcats completely in the battle group. They drink too much gas and they don't carry enough weapons.

I'd studied the charts of the area extensively and knew the approach to the IP was surrounded by low hills and a couple of higher peaks. Sheila had used her tactical decision aids to plot in the best course, allowing for evasion of the imaginary SAM sites that ringed the area and giving me some room to maneuver in case we ran into any surprises. I'd looked it over and signed off on all of it, although in truth she was the better mission planner of the two of us.

As soon as the cockpit was secured over our seats, Sheila said, "You want to tell me what all that was about?"

"Well, we still want to make sure they haven't tampered with anything," I said, deliberately misunderstanding her question and answering as though she was referring to the extended preflight. "Can't be too careful around these Russians, you know."

"You're the one who ought to be careful," she snapped. "And don't think the admiral doesn't notice you playing patty-cake with that Russian. Didn't Lab Rat warn you about that? When are you going to quit thinking with your little head?"

"There's nothing going on with her," I said hotly. Partly because it was true, and partly because it pissed me off that there wasn't. Anna had given every indication that there could be, and I was a little annoyed that the current circumstances—like being inside Russia, for God's sake—prevented me from following up on the clear signals she was giving off. The things a man has to do for his country.

"Besides, what about you and Brent?" I pitched my voice a little bit higher as I said his name, imitating her Minnesota accent. I've always been good at that, and it drives her up a wall.

"What, the career American diplomat?" she snapped. "And just what could be suspicious about that?"

"Oh, nothing," I said airily. "He sure seems to be sucking up to you, though."

"Sucking up? Since when do you care who I talk to?"

"And since when did you become my own personal hall monitor?" I demanded.

That settled it for a while. The yellow shirt gave me the signal to taxi, and I let off the brakes and jammed the throttles forward, not caring if it jolted her in the backseat. After all, she'd agreed on one thing—I got to drive, not her.

Sheila subsided into an angry muttering, but I could feel her movements in the back of the aircraft—sharp, short, and staccato. Clearly, she was pissed. That made me come to my senses a little.

"Listen, it's none of my business," I said. "Let's just forget about it and fly the mission, OK?"

"I will if you will," she answered, a sweetly saccharine note in her voice. "Just be careful about which stick you're grabbing up there, OK?"

"That was a shitty thing to say," I snapped.

"Can dish it out but can't take it?"

I gave up my attempt to restore harmony in the cockpit. Regardless of how she pissed me off, Sheila was a pro. Let her deal with her own snit, as long as it didn't affect the mission. I took off well short of where I had the time before, rolling into the air with a sharp, crisp motion. I grinned, wondering whether Sheila or Tombstone would give me the most grief if I pulled a hot-shit approach when we came back in, waiting until the last minute to lower my landing gear. Sheila, probably, I decided. Based on Tombstone's earlier reaction on our first engagement with Illya, he'd probably find at least some public reason to claim it had all been part of the plan. I knew Sheila wouldn't let me off so easily.

We ascended to eleven thousand feet, circled for a moment, then at the signal headed off for the IP. The Tomcat was its normal, beautiful self, purring under my fingertips like—hell, don't start thinking like that, I told myself. This was a Tomcat, not a cute little Russian agricultural spy.

I descended smoothly to six thousand feet, following Sheila's directions smartly, almost anticipating each command. The heads-up display was feeding me information from her plot, showing me when the turns were coming up. The radar detection envelopes of the imaginary SAM sites were painted in yellow on the display, indicating that they were all in normal search patterns. If and when the game controllers decided we were entering the fringe of a detection envelope, we might see the indicators turn red as they switched into a track mode.

"Down another one hundred feet," Sheila ordered. "Put a little bit more of the hill between us and the site."

I complied immediately, nosing down even farther to the ground.

Now, this was more like it. No imaginary deck to come up and smack me in the face, just the sheer pleasure of flying low enough over the countryside to get a good look at it. Even at almost Mach One, you can make out the general details. It seems like you're going so much faster when you're this near to the earth.

Now, what I really like is flying nap of the earth, so close that you can almost reach out and touch the trees. The Tomcat, at least on the later variance, has excellent terrain-following radar that can keep you locked at practically any altitude near to the earth. The only thing you have to watch out for then is power lines and telephone poles, which can increase the pucker factor by the next order of magnitude during night bombing runs.

"Problems," Sheila said. The yellow envelope of the easternmost SAM site turned red on my display at the same time. Her ALR-67 receiver beeped out its warning.

"I thought we were low enough," I said.

"We are—it shouldn't be getting us." Sheila's voice was calm, a shade more terse than normally.

"Well, evidently it is," I said. This is one of my great failings as a member of the team, my tendency to point out the obvious to someone who already knows it.

"You think I can't see that?" she snapped. "Get down a little lower—you comfortable with that?"

"Your wish is my command." I nosed the Tomcat down, a gradual descent rather than a sharp one this close to the ground. Finally, at two thousand feet I steadied up. "How's that?"

"It's still got us—I can't figure it out—wait! It's got to be there." She clicked in a targeting symbol that was reflected immediately in my heads-up display. "It's part of the game," she explained rapidly. "It's got to be—an unbriefed SAM site, just to test our reactions."

"Well, get me the hell out of here," I said. "I'm not carrying any HARMs."

HARMs are specialized missiles that weren't part of our normal load out. Instead of being heat-seeking or IR, a HARM would home in on a hostile electronic emission and blow the hell out of the transmitter. Sometimes it was just a soft kill, but a soft kill was good enough. You'd knock out the radar in a SAM site and the crew, if there were any left alive, would be reduced to manual targeting. It's a hell of a problem against a high-Mach aircraft.

"Hard right—you see those hills ahead? Cut in between the two middle ones. I think that'll give us shielding, but we won't be in the envelope of the northernmost site."

I complied, following her directions as quickly as she put them into the heads-up display processor. "Will we get there on time?"

"I think so—goose it a little bit, will you?"

Now that was impressive. I knew that in the backseat Sheila was quickly recalculating our inbound route, redoing the time-distance problem in her head without the assistance of the detailed planning charts she had earlier. But I had some degree of confidence—if anybody could pull it off, she could.

"Back to two three zero," she ordered.

Sure enough, as soon as I executed the last turn, the red

fire-control radar signal subsided into a cautionary yellow. Nothing else lit up either, indicating we were clear of everyone's detection envelope. I breathed a sigh of relief. "How far off are we, timewise?"

"About ten seconds. I think we can make it up."

I eased the throttles forward a little more, exceeding our briefed speed. The terrain was still familiar, although I was seeing it from a different angle than we'd planned. Our computer-aided decisioning tools are really incredible these days. The bombing run simulator allows a pilot, in essence, to prefly a mission, maneuvering the computer screen with his joystick through the terrain surrounding the IP. You can program it to paint in SAM sites and detection envelopes too. Back on the *Jefferson* when we first briefed this mission, I spent a fair amount of time on the computer flying all around the briefed IP. I knew this alternate route pretty well, at least enough not to be confused by the change in terrain.

"Ten seconds," Sheila warned. "Descend to eight hundred feet."

Now, this was more like it. We were skimming along now, still well clear of the forest and the low surrounding hills, but my sensation of speed increased dramatically.

"Five seconds." I could see it now, just as it had been briefed: the concrete bunker surrounded by a number of trucks, obviously old derelicts that they pressed into service for realistic training. I made a course correction, lining up solidly on the bunker.

"Two seconds," she said.

I kept my finger poised over the weapon selections switch. One-Mississippi, Two-Mississippi. I toggled off the bomb.

The Tomcat jolted upward as five hundred pounds of dumb steel left its wing, and I corrected immediately to maintain level flight. As the weapon peeled up, I jerked the Tomcat up hard, rolling away from and out to the side of the missile's lofted flight path. This close to the ground, it's important to put as much distance between you and the impact point as quickly as possible so that you don't get caught up in the shrapnel or blinded by the cloud from the explosion.

"That looked solid," Sheila said from the backseat. I could hear the relief in her voice.

"Good job putting us back on course," I said.

I felt the Tomcat burble as it descended, returning to ground from the realm that was rightfully hers. As I started my lineup, I saw the MiG parked on the flight line, heat still wafting off its wings, a bird of prey on the ground.

We ran through the shutdown checklist quickly but thoroughly. An enlisted man mounted the boarding ladder to help us out of our ejection harnesses, and it wasn't until his face was close to mine that I realized he was one of our own.

Sheila left the aircraft first, but I wasn't far behind. I jumped down off the aircraft, skipping the last step, and started my triumphant approach on the waiting gallery. Brent, Sheila's diplomatic trained dog, and Anna, my very own personal Russian spy, were waiting.

As was the MiG pilot, that asshole that had tripped me just after we'd arrived. He wasn't any better looking on the ground than he had been in the air.

"Nice going, buddy," I said, and offered him my hand. "Too bad you were off course."

These Russians, man. What sore losers. The guy spat out a stream of Russian at me and started to grab me. Sheila and Brent intervened. I started toward the guy, then caught sight of Anna's pale, stricken face. "What, we got some sort of cultural misunderstanding here, Sheila?" I said. "You think that new boyfriend of yours can explain just what the hell's going on?"

Brent still had one arm on the Russian puke's upper arm. The guy was struggling—like I said, real sore losers. "It's you who're going to have to do some explaining, mister. Big-time and now."

I laughed. "I'm supposed to let him win? That wasn't part of the deal, no way. If that's what diplomacy is about, then you can just—"

Sheila turned around and clamped one hand over my mouth. Say what you will about the chicks, this one had a grip that wouldn't quit. She found the same spot in my gut that she'd roughed up before and planted her elbow there again. Harder, this time.

"Shut the fuck up, Skeeter, and let me handle this." When she gets that tone of voice going, she gets dangerous.

I shut up. Sheila turned back to Brent. "Explain." At least there was no lovey-dovey stuff in her voice that time.

"Your young hotshot there needs to learn to read a map," Brent spat out. He jerked back on the Russian one last time, then relinquished his grip to a couple of other Russians. He took a moment to straighten his tie and jacket, and probably unwind the underwear that was in a knot.

"I navigated. I had to make a last-minute course correction to compensate for a SAM site, but we were right back on the proper approach within seconds." I had a feeling Mr. Smoothy wasn't going to be making much more progress with my backseater.

"Then you made a mistake. There wasn't a SAM site in this scenario."

"What's the point of it as a tactical test if every possible checkpoint is briefed? That's no way to train," Sheila shot back. But I could see from the look on her face that our thoughts were running in parallel. Judging from both Brent and Illya Kyrrul's reaction, something hadn't gone right.

More than that. It had gone very, very wrong.

"You were off the briefed approach by more than five miles," Brent said. He shot me another one of those looks that clearly indicated who he thought was at fault, despite Sheila's explanation. "Remember, this is a Russian training exercise, not Top Gun school in the States. Every evolution is briefed. No surprises."

"Then what was with the SAM site?" I asked. Both of them glared at me. Fine. I was flying the damned aircraft and I couldn't ask a simple question?

"You were way out of line," Brent said. "You were in the airspace around a research facility. And when you pulled your little jaunt off course, you got even farther away. What you hit was not a target. It was a small agricultural village."

"No." Sheila's voice was stunned and cold. I could understand why, if what Brent was saying was true.

But it had to be true, didn't it? After all, he was one of ours. We might expect the Russians to lie to us for some reason, but this gouge was coming from our own people.

"You didn't happen to wonder why there were people walking around outside?" Brent snapped.

"I didn't see anyone," I said, already feeling like I ought to be able to come up with some sort of plausible alternative explanation. What he was saying just didn't make sense. There was no way that Sheila was that far off the briefed plan, no way. "And I did a flyby for BDA and I didn't see any indication that that sight was anything other than a good ol' target. Here—look at the charts." I started pulling out my briefing sheet from my kneeboard, the handy device that snaps around your upper leg and holds all the mission briefing crap. "Look."

Brent brushed the chart away. "You hit a civilian village. There's no way around that one, mister. And I don't care what you say—after yesterday, we all know how careful you are about regulations and briefed restrictions."

"But look." I tried again, waving the chart around in the hope that I could get someone—anyone—to look at the info we'd been given for mission planning, our approach plan, and every other detail. "Look."

Stone-cold impassive Russian faces stared back at me. It finally sunk in that no matter how right I felt, Sheila and I were in big big trouble.

"Was . . . was anyone killed?" Sheila asked. "How much damage was there?"

Brent studied her for a moment, then shook his head. "You were lucky. Everyone was out in the fields, watching for the aircraft to fly by. When they saw you making an approach on their village, they ran. The damage to the structures is pretty bad, but no one was killed."

I felt a surge of relief, then suspicion. "Wait—everyone was out of the houses and buildings? Absolutely everyone? No one stuck in the can, or working overtime, or trying to filch something? Even the crooks were out watching?" My turn to shake my head. "Doesn't compute, buster. Don't tell me you're buying that load of crap."

"You bet I am. And you better, too. Because if one person ends up dead, one person seriously injured, there's going to be all hell to pay. You can count on it. So irregardless of how improbable you find it, you count your lucky stars that they were all outside."

I was just about to tell him that irregardless isn't really a word—what he meant was regardless, and if he had any sort of education beyond which fork to use on salad and which one to stick up his butt, he'd know that. I'd almost gotten the last comparison worked out when the Russian pilot got free from his buddies.

Kyrrul bolted past Sheila and Brent like a tornado. I started to move too late.

The first punch landed square in my gut, knocking the air out of my lungs. I doubled over, caught the second punch with the underside of my chin, and felt my feet leave the ground.

Russians were all over us now, pretending that they were trying to pull Illya off of me, but it sure as hell didn't feel like it. Trying to help me up, they kept nailing me in the gut again. Somebody stepped on my fingers, and another one landed a boot in my ribs.

I shouted, and finally made it to my feet. My lungs were starting to work again. Sheila and Brent were peeling the Russians off of me one by one, but making slow progress.

"Stop it. Now." The voice was so cold it froze every one of us where we stood. It took a moment for it to sink in with me that it was Admiral Magruder.

Another command echoed out in Russian and, if I had to guess, said exactly the same thing. No one was moving now, not even Illya.

I tried to straighten up as Admiral Magruder walked up to me. He might have found a clever way to cover up the altimeter/altitude screwup, but I had a feeling this one wasn't going to go away that easily. I made it straight enough to at least look like I was standing at attention.

Admiral Magruder bent down close to me. He's a little

taller anyway, and I was hunched over. "Shut up. Not another word, you understand. Follow me."

I know orders when I hear them, and I was relieved to have to obey those. If he could get me off that flight line without being lynched, I was going to be real grateful. And surprised.

We made an interesting little parade. Admiral Magruder leading, me limping along behind and trying not to vomit. Sheila was behind me, sort of keeping one hand on my back to make sure I didn't keel over. Behind her was Brent, I think, although I couldn't have sworn to it. Gator Cummings, who'd turned up somewhere around the same time as the admiral, brought up the rear. Anna had disappeared into the crowd sometime after the first punch was thrown.

The admiral herded us all into a military transport vehicle of some sort, the Russian equivalent of a Jeep or Humvee. We rode back to his quarters in silence. He motioned us out of the vehicle and we followed him into his quarters. He still hadn't said a word.

Finally, back in his sitting room, the admiral seemed to calm down. He pointed at a chair. I sat. Next thing I know, he's handing me a stiff drink. I took it, held it for a minute, not entirely sure that he really wanted me to drink it.

"Drink. It's not poison. I brought it with me." The admiral's face didn't even flicker, although everyone except maybe Brent knew how much against most Navy regs that was.

I drank. Bourbon—not my favorite, but it'll do. The liquid coursed down my throat, smooth and friendly, and finally hit the pit of my much-abused gut.

"The rest of you?" the admiral asked. He received a chorus of no's from Brent and Sheila. He poured one for himself, then sat down on the couch across from me. "Tell me what happened."

I let Sheila do the honors while I nursed my bourbon. She got it all right, but left out a few details. Like what an astounding job she'd done getting us back on the proper approach path. I filled those in, and was kind of hurt when she looked like she didn't appreciate my help all that much.

"I see," the admiral said after she'd finished. He shut his eyes for a moment, then said, "And what is State's opinion?"

Brent mumbled something about diplomatic relationship, the usual crap you hear from State. The admiral listened to him for a while, his eyes still shut. He was so still that I thought for a moment he'd fallen asleep.

Then he sat straight up, nodded at Brent, and said, "Thank you for your assistance. We'll take it from here."

"Admiral, I—"

Evidently no one had ever explained to Brent about arguing with admirals. There's really just one rule—you don't.

"That will be all." The admiral said it quietly, but he made it damned plain to these military ears that Brent was expected to pop tall then quickly haul butt. I was hoping the admiral might have to make it even clearer than that, but Brent disappointed me by getting the word. He was out of there with a quick "we can talk tomorrow," and then the door shut behind him.

For once, I was smart enough to keep my mouth shut. I opened it once, caught Sheila's look, and figured out that I'd been right the first time.

Finally, the admiral spoke. "For what it's worth—not much right now, I suspect, not at least to the Russians—I believe you. Something went wrong, just as it did with the altimeter. When we finally track down the error, it'll be something that we didn't understand—a distance in meters instead of yards and miles, something the Russians can use to absolve themselves of the blame."

"Why?" Thank God Gator asked the question. Sheila and I were in too much trouble to be talking. "Why would they invite us here and then set us up?"

"I can think of a couple of reasons," the admiral answered. For a moment, something dark darted behind his eyes, a look of grief and pain that I'd never seen on a flag officer's face before. Just a flash, then it was gone. "Some of them concern the United States and our diplomatic relationship with Russia and the former Soviet states.

Nothing like being magnanimous about a screwup to make us in their debt."

"I don't call getting beat up magnanimous," I said.

"A little higher level issue than what happens to your carcass," the admiral answered. "There are other reasons as well, some of which may concern you. And some of which may have to do with me alone. I don't think we need to go into them right now. But until we're back safe on an American flight deck, I want your mouths shut. Completely. Not even a 'no comment.' You understand?"

The admiral drained his glass in one gulp, and I followed suit. Then he stood, a clear dismissal. We trooped back out front to find the transport vehicle and a driver waiting for us.

We didn't talk on the way back to our quarters. The driver dropped Sheila off at the women's quarters, then Gator and me at our building. Once we were inside, I turned to Gator, wanting to get his take on it.

Gator held up one hand. "Not here. Not inside. Go to bed, Skeeter. You've got a couple of long, quiet days ahead of you."

I could see his point. I mean, everything we'd ever heard about Russia indicated that they probably had the whole building wired for sound. Maybe the admiral's quarters, too, although come to think of it, we hadn't discussed anything too damned sensitive in there, either. Just those vague allusions about it having to do with him alone maybe. And maybe he had some toys from Lab Rat, something that would tell him if his quarters were bugged or something.

Whatever. The one thing that worried me wasn't something that any RIO could give me much help with. I mean, whatever good they are in the air, in the end they're just passengers.

So far, I was two-for-two for screwed-up missions. I was the pilot, I was the one responsible for getting us where we needed to be to execute the mission. And after a hosed-up altimeter and bombing run, all I could think of was—what next? The next time, would it be something in the jet engines themselves? Maybe a little FOD planted somewhere that could get sucked into a turobfan and blow it—and us—to bits? Or something in the hydraulics, a pinhole leak that wouldn't show up until we'd been airborne for a while.

Well, whatever it was, I'd have to be ready for it alone.

I finally got to sleep, cold shower and all. The weather woke me up at 0300, wind battering against the glass, billowing the thin curtains hung on either side of it. The rain came next, hard and pelting. Rain—hail and sleet more likely, as cold as it had been today.

I pulled the blankets back up over me, snuggled down and tried to get warm. Still too cold to sleep. I finally got up and pulled out the rest of my clothes from the flight pack and carefully arranged them on the bed as an additional layer. A few minutes later, the weather still battering my quarters, I drifted off again.

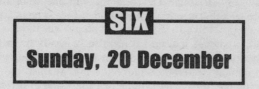

SIX

Sunday, 20 December

0400 Local (+3 GMT)
USS Jefferson
Off the northern coast of Russia

Commander Lab Rat Busby:

Someone was banging on my stateroom door. I groaned, rolled over, and pulled the alarm clock around so I could see it. Zero four hundred—what the hell? I was due at least another two hours of rack time. Six whole hours I'd planned on; worked hard all day so I could get to bed around midnight. I felt old.

The hours, the sheer length of the day when you're on an aircraft carrier, is something few civilians will ever understand. When you're twenty-one, it's no big deal. Sure, it's a shock when you first join the Navy, but everyone around you is keeping the same insane hours, sleeping racked out on the floor between flight cycles, and after a while you start thinking it's normal. But the years creep up on you and it gets harder and harder to keep up.

Another assault on my door. No way to ignore it, pretend that I was still asleep. I stumbled to the door, barely coherent and damning the day that I ever decided to join the Navy, barking my shin on the desk. I yanked it open. "What?"

It was Wilson, my leading petty officer. He had a concerned look on his face and a sheet of messages in his hand. He pulled the top one off and held it out to me.

"You couldn't call?" I asked. A stupid question—almost everything in CVIC is so highly classified that even thinking about it outside of the intelligence spaces will earn you a lengthy prison term.

"I knew you'd want to see this right away." There was a carefully neutral expression on Wilson's face. He was accustomed to waking me up and knew I'd be apologizing in a few minutes. It didn't bother him.

I took the message, already ashamed of my own peevishness. It wasn't Wilson's fault—in all probability, I would've been very annoyed in a few hours if he hadn't woken me up. "When did this come in?"

"Four minutes ago," he answered. "Like I said—I thought you would want to see it immediately."

I nodded, almost completely awake now. It's a skill you learn onboard a ship, the ability to go from dead asleep to awake. "You did exactly the right thing."

Thirty seconds later, I was dressed and trotting down the passageway to CVIC.

The message had been clear—the USS *John Paul Jones* was holding contact on a U.S. nuclear submarine. Against all odds—and all intelligence—we had one in the area. The more I thought about it, the more it started to piss me off. Captain Smith, Batman—hell, even Tombstone—didn't any of them realize that the only people we were supposed to keep secrets from were the bad guys?

Somebody knew that we had U.S. submarines in the area. Knew, and didn't bother telling us about it. No matter that I've got gear classified to the highest levels in the nation, that I've got safes, security, steel doors, and a background investigation that's like getting an enema on your entire life—no, someone hadn't wanted to trust me with this information.

SUBLANT knew, of course. Who else? USACOMM? Probably.

How about the subliaison on the *Jefferson*? Maybe. Not likely. Once he was attached to the carrier and not to an underwater brotherhood command, he'd be out of the loop. Tainted, I guess.

Captain Smith? Batman? Both of them? Now, that was a real probability. Even SUBLANT wasn't stupid enough to have subs prowling around an aircraft carrier without telling someone in the area.

And why wasn't that someone yours truly?

When I finally got to CVIC, the spaces were already filled with intelligence specialists, the regular watch section augmented by an additional team of acoustic specialists.

"Where is she now?" I asked as I burst into the room.

The lieutenant watch officer was right on top of things, as well he should be. He was seated at the consoles. He looked up as I came in, then return to his task.

"What's happening?" I asked, sliding into the chair next to his. He finished two keystrokes, then turned to me.

"Good morning, Commander. Six minutes ago, one of the S-3B torpedo bombers, Hunter 701, gained active sono-buoy contact on an unknown submarine. Given the location, they initially called it a Russian boat. A few minutes later, they gained passive contact as well, and reclassified the contact as a U.S. submarine. The *J. P. Jones* is holding contact also."

I studied the display of slanting lines and swirls in front of him, not trying to pretend that I understood every bit of data. I didn't this—not really. Translating the details of a lofargram was an arcane science that my enlisted techni-cians spent years learning to do.

"How close is she?" I asked.

"Not far," Wilson supplied. He pointed at a narrow white space between two contact positions. "I make it less than five miles. And closing."

"And it's not a Russian—it is one of ours." The watch officer looked away.

"We don't . . ." I stopped, suddenly realizing what the uneasy evasion I'd gotten from the admiral meant. We did have submarines in the area. And only he knew about it.

For a moment, my temper flared. What was the use of having an intelligence officer if the intelligence officer didn't even know the locations of our own ships? Sure, I understood security—there might have been very good reasons to tell Batman about our submarine and not me. Intellectually, I could understand that. Nevertheless, it pissed me off.

"Shit," Wilson said softly. He had an ear cocked in the direction of the loudspeakers mounted on the forward bulkhead. "And that's not all."

The noise of the radio circuit speakers is so much of a part of life onboard the ship that you tend to tune them out, focusing only on what you need to know right then. Absorbed in the question of what the hell a U.S. submarine was doing in the area, I had not been paying attention to the USW control circuit.

Hunter 701's TACCO was screaming bloody murder. His sensors were showing three new submarines within fifteen miles of the carrier. They were all making flank speed, headed directly for us and the datum of the U.S. submarine we had just located.

I picked up the internal telephone system to call CAG. The title CAG is actually a misnomer. When aircraft first started going onboard ships, the man in charge of all the squadrons was called commander, air group. In modern naval aviation, the correct title is commander of the air wing. However, since those initials spelled out CAW, it's unlikely to ever catch on as the acronym.

The CAG is always a senior Navy captain, an aviator by trade. He owns all the aircraft assigned to the carrier. In conjunction with the ship's captain, also a senior naval aviator, he provides the aircraft and mission scheduling necessary to fulfill the carrier battle group commander's wishes—in this case, Admiral Wayne. The aircraft carrier's captain owns the repair facilities, the deck space, and the support crew that runs the flight deck. The CAG owns the squadrons themselves.

"Tell the officer of the deck to come around," I added. The OOD would be responsible for maneuvering the aircraft carrier in order to generate wind across the deck. With this many submarines in the water, the admiral was going to

want wall-to-wall S-3B and helo operations in progress until
we sorted out the good guys from the bad guys.

I could hear the announcement now, coming out of the
1MC, the ship's general announcing system. Then the feet
pounding down the decks as sailors and officers scrambled
for their assigned positions. Within a couple of minutes, I
knew, the control tower looming ten decks above the water
level would be fully manned.

Getting additional aircraft and helicopters in the air was
the ship's problem. Mine ran a good deal deeper than that.
I left CVIC and headed down the passageway to see
Admiral Wayne.

I found the admiral in his flag plot, studying the large-
screen display that dominated the forward part of the room
and conferring with his tactical action officer. The cause for
their concern was clear—symbols indicating hostile submarines and subsurface contacts cluttered the large blue
display. Another symbol, labeled Hunter 701, was orbiting
overhead. I could hear the engines of more aircraft spiraling
up above as the ship launched more USW aircraft.

"My people say one of those is ours," I said. I studied the
display for a moment, trying to determine which one it was.
I had the uneasy feeling that it was the one in the center of
the pack, and not the submarine closest to us.

There's no money to be made in expressing your annoyance to your admiral. It's called a collar count—the one
with the most weight wins. Always. No matter how right I
might be, how justified in the civilian world in being
annoyed, this was one battle I would always lose.

But an experienced officer knows how to express his
displeasure without being disrespectful. It's all in keeping
your voice carefully neutral while letting the words convey
the difficulty of fulfilling one's duties when operating under
less than full information. I knew Batman would get it—
he's been playing this game far longer than I have.

"Looks like one of ours," I said. Batman would know I
was thinking about our earlier conversation, the one in
which he'd assured me there were no U.S. submarines
accompanying us.

He got it—I could tell immediately from the look on his face—a slight stiffening of his cheeks and the twitch of the corner of his mouth. But still, he said nothing.

I took a step closer, and lowered my voice. "What do you want me to tell SUBLANT—if anything?" I was referring to the top secret circuits, cleared for the most sensitive information around, that I had access to in CVIC.

"Nothing—for now," the admiral answered quietly. "Anything we know, they know."

"Including the fact that their submarine may be in trouble?" I asked. I pointed at the large-screen display. "I don't think she was counting on that much company."

Batman shook his head, his face still impassive. "They knew what to expect, coming up here. We'll give them what support we can, maybe try to scare the little bastards off. But nothing overt, nothing that can be interpreted as a hostile act." He turned to face me now, and I saw the concern in his eyes. "There's too much at stake, Lab Rat. Too much, right now."

"What do you mean, too much at stake?" I asked. "We're on a friendship mission, a cultural exchange military style, if you will. Isn't that right?"

And again, the admiral shook his head. "That, yes. But there's more to it than that." A brief, wintry smile crossed his face. "You've already found out I'm not telling you everything. Let's just leave it at that, shall we?"

In between the admiral's comments I could hear the questions, orders, and concerns of the Hunter 701 pilot coming across a tactical.

She's going deep, she's going deep. Put another two sonobuoys on her. We can't lose her now, not while—

"But what does that mean, Admiral?" I pressed. "Just how deep are we in this?"

"Deep enough," the admiral said. His eyes were fixed on the speaker.

Admiral Wayne was a Tomcat pilot. He had been one for twenty years, flying wing-to-wing with Tombstone Magruder for more tours than I cared to think about. We knew a fair amount about USW—most admirals do—but it certainly wasn't his speciality. Watching him now, I could almost see his mind mapping out the possibilities, tracing the actions and tactics of the Viking pilot against the submarines.

Where the hell are those other Vikings? Jesus, we have more than we can handle in here! TAO, what the hell is—?

"She can't go that deep," the admiral said, almost to himself. "It won't make that much difference—not here. The Russians know that. Surely the skipper knows it, too."

I knew what the admiral was talking about. The ocean up here was a barely liquid frozen slab of water, dense, with a uniform temperature and gradient that created a perfect isothermal layer. Sound waves were affected only by the depth of the water, since the temperature was constant. But the water was not deep enough to create truly long-range transmission paths. Indeed, playing USW in these frozen waters was truly a challenge. The temperature and depth profile combined to create convergence zone transmission that bore no resemblance to its cousins in warmer climates.

Somebody better tell that boomer to get out of the way. Sierra 002 is headed right up her ass. Damn it, can't we get word to them somehow?

The submarine symbols of the large-screen display moved with chilling slowness. The blue symbol, representing the friendly submarine—or at least we believed it was the friendly—was tracking south, apparently oblivious to the company in the water. The Soviet—excuse me, Russian—submarines were vectoring in from the north, east, and south, slowly and inexorably boxing her in.

Surely she must know. One of the unvarying rules in the undersea warfare environment is the reciprocity of sound. If you can hear them, then they can hear you—like the signs you see on a tractor's rearview mirrors that warn *If you can't see me, I can't see you.* If the Russians' submarines could hear the U.S. submarine well enough to track her, then the U.S. submarine must know that the Russians were there. *Must*—the superiority of our acoustic gear in terms of sensitivity and processing ability was just too great.

But then why weren't they doing anything? Attempting evasive maneuvers, making a course change, even getting the hell out of the area? Did they think that the carrier and her air wing would protect them? Hell, we weren't even supposed to know she was here!

But then again, it could be one of those massive operational screwups. The submarines were told one thing, we were told another. In our case, that would be nothing. If the powers that be had let a U.S. submarine enter these potentially hostile waters without telling her of the true tactical situation, it was criminal. Someone would face the long green table over this, I was sure.

Just as long as it wasn't me.

If she shoots now . . .

The pilot's voice, which had earlier been rising to almost a frenzy, sounded almost resigned now. He had torpedoes on his wings, but no shot. Not this close to a friendly. Even absent a formal declaration of a no-attack zone, he could not in good conscience put a weapon in the water this close to an American submarine.

"But what the hell are they doing?" Admiral Wayne said. He turned to me, a puzzled look in his eyes. "Sure, they're closing on her. But there's no indication of hostile activity yet—at least, not anything I'm willing to classify as that. They are in their home waters, and we're operating without any notice to them. Just what the hell am I supposed to do?"

Within the minimums now.

I could see from the screen that the Hunter pilot had assessed it correctly. The Russian submarines were now well within torpedo range of their prey.

But would they fire? What possible justification would they have for attacking a U.S. submarine, even in these waters? For all that she was in their home waters, our submarine was outside the twelve-mile limit, well within international waters. Bad manners, extremely bad manners, but not an act of war.

Want some company up here?

The flight deck above my head had been silent for several minutes now, so I should not have been surprised when the new voice entered the tactical net. It was another S-3B, one of the alert aircraft that had been on the deck just moments before.

Yeah, come on. Let some other people play here, too.

And the third voice, this one as uncertain and erratic as a young man going through puberty. In the background, I could hear the hard thump of a helicopter's rotors. I knew Batman was as relieved as I was.

There are not many things that threaten the submarine as much as a couple of ASW helicopters working in conjunction with a long-range Viking aircraft. The helicopters are equipped with dipping sonars, and an acoustic transducer that is lowered from their underbelly by a long cable. The operator can select the depth, positioning the receiver in exactly the same layer of water as the submarine.

A tactical display was catching up now, showing the location of the two ASW helicopters as well as the additional S-3B. A potent force, enough to deal with three Russian submarines. Would be, except for the small problem about putting weapons in the water.

No, don't do that. You can't—damn him, he's closing!

There was a new rate note of alarm in the first pilot's voice.

Home Plate, Hunter 701. Sierra 002 is showing down Doppler. He's heading away from us, and away from the U.S. submarines—and toward you.

"General quarters!" the admiral snapped. The TAO was a microsecond ahead of him. Before he even finished the order, the hard, incessant bonging of general quarters filled the ship.

Finally, the U.S. submarine reacted. She almost looked uncertain, changing course slightly several times, before staying up on her original course. She continued south for several minutes, then made one final turn. Back toward us.

"What in the hell does she think she is doing?" the admiral muttered. "The safest place to be right now is far away from the carrier."

"Maybe we're not the only ones with secret orders, Admiral," I said, suddenly aware of the possibilities. "You knew about the submarine—I didn't. Maybe the sub skipper has orders you don't know about. Like to protect the carrier."

"I don't need a submarine with this much airpower," the admiral snapped.

"The best submarine hunter is another submarine," I pointed out quietly. "You've seen that before."

The admiral stared at something I couldn't see in the corner, growling softly at me. I kept quiet. Finally, he said, "We stick to the original plan. Whatever that submarine is doing, that's their business. And the same thing goes for the other submarines now—as far as I can tell, they have made no overt or hostile actions. And I am not about to start an international incident by getting too nervous too soon. After all, we're here on a friendship mission."

Some friendship mission. I could still hear feet pounding down the passageways as the ship set general quarters. It takes time, sometimes too much time, to mobilize six thousand sailors to their battle stations. Ten minutes—anything less is considered good.

As the minutes dragged on, the admiral appeared to reach a decision. He turned to the TAO and said, "Every ship in this battle group remains at general quarters, until I see that submarine moved out of torpedo range. After that, you tell those skippers to stay in at least condition two. I don't want any surprises, people."

"I wouldn't say we're the ones being surprised, not at all," I heard myself say. There was a small, shocked silence inside the flag plot.

Then the admiral laughed. It was not a particularly pleasant sound. "I guess not. We're rather the ones that started this whole thing, aren't we?" He pointed at the tactical screen, indicating the U.S. submarine. "Or at least—she did. But if I'm going to be able to keep up my part in this operation, we have to act like nothing is happening. Like it's a goodwill mission, that there's nothing unusual about submarines making a run on us. After all, it's only for another week."

Another week. I remembered the meteorology report I'd seen the day before. The weather guesser warned all hands to stand by, that colder weather could strike virtually anytime. The storms that blew out of the north were unpredictable, difficult to anticipate.

I glanced at the camera showing the flight deck and, beyond that expanse of metal, the cold ocean around us. Even on the low-resolution camera, I could see the thin crust of ice forming on the horizon, the beginnings of the winter ice that would block this port in solid until the next spring.

The icebreakers, of course—as a condition of participating in this mission, the Russians had guaranteed us primary use of their potent icebreaker force.

And just how long would that last? We had both thus far violated the basic rules of our agreement to prevent incidents at sea, with almost fatal consequences. Although no one had taken a shot yet, the admiral had six aircraft airborne just itching to fire a torpedo, a friendly fouling his field of fire, and Russian submarines up the butt.

Just what was it that the admiral was not telling me? First had been this presence of the U.S. submarine, and now it was this ill-defined and barely-hinted-at question of bigger stakes. We were supposed to be operating in support of the friendly competition, in short, not reverting to our old Cold War tactics against one another in the Soviet Union's old backyard.

Just what did Admiral Wayne know? And, even more importantly, when would he tell me?

The answers would probably be: everything—and when hell froze over.

From what I could see on the flight deck camera, that's exactly what was about to happen.

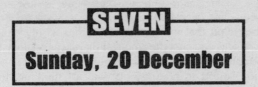

SEVEN
Sunday, 20 December

1300 Local (+3 GMT)
Arkhangel'sk, Russia

Vice Admiral Tombstone Magruder:

Over time, reality and dreams mesh until what remains is a mixture of truth and imagination. It taints one's reactions, coloring how one views current events and set scenarios. All reality is anecdotal.

The same can be said for what I once thought about being a flag officer. I had power, the power to do good. The power to affect the outcome of conflicts, to shape the squadron—and later a carrier battle group—in the way that I thought most effective to form a cohesive fighting force.

Much of that happened. I had had command of the superb fighting squadron, VF-95, the best Tomcat squad that ever existed. And command of Carrier Battle Group 14, one of the most grueling, challenging tours of my entire career. I had learned it was much easier to do the fighting and dying yourself than to order other men and women out to do it at your command. I hadn't expected the feeling of helplessness watching them launch, knowing that some of them wouldn't come back. Nor had I known then that so much had been kept from me, that the government had failed to live up to the promise that I made to every aviator who flew combat missions at my command: that we would get them out. How could I make them believe me, when I knew I had believed—and been lied to.

The cockpit that was once as familiar as my childhood bedroom was now just the smallest bit disconcerting, at least in the first few seconds after I strapped in. I had to make a conscious effort to readjust my way of thinking, to once again become the fighter pilot that I was. But in as few odd, painfully nostalgic moments, I stripped off the outer veneer that circumstances forced me to wear, and within seconds was as at home with the knobs, buttons, and flight controls as I ever was. In a way, it was like being born again.

But would I have changed my career path if I could have? Probably not. Competition is ingrained in every pilot from the moment he or she steps into basic training. You claw your way to the top of your class, knowing that if you are the best, the very best, you will have your choice of aircraft when you graduate. Later, as a junior officer, you learn what the checkpoints are—what tours of duty are considered desirable for promotion competitiveness, what assignments spell out a dead end to your career. We scramble and scratch for the former, and to avoid the latter, fully indoctrinated in the quest for power we call building a career in naval aviation.

No one ever tells you, though, that getting what you think you want will strip you of the one thing you truly desire, the reason you chose this odd, demanding career path in the first place. It's gradual at first, the way you find more and more of your time taken up with leadership, paperwork, and developing new subordinates. These duties etch into your flight schedule time, until you finally find yourself putting notes in the Snivel Log, asking the schedulers not to assign you to flights during particular times. The transition of turning into a desk jockey is a gradual slippery slope.

Batman was one of the few men I knew who managed to alternate tours in Washington, D.C., while still maintaining his cockpit proficiency. True, a number of his shore duty tours had been squadron, or attached to the naval test pilot facility in Maryland, but he managed to put in his fair share of time in the Pentagon. Now, in command of CBG14, he was back at sea.

So when the inevitable invitations to tour other Russian facilities in the area came, I was not surprised. Not even dismayed. I accepted as many as I could, feigning good grace and eagerness to see the latest in Russian technology. But in truth, I would rather have been flying every second, and considered those political necessities a complete waste of time.

Not that we would have been doing much flying anyway. A storm had blown in from the north with a vengeance, grounding all but the most determined or critically necessary flights. There was no justification, not in my mind or in the Russians', for allowing either my Tomcat or their aircraft into the air.

According to their meteorologists, the weather would linger for three days. My calendar quickly filled with a host of social and political obligations. Gator, Skeeter, and Sheila would probably spend the entire time drinking vodka and getting to know their counterparts. I just hoped they'd keep their mouths shut. I'd rather have kept them with me, kept their collective mouths under close control. Whatever was going on with the Russians tinkering with scheduled competition evolutions, we were best off keeping it to ourselves now.

I had a host of possible bases to visit, but one in particular caught my attention. There was a naval aviation training facility located far to the south—in Ukraine, actually. Kursk, a city located in the center of Ukraine, and one with a long military history.

Kursk had been a bloody, brutal battlefield during World War II. The Germans, plowing north in their tank battalions, had met a grim and determined Russian force there. It was winter—cold and brutally harsh. And German troops, unprepared for the snow and ice and frozen mud, floundered and stalled. The small, determined Russian force met them.

Met them and killed them.

Tourists could still see the old gun emplacements, rings of stone now grown over in the fertile soil that had earned the

Ukraine the name of "Breadbasket of Europe." But underneath the inches of lush red topsoil, the blood of Russians and Germans ran deep.

One in ten Russians had been killed during that war. It was a price Americans have never paid on their own soil, and the results of it they will never really understand. It makes a nation rabid over the prospect of enemy boots on home soil, scars the nation's psyche in a way that the Vietnam conflict just barely scratched ours. Their experiences in World War I and World War II did much to shape the Russian—or Soviet, if you will—mentality, and I think that in our years of foreign policy, in shaping our nation's conduct toward them back then, we never fully understood the impact. America, splendid in her geographic isolation, has never known enemy soldiers on her land, has never seen brother, son, and neighbor cut down by foreign troops, has never known the rumble of enemy tanks on Main Street, U.S.A.

Not that I am advocating it as a national experience. But we have been blessed, and I wonder sometimes how much of our population truly understands how great that blessing has been.

Like many senior military officers, I am an avid history buff. It is true that those who know history are doomed to repeat it. Technology simply puts a different face on old tactics and strategy. Kursk has always been of particular interest to me, and I welcomed the chance to get to see it up close and personal.

But there was another reason that Kursk fascinated me, one that I had not shared with my Russian hosts. I would not have been surprised to learn that they already knew about it, but I had no intention of confirming their intelligence. If their intelligence network was worth anything at all, then they knew most of what had occurred to me in the last year.

It had been an opportunity I could not pass up. I was between tours, awaiting an available officer billet, and even contemplating the possibility of retiring. My wife, Tomboy, had pointed it out to me first.

It was my father. As I grew older, and contemplated

starting a family of my own, his loss became more and more of a void in my life.

Within the Pentagon, my increasing obsession with the fate of my father was a well-known secret. Only my uncle really understood what it meant to me and had understood my sense of outrage and betrayal. Russia—in the last year, it had become an obscenity to me. I had nightmares about it and woke up yelling. That he could have been shot down I understood. That's the risk you take when you fly combat air. But *Russia*! Being here myself—making pleasantries with men who might have interrogated my father, finding that I had something in common with the aviators—was a difficult path to walk. I wanted to hate them all, to make them pay the price for what their predecessors had done. But I couldn't, not now. Finding out the truth meant playing the role I'd chosen, and I was determined to do it well.

Around two o'clock that afternoon, the weather broke for a few hours. We boarded a transport plane and headed south. After about an hour, we broke through the weather completely, and the rest of the trip was as smooth as glass.

Like most pilots, I am a terrible passenger. I know too intimately what can go wrong with these fragile constructs of steel and fiberglass that we put in the air. Even the mighty Tomcat, forever my favorite aircraft, is a fragile thing compared to the forces of nature. A single, small bird sucked into the intake, an invisible hairline fracture in the bolts holding engines to wings, or any one of a number of small mechanical failures can spell disaster.

At least in the Tomcat, the passengers—the pilot and the RIO—always have the option of punching out, of taking their chances with the ejection system, hoping that they have enough altitude to survive departing the aircraft in flight. Not so with commercial jets.

This one was luxurious by military standards, even more so for Russian aircraft. I was offered vodka, caviar, and a host of other hors d'oeuvres. I passed on all—the violent buffeting we experienced penetrating the frontal boundary coupled with my paranoia when in Russia combined to kill my appetite.

Three hours and twenty minutes later, we touched down gently on the airstrip at Kursk. I stared out the thick plastic double-paned cabin window and saw the normal welcoming horde of dignitaries, officers, and troops. Injury to insult— first a passenger, now more of the duties that I neither wanted nor enjoyed.

There's a sameness to military bases around the world. Flying combat aircraft generates certain necessities of function: fuel, a place to store it, and vehicles for transporting it to the aircraft; a means of controlling the arrival and departure of those aircraft—the control tower; maintenance facilities, gear for repairing and towing aircraft, access ladders, and accommodations for the soldiers or sailors who use the gear. No matter where they are located, all airstrips look the same, whether eighteen hundred feet of concrete runway or a rutted dirt track in the middle of the jungle.

We got through the formalities with a minimum of fuss and bother. I was introduced to the commander of the air base, a host of officers, and the local civilian dignitaries. I managed it all with what I thought was a good grace, dredging up the details of some of their biographies and even managing to pat one young tyke, the son of the mayor of Kursk, on the head. So this is what it came down to, this business of being an admiral—shaking hands and kissing babies.

Finally, free of the formalities, I was escorted by a small honor motorcade to the visiting dignitaries quarters, safely ensconced in the back of the Zil limousine and flanked fore and aft by military vehicles and motorcycles.

There was another reception planned for that evening. Another one of those long affairs where I tried to remember everyone's name and anything of importance he or she said while the Russians tried to weasel tiny bits of operational information out of me. In the weeks afterward, I knew a team of Russian intelligence experts would be scrutinizing my every word, looking for nuances of American policy, operational capabilities, and just about anything that could conceivably give them an edge over my battle group.

Attending one of these functions is truly like walking into the lion's den.

Except maybe tonight.

I had two hours before the reception began. It would be followed by a formal dinner, complete with many courses and determinedly hospitable dinner companions. Somewhere, hidden in this throng, there might be one person I truly wanted to talk to. The one who had gotten word to me via the network of MIA/POW families, who for some strange reason, either national or individual guilt, was providing information to us.

I'd thought I'd known who it was. And I'd been wrong.

It was Brent, who'd been currying favor with Sheila as an excuse to hang around our group. Brent, ostensibly with the State Department. Brent, who'd taken me aside for a quick whispered briefing and the promise of more information, and who'd identified himself finally as my in-country contact.

Brent, the spy.

The arrival of Anna on the scene had thrown both of us into a bit of a panic. According to Brent, she was far from the simple agricultural spy she held herself out to be. She was a top agent with internal security, one vetted for only high-level assignments. I supposed I should have been flattered that she was assigned to follow me around.

I would be meeting another man tonight, one that Brent had had many dealings with in the past. A man deeply involved in passing information on former POWs to American authorities. Whether or not he personally had seen the photographs of my father, he was responsible for getting them to me. And I had it on good authority that he might be at the dinner tonight. It would merely be a matter of finding both the time and opportunity to talk to him.

How would he make contact? It would be difficult, but certainly not impossible. It is a given when one is in Russia that one's quarters are bugged, that one is followed continually, and every action and chance encounter is recorded on videotape. I had no illusions that we would be able to arrange a clandestine meeting, although it seems to be the norm for espionage movies.

No, the meeting would take place in public, cloaked by the presence of other guests. My contact would find some way to make it appear normal, to avoid arousing any attention. After all, he had lived in this environment for far longer than I had.

I unpacked, waving away the attentions of the Russians assigned to me. I was introduced to my maid, an attractive young woman whose English was suspiciously good for a domestic worker. Based on her brief comments, I was left with the impression that her range of services could be as extensive as I wished, up to and including keeping my bed warm.

The transparent attempt amused me. Did they really think that I was likely to engage in sexual misconduct while deep in the heart of an old enemy? Even if I had not been married to Tomboy, and did not love her unconditionally, I would not have been tempted. Not here.

Finally, the last of the hangers-on left my quarters. I was left alone, with still an hour to spare before I had to be ready to leave. I eyed the dress uniform hanging in the wardrobe, contemplated the possibility of a hot shower, then decided what I really needed was a nap. I shucked off my clothes down to my skivvies and slid into the luxurious king-size bed. I set my alarm, granting myself twenty minutes, and immediately dozed off.

It's a skill you learn at sea, the ability to catnap on demand, grabbing precious sleep whenever and wherever the opportunity presents itself.

As always, the alarm startled me slightly. I came immediately awake, ready to deal with whatever situation was at hand. There had been too many times at sea when this was exactly how I first learned of the crisis, of the loss of aviators at sea, or some new, hostile move made by adversaries.

But this time, there were not the familiar background noises of the carrier. Only silence. Thick drapes muffled the sounds of the airstrip two miles away. It was deadly silent.

After a few minutes, I allowed myself the luxury of enjoying the warm sheets, letting my level of consciousness drift back down to a doze.

Only a few moments. I shoved the bedclothes away and rolled into a sitting position. My toes dug into the deep, plush carpet, felt thick padding under the soles of my feet. I wondered how many of the Russian people knew how their ruling class lived.

They came to escort me to the dinner precisely at 7 P.M. I was ready and waiting, outfitted in my dress whites. Broad swaths of gold gleamed on my shoulders, broken only by the three silver stars indicating my rank and the insignia indicating I was a line officer.

The short dash between my quarters and the limousine was brutal. The winds had picked up as a front moved south, and I could feel the blood congealing in my cheeks and other exposed skin, even under my heavy winter coat. Warm air billowed out of the open limousine door, condensing immediately into fog. I slipped gratefully into the backseat.

Admiral Ilanovich was already waiting for me. "Everything is satisfactory?" he said, once we'd exchanged greetings.

"Quite. Please express my appreciation to the commander of the base."

"I will, of course. You can tell him yourself this evening if you wish." The admiral shot me a sly, sidewise glance. "And his superiors, as well. At this stage in his career, it could only help."

"I thought that's what I was doing."

The admiral laughed, true amusement in his voice. "No, Captain First Rank Chelnov does not report to me. He has other, more demanding masters."

I mulled that over for a few moments before replying. When dealing with the Russians, one must assume that everything is said for a purpose. They make the same assumption in dealing with us, which is a mistake on their part. American naval officers are not so well schooled in the intricate games of political intrigue.

What did the admiral mean by that? A few possibilities

came to mind. Perhaps it was a warning, one aviator to another. Possible, but not probable. There was undoubtedly some more subtle agenda at work.

Finally, I asked, "What masters?"

That was a reasonable reaction for an American officer, one that the admiral probably expected. It would place the ball back in his court, giving him the opportunity to explain or further confuse me.

The admiral was silent for a moment. Although his eyes reflected nothing but good cheer, I knew that he was spinning this turn in the conversation around in his mind.

"Russia has always been a strange place for Americans," he said finally. "You have never understood our interlocking directories, the functional structure of our chains of command. You assume we are like you are, with command related to specific task force or functional area of platforms."

"Not me. I know better than to make those assumptions, I think." I tried to make my voice and tone match his. We were having a conversation on several levels, or at least I thought so. Either way, I was intrigued by his evasions. Why had he brought up the chain of command? I had to assume it was for a reason.

But maybe that in itself was a mistake. The complicated game of guessing and double-guessing the meaning of each other's remarks generated the labyrinth of meaning. Perhaps he was counting on speaking with a guileless American officer, not one of his own. His comment on the chain of command was then nothing more than a simple professional statement, one intended to educate a foreign officer not familiar with Russia.

Or to prepare me for something that would happen later that evening?

On the other hand, it could be that he knew how well I thought I understood Russian psychology. He might be playing to that, counting on my ability to discern his hidden agenda without stating it openly. A far more flattering interpretation, and he might be counting on that as well, that I would interpret to my own favor.

Chain of command—this complicated multileveled discussion had all been generated by my simple remark about my quarters. If this were any indication of what I would face tonight, I would have to be particularly careful with my conversation.

The reception hall was a series of connecting rooms immediately to the right of the officers club. This time, the limousine had stopped just a few feet away from the entrance, which was an enclosed walkway. It was cold, but the bitter wind blowing out of the north was cut off.

The crowd thronged around me, many of the faces familiar from the earlier reception line at the air base. I greeted those whose names I could remember, silently bemoaning the fact that I had not brought an American aide with me. He or she would've been at my side, slightly behind me, coaching me on names, easing the crowd along.

I managed as best I could, committing some social errors no doubt, but surviving. A glass of vodka was thrust into my hands. I held it by my fingertips, feeling the cold reach out to me through the thick glass. Russian liquor is like its weather—it's made me wonder why the English still drink warm beer.

"You would care for champagne instead?" the admiral asked, obviously noting the fact that I had not immediately bolted down the vodka. "Or perhaps American liquor?"

"It looks to be a pleasant evening," I said mildly. "My capacity for liquor does not match that of the average Russian." At once I regretted the remark, hearing in it the possibility of insult, implying that Russians were drunkards.

To my relief, the admiral laughed heartily. "We know that about Americans," he boomed. "That is why I insisted on a supply of your own liquor as well."

I demurred to that as well, and turned my attention to the crowd. They were still milling around, obviously waiting for a chance to greet me.

I had my own reasons for wanting to meet at least one of them.

There seemed to be at least three hundred people packed into the room. An hour later, my hand felt like it had shaken hands with all of them at least twice. There was still no sign of a contact—no meaningful glances, no whispered request to speak later in private. I began to doubt. How could he ever arrange it under the scrutiny of all these military and civilian officials?

Just then, a man drifted out of the crowd and stood before me. Muscle corded his arms, and I had a sense of easy, lazy grace, controlled power that could explode into motion upon provocation. He held out his hand and said in passable English, "Good evening, Admiral. Vladimir Vylchek. I am in charge of the sports programs for this district. The athletic teams, conditioning for new pilots—all phases of it. I understand you are a runner?"

I nodded, containing my curiosity. Now, just where had he gotten that piece of information? Yes, I often took advantage of clear weather and no flight operations to work out on the flight deck, but I was purely in the class of most amateur athletes. I ran because it was good for me.

"I notice for your schedule that there is some time free tomorrow morning. I, too, am a runner. Perhaps you would care to join me for an early workout?" he asked.

Was this my contact? I had hoped Brent would be in view when it happened and be able to give me some subtle signal. Nevertheless, the offer seemed just too much of an opportunity to pass up. "I would. Thank you for the invitation."

Vladimir looked pleased. "A few additional precautions you may wish to take," he said. "The weather is much colder than you are used to. Gloves and a face mask are helpful. If you do not have them, I will be happy to loan you an extra set of mine."

I continued smiling, stifling the groan crowding in the back of my throat. Just the thought of exercise in this weather was more than I wanted to contemplate. "Good suggestions," I agreed. "Fortunately, I have my own equipment. What time shall I be ready?"

"Will five o'clock be too early?"

"Come now, Vladimir," the admiral broke in. "Surely you are not proposing to take our guest on a three-mile run in the dark in this weather?" He gestured vaguely around him, encompassing the weather outside the stuffy reception hall. "I really do think—"

"On the contrary, Admiral," I said firmly. "It is not everyone's idea of fun, but I am rather looking forward to a stiff workout in the morning. Too many days of flying, of traveling—perhaps we could finish with a sauna?" I turned my back to Vladimir. "I understand that is a Russian tradition."

Vladimir nodded vigorously. "Of course. We have excellent facilities on the base itself—if you have not experienced a true Russian sauna, you are in for a remarkable treat. It will be the highlight of your visit to Russia, I promise." He beamed congenially, obviously delighted at my acceptance.

"At five o'clock, then," I said.

Vladimir drifted back off into the crowd with one last friendly wave. I heard the admiral grumbling beside me in Russian. Then he turned away from me and spoke with one of his aides. They held a brief, whispered conversation in Russian. "Do not feel obliged, Admiral Magruder. Vladimir is well known to us for his obsession with running. But none of us would think the less of you if you decline."

I regarded him levelly for a moment. Was there some reason the admiral wanted to keep me away from Vladimir? Or was Vladimir the contact man I had been seeking? If so, a morning run in this cruel climate was not too stiff a price to pay. "On the contrary, Admiral. I'm sure it will help clear the cobwebs from my brain. Perhaps you would care to join us?" I felt safe in making the offer, since the admiral was clearly not one of Vladimir's students. Probably the last time he had run had been when the limousine was too far from a heated walkway.

"We will provide security for you, of course," the admiral said, a small bit of anger breaking through his mask of friendliness. "I'm sure there are men among my guards who will be delighted at the prospect of an early morning run with Vladimir."

I waved a hand grandly. "I would not dream of imposing on them. Surely we will be perfectly safe if we stay around the base. After all, in these days, what have we to fear from one another?"

"I cannot allow that," the admiral said firmly. "If anything happened to you, it would be my head."

"To the contrary, Admiral. I must confess, being constantly followed and escorted everywhere gets a bit weary for an American officer. I am sure you have had the same experience during your visits to America. Quite frankly, I relish the idea of spending some time alone running."

"But what if—"

"Are you saying it is not safe on this base?" I let the question hang in the air, implying as it did a lack of diligence on his part.

"We are perfectly safe," the admiral snapped, all pretext of bonhomie now gone from his voice. "But surely you must know there are certain restrictions on all senior officers— both in your country and in mine. One must not take chances."

"Then perhaps that is something that you must learn from us as well," I said softly. "In my country, you would be quite safe walking alone on any military installation." Privately, I was not as certain of that sentiment as I would like to have been, but I was not about to back down now. If Vladimir was my contact person, then I had to meet with him alone. Had to.

"You will be followed by men in a transport, then," the admiral said, his voice surly. "Surely you cannot object to that. In case of a cramp, the effects of the weather—for health purposes, you understand."

"Very well, then. Now, the undersecretary for naval aviation—I met him earlier, but I have not seen him tonight. I was hoping to discuss some of the finer points of carrier aviation with him."

The admiral relaxed visibly. "Of course," he murmured. A few quiet words to his aide and I was escorted off in search of the man.

In reality, I had no particular interest in speaking to the undersecretary. However, I had known the words that would arouse their interest. By this time, they were finding it tedious trying to get me talking about technical matters, and the possibility that I would divulge some interesting details on American carrier construction, particularly the catapults, was too tempting to bait.

I managed to finesse the rest of the evening without mishap, unless you count having to dance around the finer details of catapult construction with the undersecretary. As I smiled, made small talk, and tried to keep names associated with faces, one thought kept intruding.

Who was Vladimir? Was he who I hoped he was?

EIGHT

Monday, 21 December

0900 Local (+3 GMT)
USS Jefferson

Commander Lab Rat Busby:

Trouble rarely begins during the daylight hours. Even as humans lose track of their circadian rhythms, confusing day and night in the endless cycle of watches, duty, and meals onboard a carrier, disaster always seems to know precisely what time it is. It happens in the early morning hours, and more often than not, the people that must deal with it are awakened by watchstanders pounding on their doors.

This time, it was different. And that worried me.

It was nine o'clock in the morning, and I had been at my desk for almost three hours after a hasty breakfast consisting primarily of cinnamon rolls and coffee. The sugar and caffeine were beginning to wear off, and I was starting to count the hours until an early lunch. I had the speakers in my office turned low, merely background noise. The normal tactical chatter surrounded me, filtered out of consciousness by my brain.

Ever since the first detection of our Russian submarines, we had kept a continuous antisubmarine patrol in the air. One of my speakers was dialed up on that circuit.

It was the tone of the pilot's voice more than the words he said that first caught my attention. I knew him, as I knew most of the pilots, and it wasn't often that he got excited. Not in public, at least.

Commander "Rabies" Grill was one of the most experienced S-3 pilots onboard. While we were in the Spratly Islands, we had had our first encounter with an enemy submarine firing surface-to-air missiles. He rotated off *Jefferson* a few years ago, and had returned just two months ago, selected for full commander and headed toward the prospective executive officer—PXO—slot with VS-29. His flight crews complained about his love for country music, and said he was fond of singing to them during extended flights. I had heard Rabies singing, and I pitied them.

Even now, I wouldn't have called his voice excited. Just out of character—enough to catch my attention.

"Home Plate, this is Hunter 701. Is our bird sweet?"

Rabies was asking if his data link with the carrier was up and working. An odd question, since aircrews usually didn't worry about data links unless the carrier was bugging them. I glanced over at the data console to see for myself.

The symbol for the antisubmarine warfare aircraft was clearly displayed, moving in a circular orbit approximately forty miles northeast of the carrier. There had been some concerns earlier that day about the ice moving and the meteorologist had recommended moving to the north to stay in open water. If ice started forming, the sonobuoys must be able to break through it to reach the water, but the ice would prevent the antenna from deploying and transmitting the information back to the aircraft.

When Rabies had reported on station, he had noted that the water was essentially open at that point. However, the ice did indeed appear to be forming up to the south of his briefed pattern, and he was worried about problems later in the mission.

Now it looked like he had other things to worry about.

"Roger, Hunter 701. Good data link." The operations specialist's voice was calm and unconcerned. "Problem on your end?"

"No. Just wanted to make sure it was good for you, too."

The operations specialist rolled his eyes over the risqué remark. "You need to talk to the USW module—we're sweet and hot on number six, and I'm not hearing you talk to me about it."

"Hot?" The operations specialist now sounded interested. I could picture him leaning forward over his console, picking up his white grease pencil, and preparing to scratch notes on his radar screen as he watched the symbol representing the aircraft he was controlling track across it. "How hot?"

"How does positive acoustic contact on a Victor and an Akula strike you? That hot enough?" I could hear the undercurrent of cool amusement in Rabies's voice. Rabies might take the brunt of some good-humored teasing within the squadron, but unlike most pilots, he was no slouch when it came to USW. Most pilots left it to their TACCOs, but Rabies knew more about it than just the tactical implications of getting his aircraft from one spot to another, of positioning it to drop sonobuoys where the TACCO wanted them.

"How close are they?" It was the TAO's voice now, breaking in on the interchange.

"Look for yourself," Rabies answered. "You said the data link was good, didn't you?" He left unspoken the possibility that the TAO couldn't read. But implied it quite clearly.

The circuit fell silent for a few moments. I could imagine the panic that was starting in CDC, the squawking over the bitch box, the calls going out over the ship's internal telephone system. Within a few moments, the TAO would have talked to the flag TAO, who would call the admiral. I glanced at the clock on the wall. Admiral Wayne was a believer in intelligence. Any second now . . .

The phone rang. I picked it up myself. "Busby."

"Get down here." The admiral's sharp Boston voice was unmistakable. As was his immediate reaction to new data on the missing Russian submarines. "You have been listening, I take it? Judging from the speed at which you answered the telephone, one might even suspect you had anticipated my call."

Admiral Wayne and I had been on three cruises together. If I could not anticipate his wants by now, I truly was a sorry intelligence officer. "Of course I'm listening, Admiral." I left unanswered the rest of his comment.

"Do you know anything about this? Anything more than we've discussed?"

Another odd question, coming from him. By now Admiral Wayne should have known that anything I knew, he knew.

But maybe not so odd, given what had happened before. After all, Admiral Wayne had known about the American submarines in the area. And he had not told me. It was a simple matter of mistrust breeding mistrust, and one of the reasons I prefer to have no secrets from my admiral.

But RHIP—rank has its privileges. I hauled my skinny butt up out of my chair and headed for TFCC.

As soon as I stepped into the small compartment located immediately off of the admiral's conference room, I knew this situation had gotten worse in the few moments it had taken me to walk down there from CVIC. In addition to the normal watch standards, there were three submarine officers in TFCC. I knew one of them well, Commander Hank Fowler. He was attached to the admiral's staff as the submarine community representative. I had found him to be a normal type of submariner—that is to say, extremely bright, lacking in social skills, and having a utterly odd, dry sense of humor.

Submarines have three rules: $I = E/R$, $P = MA$, and "You can't push a rope." They are generally funny as hell, if you can get past the weirdness.

I stuck my head in SCIF, the Specially Compartmented Information module located immediately next to TFCC. I doubted that there was anything new to be learned there, but I wanted my people to know I was in the area. That way, they could find me if they needed to.

Two seconds—that's all it took. Then I stepped inside TFCC. I moved just barely inside the heavy steel hatch that separated the compartment from the conference room, which opened onto a small vestibule. I made eye contact

with the admiral, then settled in to wait. He knew I was here
and he would yell if he needed me.

Immediately, I knew we were in trouble. Not the carrier,
but the submarine traveling with our battle group.

At the depths at which they operate in order to remain
concealed, submarines have very few options for communication. They can launch a transmitter buoy, which will
reach the surface and broadcast their message to anyone
listening. Noisy, and it gives away the submarine's position.
If she's got time, the submarine can come shallow, send the
message to the satellite, and back down to us directly. But
there are disadvantages to giving up the protection of depth
as well. Finally, there was the low-frequency option. The
submarine carried an acoustic generator that could broadcast low-frequency tones. In addition to using her underwater telephone, code-named Gertrude, she could transmit a
series of tonals that would pass a coded message to any
platform with the appropriate receiver. However, without
the code book, the message could not be unscrambled.

Most USW assets now carry some form of recording
equipment. While they may not be able to decode the signal
immediately, they can transmit the frequency information to
the aircraft carrier.

And we can decipher it. Oh yes, we can. And the chaos
that I was seeing in the flag plot right now was evidence of
that.

"How bad is it?" Admiral Wayne demanded. He was
nose-to-nose with Commander Fowler.

"About as bad as it gets." Hank was as worried as I'd ever
seen him. "There's triple redundancy built into every
system, but even that sometimes isn't enough. If three
reactor coolant pumps are down, she's got problems." He
shook his head, acknowledging the effect of Murphy on any
sensitive military mission. "If it had to happen, you have to
figure it would be here."

"How many does she have onboard?" the admiral asked.

"Four—with a couple of emergency measures built in as
well. There are things that they can do, Admiral, and they
may be able to fix some of it. But I have to tell you, being

at depth, I wouldn't want to try. Too much goes wrong, you have to shut a reactor down—and there you are. You have to use your batteries to come shallow, then maybe you don't have enough power to restart the reactor later on. And there you are, stuck shallow in Russian waters."

Finally, the admiral turned to me. "Anything to add?"

I shook my head. There was no additional intelligence data I could provide, nothing that would matter in this situation. There were submarines in the area, nasty tough ones, and our boat had problems

The admiral stared at the large-screen display as though he could will it to change. The geometry of the attack was perfectly clear there—our submarine, theirs, and the carrier battle group. "It's always a trade-off, isn't it?" He shook his head. "We can provide some additional protection for our own ship by moving the destroyer in closer to her, but that's likely to tip our hand. They'll know that we know, and we will know that they know that we know. Oh, what a tangled web we weave . . ."

"When first we practice to deceive," I said, finishing the quotation. Between Murphy and Shakespeare, I figured we summed the situation up pretty well.

The submariner spoke then. "There is one other possibility." Whatever it was, I could tell by his expression he didn't like it. "They do carry a certain amount of spare parts, as well as some crackerjack mechanics and engineers. I've seen a submarine machinist's mate completely rebuild a main coolant pump while we were on a mission. It was amazing—when we got back to port, the company that built it damn near cried. The tolerances were all off, he'd jury-rigged some gaskets, and it worked like a charm. And quiet—quieter than the original. I think they offered him a ton of money to leave the Navy, but he didn't."

The admiral looked skeptical. "So you think they can fix it?"

The submariner nodded. "Even if they can't, they can still operate with one pump. Not as fast, not as long. And no captain is going to like it, operating without triple redundancy. But they can do it for a while—maybe long enough to get another pump fixed. If you want them to."

Admiral Wayne stared at him for a moment. "It always comes down to this, doesn't it?" he said softly. "For the skipper on that sub and for me. How far are we willing to go to finish the mission? What do you think he's going to want?"

"I think he is going to want to finish the mission." Fowler smiled a little, and I caught a glimpse of the kind of decisions he must have had to make during his command tour. "The first thing they make sure of in sub school is that you're not afraid of the deep water. Or claustrophobic. If I were that skipper, knowing what my mission was, I'd want some peace and quiet so I could take a shot at fixing at least one of the pumps. Remember, he's not screaming for rescue right now. He's just advising us of the situation, letting us know what he can and can't do. If he needs help, don't worry—you'll hear about it."

"If you were him, where would you like to be?" I asked.

Fowler pointed a stubby finger at a series of lopsided, stretched-out circles. "There. That looks to be the nearest thing I've seen to an undersea canyon in this part of the world. Deep water, and the canyon will trap most of the sound. It's the closest thing to a hideout around."

"Not much place to run, though. Not if that Akula gets a sniff of her."

The Akula was the deepest-diving submarine in the Russian inventory. It was also the fastest, capable of speeds exceeding thirty-five knots, far faster than anything we had in the water. Even our new Seawolf couldn't chase her down.

Admiral Wayne nodded. "That's the plan, then. At least for now." He turned to me. "Get on your secret line to SUBLANT. Get them to tell that submarine to lay low and fix it. We're here in case they need us, and I can have that destroyer in their immediate vicinity if they need protection. But for now, we stick with the game plan."

"What do we tell Rabies?" I asked.

"Why the hell should I tell him anything?" Admiral Wayne looked annoyed.

"Because sooner or later he will be back onboard," I said. "Sure, I'll tell him not to talk, but too many people have already seen what's going on. There are a lot of smart people on this aircraft carrier, Admiral, and most of them don't work for me. They'll be asking questions—and we need some answers."

The admiral sighed. "It's not like they're going on liberty and will be shooting their mouths off in bars, is it? Why do I have to tell them anything?"

Because it will get us in trouble if you don't. Just like now—you knew about the American sub with us and you didn't tell me about it. Secrets ought to be what we keep from the enemy—not from each other.

I didn't say that, of course. There was no need to—the admiral knew it as well as I did. Instead, I said, "Morale, sir. Rabies is a smart officer—he'll figure it out soon enough."

The one thing you never want to say onboard a carrier is *What else can go wrong?* As soon as you do, something else will. I saw Admiral Wayne start to say the words, felt a mild pulse of fear, then looked back up at the large-screen display.

Sometimes it wasn't even necessary to say it—just thinking it was bad enough.

Two enemy aircraft had just appeared on the far eastern quarter of the display. In these close quarters, they were well within our weapons range, as we were within theirs. Not that anybody was thinking weapons—of course, this was a goodwill mission. Some war games, sure, that sort of thing.

"I'll be in SCIF," I said abruptly. In two steps I was back in my own domain. The admiral followed me. I pulled the heavy steel hatch shut behind us, locked it, and went immediately to the sensor operator. "Anything?"

"Just those MiGs that launched. So far, they're following the same patrol pattern as the earlier missions." The technician looked at me, then returned his gaze to the screen. "We have some reason to worry about them?"

I shook my head. "No video downlink?"

Video downlink was a method of communication between an aircraft and a submarine or surface ship. It was one of the most critical bits of SIGINT, or signal intelligence, that we could detect. VDL was used for passing targeting information from the aircraft, who had a farther horizon, to the shooting platform. If you think there are no submarines in the area and you start detecting VDL, you know you've been mistaken. In this case, if we detected VDL, we would know that the MiGs were talking to the submarines chasing ours.

Or worse—that the aircraft were passing targeting information on the carrier to one of the submarines. If they were carrying the new 28mm torpedoes, we were in serious trouble. One shot right under the keel could sink an aircraft carrier.

"Might be nice to get me some help over here," Rabies's voice said. "I'm a little short on air-to-air missiles right now."

I saw what Rabies was worried about. The two Russian aircraft were rapidly approaching his location. The S-3 has a maximum speed of 450 knots. The MiG could do about three times that—not a fair contest. Furthermore, the S-3 carried only torpedoes and a few antisurface weapons, nothing capable of taking on a determined fighter. There was no contest.

"Where is our CAP?" the admiral snapped. "Damn it, get that man some help!" Before he could even finish his sentence, I heard the air traffic controller in CDC talking quietly, urgently, with our airborne fighters. The symbols on the screen changed direction immediately and streaked north from their position south of the carrier battle group, interposing themselves between the carrier and the intruders.

Something cold in my stomach went sour. It wasn't going to start this way, was it? With nerves rubbed raw on either side, aircraft approaching each other too fast for rational thought, missiles fired before anyone truly thought out the consequences?

"Rabies, get your ass out of there," the USW controller said urgently. "Come on, man . . ."

Rabies's aircraft was now turned away from the MiGs, beating feet back toward the carrier. But the Russian aircraft were far closer to him that our own fighters were.

What had we been thinking? Leaving him out there alone? Or had the admiral reasoned that putting up fighters to escort him would escalate the tensions, that there was no real danger to an unarmed S-3 Viking supposedly conducting safety of navigation operations? I was beginning to doubt that we could ever have sold anyone on that particular explanation for disobeying the prohibition on USW missions.

No matter. At this point, the situation was critical.

Admiral Wayne grabbed a microphone from the overhead, the one hardwired into the tactical fighter net. He stared at the two friendly fighter symbols on the large-screen display as he spoke. "This is the admiral," he said. "Listen up."

"Tomcat lead, Admiral. I'm listening." The lead pilot's voice was cool and collected. "We're about to have us a situation here. Any guidance?"

"I'm not going to second-guess you on this," the admiral began. "At the first sign of any hostile activity, you nail their asses. But don't jump the gun."

There was silence from the aircraft. I could tell what they were thinking—*Gee, thanks, that helps a lot, Admiral . . .*

For what it was worth, I agreed with them. But what else could the admiral tell them? Don't take the first shot at the Russians—but don't let the Russians take it either.

It was deadly silent inside CVIC. No one moved, as though to do so would disturb the pilots forty miles away. Most of them were pilots themselves, and I could see that they were imagining the situation inside the cockpit. Playing out their reactions to the MiGs, figuring out how they would handle it themselves. Hands moved, almost involuntarily, reflexively fighting the battle taking place on the screen.

It was difficult to breathe. The tension inside TFCC was palpable.

The aircraft symbols on the large-screen display moved slowly, creeping millimeter by millimeter across the projection. Altitude and speed indicator numbers clicked over silently on the data display at the TAO's right hand. Rabies was hauling ass, buster—as in "bust your ass getting here"—toward the boat. The MiGs were right on his tail now.

"A little too close for comfort," I heard him grunt on the speaker. No shit. The MiG symbol was so close to that of the S-3 that the two were merging. Rabies must be able to see him, practically feel his breath down the back of his neck.

"Little bastard is all over me," Rabies continued. "He and playmate—we got one directly overhead, and I think the other is right under us. They're swapping places—the turbulence is hell. Where the hell are those Tomcats? Damned fighters—never around except during meal hours."

Admiral Wayne keyed the microphone in his hand. "They should be almost to you. Have you got a visual yet? Same altitude, dead ahead."

"No, not yet. TACCO's got them on LINK, but I don't—wait, there they are."

"Expand the picture," Admiral Wayne ordered. The TAO's fingers danced over the keyboard, zooming out on the one small piece of sky crowded with fighters and one lone S-3. The scale grew larger, reducing the area displayed on screen. I could see them now, the two fighters moving slightly away from the S-3, the two friendly Tomcats boring in on them.

Our Tomcats were in combat spread, one high and one low. It was an effective fighting formation, and one the U.S. Navy had perfected over the decades.

"Doesn't look like they're going to scare that easy," Rabies said. "But as long as they go pick on someone their own size, I'm happy."

"Rabies, get the hell out of here," a new voice broke in. "We'll take it from here."

"What the hell do you think I've been trying to do?" Rabies answered. "Play patty-cake?"

The lead Tomcat pilot arched in toward the MiGs, bearing down on them with the rest of his flight behind him. Just as they were within short-range-missile distance of the MiGs, the Russian aircraft veered away. The Tomcats followed them, closing on their tails now, in perfect firing position, but the MiGs ignored them.

"What the hell was that all about?" the TAO wondered aloud. Batman just grunted.

We watched until the MiGs were back in Russian airspace. The Tomcats broke off as they reached the twelve-mile limit and turned back to the boat.

A training mission, perhaps. Or maybe just a reminder. We might never know which one.

"Admiral?" I asked. "Sir, about the American sub-marine—"

"No discussion," Batman ruled.

"One other question, then?" I asked.

"Shoot."

"What do we tell Tombstone about this? The subs, the MiGs?"

Batman was silent for a moment, then said, "Nothing."

NINE

Monday, 21 December

Vice Admiral Tombstone Magruder:

Vladimir was right on time. I'd already dressed and stretched out, and was ready to go.

"It is very important to keep moving," Vladimir said, running in place just outside the front door. "Even if you slow to walk, you will stiffen up too fast. Run—we will not go far, just three miles perhaps. This will be acceptable?"

"Three miles is fine." I could feel the cold seeping in through the long underwear and head covering. "I'll keep up."

At first, it was excruciating. The cold bled up through the soles of my running shoes, through two pairs of socks, and I lost feeling in my feet. Vladimir appeared unaffected, so I pressed on, struggling to extract oxygen from air so frigid it felt sterile.

Fifteen minutes into the run, I started warming up. A sense of well-being and euphoria flooded me, all the more startling for the circumstances. Vladimir set a brisk pace, but not a difficult one. Eight-minute miles, I figured. But from what I could tell, he'd made one small mistake in his English. This was not three miles total, it was three miles out and three miles back.

No matter. By now I could feel my muscles sliding easily over me, and I'd learned the trick of taking shallower breaths as my body settled into the rhythm of the run.

One of those ungainly Russian transports followed us but stayed well back. The noise of its engine was annoying in the cold, silent, dark morning, but it gradually faded to background as Vladimir cut off the road and led the way into the woods down a path too narrow for the transport to follow. When I could barely hear the Russian truck, Vladimir slowed to a walk.

"We have not much time," he said, his voice slightly ragged from the run. "Your father—there are circles within circles here in Russian, Admiral. Too many sides are trying to play this card with you."

"And you?"

He gave a short laugh. "You can trust me—I sent the photo." I'd not mentioned it to anyone other than my mother and my uncle, and I felt relatively sure they'd kept it quiet. "But you have no way of knowing that, do you?" he continued. "No reason to believe me. Still, later today someone will try to convince you that you are meeting your father. Please, test the man they present to you. Convince yourself—do not let them convince you with their statements alone."

"Where is he, then? And why will they try to deceive me?" I asked. The anger that was always below the surface surged back. I wanted to smash his face into the cold ground, feel his neck crushed between my hands.

Vladimir shook his head, and picked up the pace again. "It will take some time to arrange it. But first, you must let them make their play for your belief. Otherwise, you will not understand when I show you."

I reached out and grabbed him by the arm, spinning him around. "Who's working with you? Anna? Brent? Ilanovich?"

Vladimir pulled away easily, and I was aware of the immense power in his sculpted muscles. "All of them—but sometimes not with their knowledge. They think they do one thing, for one reason, but it has . . . repercussion." He paused, as though uncertain of the word. "Ripples."

"Who will try to trick me, then? Can you at least tell me that?"

Vladimir shook his head. "When you see the truth, you will know it. You are closer to it than you know. I have shown many families what has happened, and they all know. You will, too. Now, let us finish this run before we both turn to cement in the woods."

We reemerged from the woods onto the road and turned to head back to the quarters. I tried to regain the easy sense of timelessness I'd had on the first leg of the course, but the questions Vladimir had raised in my mind would not be silenced. When we finally reached the barracks, I was more troubled than when I'd left. Vladimir refused to answer any questions, thanked me for accompanying him, and let my security detachment take charge and hustle me back inside.

I showered and breakfasted lightly on the fresh pastries and fruit that had been delivered at my request. By now, I should have been accustomed to the intricacies of dealing with Russians, but if anything I was even more frustrated. Why would my search for my father raise so much interest—and for evidently different reasons—in various factions in Russia today? I could understand wanting to keep it a secret, to hide the fact that they'd done what they'd denied to the world. But if what Vladimir said was true, then more than one group wanted to be the ones who fessed up and tried to repair the damage. Some sort of maneuver by someone to demonstrate that they were the new Russian leadership determined to atone for past sins, I finally decided. My own personal agony was merely a pawn in some deeper game.

Was it even possible that my father was still alive? It had seemed so eighteen months ago when I'd first met the Ukrainian officer. In a way, I had believed it more readily then than now.

Perhaps it was something like the way an aviator never really believes he's going to die in his aircraft. Sure, it happens to others, pilots who aren't as careful. Or as good.

Or as touched by the gods, as most pilots seemed to feel.
Under the same circumstances, you're certain you would
have been smarter, faster, tougher—seen the problem earlier, done the right thing the first time, or, barring all that,
you would have been smart enough to punch out before it
was too late. Sometimes, that attitude bleeds over into the
rest of your life.

But no matter how good I was, this was all out of my
control. It was like sitting in the backseat if you didn't
have an ejection handle—which, thank God, a Tomcat RIO
does, a little fact that has saved my ass more than once—
with a pilot who's dead. You always need a way out. In
fact, that's a major teaching point in most training syllabi.
Always think one step ahead, plan what you're going to do
if things go to shit.

Maybe that's what was bothering me. That there was no
way out at this point, at least not one I could live with. The
Russians claimed my father was alive and that they would
take me to him. I had to either go see or live with that for
the rest of my life.

A knock on the door, then Ilanovich's distinct voice.
"Tombstone, my friend. I have news." I opened the door and
invited him in, already suspecting what he would have to
say.

It had been, according to Ilanovich, a matter of personal
honor to him as a Russian and as a senior naval officer.
He'd heard, of course, about my quest for my father. That
much he admitted readily, lending a semblance of sincerity
to the rest of his story. How could he, as my counterpart and
a man who respected me deeply, not only professionally but
on a personal level, allow this question to go unanswered?

I waited, holding down the anger and trying to appear
patient and interested through a thirty-minute narrative of
the difficulties of tracing down post–Cold War witnesses, of
penetrating the shrouded secrecy that cloaked even the most
innocent records in Russia, of calling in favors owed to him
dating back from his earliest days in the military. Finally,
Ilanovich concluded, he'd learned the truth. The horrifying,

glorious, shameful truth. My revulsion reached a new level at his next statement.

"Your father still lives, my friend," he said, his voice choked with emotion. "I cannot even begin to apologize— the things that happened, you understand, this is not the conduct of professional military men everywhere. The politicians, the GRU—you have my profoundest sympathies, and I will do everything in my power to correct this heinous act."

"Where is he?" I asked.

"Here—in Kursk, in a hospital. We can see him this afternoon. You . . . you will want to go, yes?"

"Of course I will." I started to try to add some words of thanks, but a profound confusion was setting in. Was Vladimir right? Was Ilanovich lying to me, trying to manipulate me for some purpose? How could I tell which one was telling me the truth?

Ilanovich evidently took my silence for profound emotions. He reached out, covered one of my hands with his own. "We will go then, at two o'clock. I will come for you." He started to say more, but something in my face stopped him. He stood, clapped one hand down hard on my shoulder, and squeezed. "I am honored to be able to do this thing, to set this right." He left me sitting there staring out at the early morning light.

It was still two hours before we were due to leave, but I was already dressed, waiting impatiently, just like a kid on his first day of school. Finally, when pacing the room was starting to get on even my own nerves, I forced myself to sit down in a comfortable chair located at one end of the room and consider my options.

First, I could simply not go. God knows there were plenty of reasons that I could come up for that one. The Navy was not going to be any too happy abut my traipsing around the Russian countryside unescorted. Any admiral in the Navy has enough classified material floating around inside his head to set back national security about fifteen years. Me more than most, given the amount of time that I'd spent on the front combat lines. If I wanted an excuse, I had a built-in one.

Then there was the small question of the rest of my detachment. Theoretically, we were in the middle of a goodwill airmanship contest. If I left, that would leave Gator Cummings in charge as the senior officer in the detachment.

Gator was a good man, no doubt about that. Smart, canny in a way that his hotheaded pilots Bird Dog and Skeeter would probably never recognize. But even though he could handle Bird Dog's ego in the cockpit, dealing with Russians and diplomatic relationships on the ground required different skills, ones I wasn't sure he was senior enough to have mastered yet.

Could he handle the Russians? Under normal circumstances, yes.

But these weren't normal circumstances. Lab Rat's daily wrap-up message had mentioned increasing tensions in the water to the north of us, and I was feeling increasingly uneasy about even being on the ground in Russia. If things fell apart, it would be a hell of a lot more awkward for the Russians to make an American admiral disappear than some more junior officers. Not to mention the two Tomcats we brought with us.

No doubt about it, there were plenty of reasons for me not to go. Any one of them would have been sufficient.

The only hard point was that I could see no way that I would be able to live with myself afterward. My uncle understood that, and it had been the only reason that he had authorized this mission at all. Uncle Thomas was made of stronger stuff than his nephew—I knew in that moment that he could have lived with the knowledge that his brother was still alive.

I couldn't. Whether it was because I was his son, or that I had some weakness Uncle Thomas did not, I could not say. Nevertheless, there was simply no way I could not go.

But that didn't mean I couldn't have a contingency plan. The resources available to me in this country were scant, to be sure. But I had a couple of tricks up my sleeve that I was relatively sure the Russians didn't know about.

I pulled my black leather briefcase up onto my lap, and paused a moment before opening it. If there was video camera surveillance in this room, then I was well and truly screwed.

I picked up my briefcase and walked over to the bed. It was still rumpled and unmade since I had not left the room long enough for the maids to take care of it. I lifted up the heavy comforter that was the top layer and pulled it over my head while still sitting on the edge of the bed.

I slid the briefcase on the bed and under the cover. If the Russians were watching, they would undoubtedly be suspicious.

Suspicious—and ignorant. They might think I was carrying classified material, drugs, or almost anything else. They might even suspect the truth.

I unlatched the briefcase and pulled out the pistol. Still under the covers, I tucked the pistol into the special pocket concealed just under my armpit. I had spent hours at the tailor making sure it would fit without showing. It would not survive even the most routine pat down, and certainly not a metal detector, but at least it wouldn't advertise its existence to a casual observer.

It might not do me any good but I felt better having it on me. And with any luck, I wouldn't need it. After all, luck had gotten me this far. If I hadn't been onboard USS *Jefferson* when Yuri had been there, I never would've heard about my father in the first place.

I paused for a moment and considered that proposition. Had it been luck and nothing more? The same capricious factor that had put my father over the bridge just as antiair search radar came on? The same thing that had kept him alive through the ejection and perhaps the countless years in Russian custody? That luck?

Or had it been something more sinister? Could the Russians—and the Ukraine for that matter—have known I was going onboard *Jefferson* that very day? At that time, I had no longer been in command of either the ship or the battle group. Predicting my presence onboard *Jefferson* would have required an intelligence gathering capability far greater than I wanted to believe they had.

But it was hard to go wrong overestimating the capabilities of your opponent. At best, it would keep you prepared for disasters that others had failed to anticipate. At worst, you simply had an additional edge on them.

Did it always come back to this, then? Thinking and rethinking, anticipating and planning, almost to the point of outguessing yourself?

I patted down the gun again, finding a way out of the circular reasoning by feeling its hard outline under my fingers.

My escort arrived precisely on time. I opened the door, expecting to see the military police, the translator assigned as my aide, and a few other pilot fish with them for good measure. Who I didn't expect to see was my counterpart Admiral Ilanovich.

"It would be my honor to accompany you," the admiral began. "And perhaps to expedite this trip should unexpected difficulties arise." He stepped across the threshold, held up his hand in American fashion, then apparently changed his mind and gave me a quick, hard Russian hug.

I started to endure the unwanted familiarity with diplomatic grace. Then I remembered the gun. I drew back sharply, the classic American startled by customs that were not his. I feigned a look of discomfort, followed by an apology of a smile. With any luck, they would buy it.

The admiral looked slightly offended for a moment, then his face moved over into a diplomatic mask similar to my own. "I forget," he said. "Our customs, they are so different. And we Russians are an emotional race. That you'll see your father today, after so many years—please, forgive my intrusion." He touched one finger to the corner of his eye, a move that I found over-the-top. From this man, this admiral, I did not buy an excess of emotion that drove him to tears. And I was slightly insulted that he thought it would work.

• • •

We left the visiting officers quarters in one of those ubiquitous black Zil limousines that are the hallmark of power and prestige in this part of Russia. I heard that Mercedes-Benz were replacing them in Moscow and other large cities, but that innovation had not made it this far north yet. Besides, there were no doubt more Zil automotive technicians than Mercedes this far north. There was something about the native Russian construction of the engine and the suspension that was peculiarly more adapted to this harsh northern climate.

Traffic was light, as it always is in most Russian cities. The average Russian citizen does not own a car, uses public transportation, and traffic jams are one of the innovations of the late twentieth century that had not yet come to Russian cities. Not that the roads would have supported them. Except for main thoroughfares, the roads were generally in bad repair, potholed and tortured by the brutal winter climate.

The buildings on either side, apart from the military installations, had a dirty, neglected look to them. Row after row of featureless cinder-block apartments, some looking half-occupied. There were few signs of human habitation—no plants in the windows, no decorative curtains, nothing to indicate who actually lived there. Combined with a lack of traffic on the roads, it gave the entire area a deserted, forlorn look.

And why should the average citizen do anything to personalize his or her living quarters? After all, they didn't own them—didn't even pay any rent, at least not in most areas. The facilities were owned by the state, provided to the citizen along with food—scarce and in poor quality—and utilities—intermittent at best and sometimes consisting only of dirty-burning coal—as a benefit of Russian citizenship. As much as anything, that is the difference between a communist economy and our own system of free enterprise. In America, you decide who you want to be and then work to earn it. In Russia, the state decided.

Finally, we pulled to a stop in front of a building only

slightly less derelict than the others. It was constructed of a lighter shade of concrete, with the same small windows and forbidding construction as the apartment buildings. A Russian bus was parked in front, rust streaking the sides and with two windows missing. It pulled away belching dark smoke, the jerky motion indicating that the transmission was barely operating.

The admiral pointed at it and said, "What you call mass transit. Very highly developed here in Russia. You notice how clean the air is? We do not have your reliance on Middle East oil for private automobiles."

"And your domestic resources are sufficient for all of your heating and industrial purposes, I take it?" I asked. Bragging. The Russian economy was in an abysmal state. The oil producing fields around the Black Sea hardly made Russia self-sustaining. Indeed, if anything, their reliance on foreign oil was even stronger than our own. And with the recent construction of a pipeline between a few independent former Soviet Union states and Turkey, with Turkey undertaking refining of the crude, Russia was surely to be hit worse than before. Only several years ago, utilities to most major naval installations had been terminated in Ukraine when Russia failed to pay for heating oil. Critical in the south—deadly here in the north.

"Our distribution system is most efficient," the admiral replied, and left it at that.

The car pulled to stop directly opposite the entrance, taking the place of the bus I'd seen pull away. A man darted out and opened the back door for us to disembark.

The wind was muted here, undoubtedly blocked by the massive rows of buildings. The cold still bit immediately, and I could feel it etching lines in my face.

It was but a few short steps into the building. I passed through a double layer of doors intended to retain as much of the building heat as possible against the icy climate, and was immediately uncomfortably warm in a long winter coat. I shucked it off and was then conscious of the thickness under my arm and the pistol snuggled there.

Was it noticeable? I slid my hands over my body, as

though checking for wrinkles in my jacket. Yes, I could feel it—it would be immediately discernible to anyone who wanted to pat me down, but the odds of that happening in a Russian hospital were not high. Or so I hoped.

We were met by a Russian civil servant, one of the institutions that Russia shares with us. In some strange way, he resembled his building—an institutionalized look, closed off and inaccessible. There was no telling how long he had held the position. Russian civil servants earn their positions by party membership and political patronage and, once in place, tend to be as long-lived as their American counterparts. Even in the post–Soviet Union era, party membership still counted for something.

Introductions were exchanged, the translator moving quickly to my side. I murmured something polite about the facilities. It was as though I could feel my father's presence radiating down from the floors above, calling to me, insisting that I see him. I glanced up involuntarily, almost expected to see the summons flooding in the air.

After I refused the traditional offer of tea and refreshments, the hospital administrator nodded understandingly. He said something quietly to the admiral, which my translator did not repeat. I turned to him. "I'd like to see my father now." I did not have to force the note of real longing in my voice—not for the man they were going to try to pass off as my father, but for the man I'd barely known as a child.

One elevator out of four worked. I boarded it with some trepidation, noting that most of the staff opted for the stairs. The hospital administrator punched a button, and, after a moment of indecision, the doors slid shut. With a shudder and mechanical groan, the elevator jerked upward.

Two minutes, much longer than the trip would have taken at an American hospital. Finally, the doors slid back, to reveal that the elevator was almost even with the floor. I stepped out hastily amid nightmares of the elevator cable breaking and plummeting to my death in that dingy hospital.

The hospital administrator said something that could only be "This way," and then led us down the passageway to a nursing station, notably cheerful and efficient-looking in the midst of so much disrepair. Both male and female nurses were standing there, evidently staged in position by an advance party. They wore stark black name tags on their shirts, quasi-military white jumpsuits. A professional-looking organization. I noted a bouquet cut out of construction paper pasted on one wall, the sole evidence of an attempt to make their surroundings look more human and less institutional.

It smelled clean and like a hospital, and the medical equipment I saw all seemed to be in good repair. There were rooms lining the corridor, not the large, open ward I expected. Perhaps just for my sake?

The hospital administrator rapped out a question to the admiral, who shook his head in reply. The administrator turned his eyes to me, his look warm and oddly full of compassion. He spoke a few sentences in a gentle voice, and waited for the translator.

"Your father is not well, sir," the translator said, speaking softly. "He suffers from dementia, the type associated with advanced age. The years have not been gentle to him." The translator paused, waiting for more. Another burst of quiet words, and a guilty, half-apologetic look from the administrator. "His injuries when he arrived in our care so long ago, they were considerable," the translator continued. "You must understand, there are some things that are very difficult to recover from. Mentally, he is often confused."

The anger again, harder and demanding now. No matter that it might not be my father, the idea that they'd expect me to understand, perhaps even forgive, the unspeakable acts they'd committed.

It took all my self-control to keep my face neutral and composed. I took a deep breath, and said, "Tell him I understand. And I am most grateful that he has warned me, and he has given my father excellent care here. There are some things even the finest medical science cannot cure, I know." *Like the sickness in your soul that could allow them to break bones, listen to the screams, and then pretend that it was simply a normal part of warfare. Nothing personal, you understand.*

They were wrong. This was very personal.

The hospital administrator nodded, a ghost of relief crossing his face, so I must have succeeded in keeping my thoughts from my expression. Ilanovich scowled, but made no comment.

Without further remarks, the administrator pushed open the door. He called out a soft greeting in Russian, then stepped aside, holding the door open with his body to allow us to precede him into the room. Ilanovich motioned me forward.

I stepped into the room.

It was warmer air, distinctly warmer than the hallway outside. I spotted a small space heater in the corner. The walls were blank, clean and pristine. The hospital bed itself looked new, the metal shiny and unmarked. The room smelled of starch and disinfectant. The sheets on the bed were gleaming white, partially covered by a light blue blanket.

The details of the room itself distracted me from focusing on the figure in the bed. Or maybe I was avoiding it. After all these years, the thought of seeing the father I thought long dead was simply too much. I was surprised to find I still harbored a lingering hope that it could be him.

I took another two steps into the room, then moved swiftly to the side of the bed as though jet-propelled. I stood there, looking down at the man, my vision now clouded with unchecked tears.

The face was Caucasian, with pale, thin skin drawn tightly over prominent bones. His eyes were shut. Ragged curls of dark brown and gray were clipped close. The ears stuck out from his head at slightly different angles from each other. The lips were dark and wrinkled, slightly closed over strong, yellow teeth. He was clothed in serviceable yet unremarkable long johns, not a hospital gown.

He was sleeping—or unconscious. Whichever it was, his breath came in long, shallow gasps. There was no trace of rapid eye movement, nor any other indication that he was dreaming. Only the slight pink flush tinting his cheeks and the regular rise and fall of his chest assured me that he was not dead.

The hospital administrator had entered the room behind my entourage, and now crossed the room to stand on the other side of the bed from me. Light streamed in from the window, backlighting him and casting a long shaft of pale yellow on the figure in the bed. The hospital administrator's face was composed, but I could hear the soothing tones in his voice as he touched the man in the bed on the shoulder. A few words—the equivalent, I assumed, of "Wake up. You have visitors."

The man came awake instantly. His breathing pattern changed, a sudden, sharp intake of air, followed by a quicker pattern of respiration. Yet his eyes remained closed, although the muscles in his face tensed slightly.

"Voy cyn." Your son, if my elementary Russian vocabulary served.

Then his eyes snapped open. They were alert with hard, cold intelligence lurking behind them. Dark brown, extra white at the edges of the iris now, almost the same color as my own. He must have seen something in my face, the recognition or confusion, because the expression quickly changed to one far less alert.

I stared at him, trying to see the man I knew only from photographs, inside the weathered husk.

The eyes, those were certainly right. How many times had I heard that my father's eyes were exactly like mine? The build looked right, too. According to everything Mother had said, my father and I were roughly the same size. We had the same coloring, the same long bones and lanky bodies. But in him, the dark shock of hair that was the Magruder family trademark had been wavy, flattened out only by a short military haircut and diligent application of greasy hair cream. My mother had laughed at that, at my father's eternal battle with his curls.

There were other differences as well, more in emotional and mental makeup that in physical appearance. According to my mother, my father was far moodier, given to those dark, impenetrable moods that I knew in myself, but also capable of wild, childlike enthusiasm. He had had a certain insouciance and an outgoing, cheerful side to his character that seemed to have passed me over. My uncle, although he had poo-poo'd my mother's description, had finally admitted that there was something to it. My father had, after all, been his younger brother.

How much of the difference had been due to the fact that I had grown up without him? I would never know, and in truth, I might simply have inherited my uncle's temperament rather than my father's.

The silence stretched out, although not comfortably. I had a sense of being observed closely, of being watched and assessed by the man in the bed. For my part, too, I was looking him over, whether trying to convince myself that this was him or trying to allow myself to believe that it could be, I wasn't certain.

Finally, he spoke. "Are you really Matthew?" The voice had a distinct Russian accent, but underneath that, underlying the fluent English words, were traces of United States. It was the voice you would expect of someone who had spent the last forty years in Russia.

I nodded. "Is it really you?" It sounded stupid the moment I said it, but what do you say to a ghost? An imposter ghost, perhaps, but even so my performance had to be believable.

He nodded. "It's been a long time. Pull up a chair, why don't you?"

The farce seemed impossibly mundane. All these years— pull up a chair? I reeled, trying to maintain my equanimity.

There was a small scuffling in the room, and a chair was produced. I reached out, touched the weathered old hand, felt the loose skin under my fingertips. The skin was warm, almost feverish. I held his hand as I sat down.

The admiral and his two guards moved closer to the bed, as though some unseen barrier had been breached. I glanced away from my father's face and looked at the admiral. "I think we would like some time alone, if that could be arranged." *And a smaller audience.*

A flash of annoyance across his face, then he nodded. "Of course—but your father is not as strong as he seems." He glanced across the room at the hospital administrator for confirmation, who supplied it quickly. "I understand sometimes he becomes . . . confused." He made a small motion to the rest of the crowd, and they followed him out of the room.

Finally, we were alone. I took a deep, shuddering breath, suddenly at a loss for words. What do you say to a man you believe has been dead for over forty years?

"It is hard for me to believe it is you," he said. "As difficult for you as it is for me, I suppose." He took the breath, and tears shone in his eyes. "You don't know how many times I thought about you—wondered what you would be like when you grew up. When they told me two weeks ago that I would see you, it— You understand, I thought I would die here without ever knowing you or seeing your mother again. I had to believe that, had to come to terms with that, in order to survive. It wasn't that I didn't love you both, more than you'll ever know. But as long as they knew that, they had power over me." He shuddered, evidently disturbed by the memories. "And now . . . your mother? Did she remarry?"

"No. And I don't think she's ever given up hoping, either. She knew I was coming, and she sends her love."

He nodded. "Somehow, I believe that. Not many women would have waited that long. Talk to me, Matt. My brother—how is he? And my parents—they must be dead by now." Despite his words, I could hear the hope in his voice.

"Grandfather, yes. But your mother is still alive, and going strong. It was . . . it was difficult for her, as it was for all of us."

He was staring through me now, seeing memories I would never share. "Tell me more."

He was begging now, or at least as close as he would ever come to it. I heard the naked need in his voice, saw the tears well up again. "It's been so long, and sometimes I can't tell what I remember and what I just wish was true. Talk to me, son."

Alarms went off in my head. I wanted so much to believe,

to have this be the truth. Yet I had spent over half my life in the United States Navy. At least three times a year, and more often when in sensitive security positions, caution had been hammered into me about counterintelligence specialists.

In the last few days, the Russians had already demonstrated that they knew far more than I'd thought about me personally. My family, my call sign, all the details that must be in their files.

Enough to coach an imposter?

"Tell me what you remember," I said.

Nothing changed in his face, yet it seemed to me that the tired, aging eyes were slightly more alert. Revulsion flooded me—and at that moment I knew the truth.

But perhaps this wariness could be the result of living in Russia for forty years? As first a prisoner of war, then later a political prisoner inside this monolithic, secretive state, he would have more experience with lies, deceit, and treachery then I had ever encountered. He knew that this was no simple question from a son to a long lost father. No, it was something entirely different, something that almost broke my heart. It was a test.

"Tell me how you met Mother." It was a story I had heard many times, and one that certainly wouldn't fade easily from his memory. If he was who he claimed to be, he would have replayed that scene millions of times in the last decades. "Tell me the story."

He smiled slightly and seemed to relax. "She was a friend of Sam's sister. She told you about Sam?"

I nodded. Sam had been his roommate at the Naval Academy, later a fellow aviator. Sam was shot down two years after my father, but there was no need to tell him that now.

"It was the Senior Ball. I didn't have a date—Sam said I was too ugly to get one on my own, so he fixed me up with a family friend." He shook his head, a bemused expression on his face. "Sam really screwed that one up. His date stood him up, so he ended up taking his own sister. And I met the most beautiful woman I'd ever seen in my life. Not that we saw many in those days, you understand. The Academy was—well, it was the next thing to a monastery most of the time. Except for the town girls who wanted to marry a naval officer."

"The Senior Ball—yes, Mother told me about it several times." *More than several, as a matter of fact. It was a standard family childhood joke, one that we told everyone. It was something you would have known from any sort of investigation into my family, since the incident had been widely reported after you were shot down. For days, the papers were filled with human interest stories about you two, your brother, me.*

The only problem with the entire tale was that it wasn't true.

My father had indeed been a senior at the Naval Academy when he met my mother. But the Senior Ball wasn't the first time, not at all.

In his day, liberty was much more restrictive for midshipmen at the Academy. During their senior year, they were free on weekends, if they did not have duty or were not restricted for a number of other reasons. My father probably had less liberty than most did. According to my uncle and my mom, he was something of a hellraiser. He spent a fair amount of time confined to Naval Academy grounds for one infraction or another.

The weekend he met my mother, my father was supposedly restricted to his room. A Volkswagen bug had miraculously disappeared from the faculty parking lot and been reassembled in a professor's office. After a thorough investigation, my father was implicated. And restricted to base with no liberty.

Mother said he sneaked out somehow. I guess he never gave her all the details, but after my own time at Annapolis, I finally figured it out myself. Ingenious—and a technique I don't want to pass on to future generations.

At any rate, my father was an unauthorized absentee. Over the fence, the wall, whatever you want to call it, he headed into Annapolis for a night on the town. After all, as a senior he was fast running out of chances to break Naval Academy rules.

He met my mother in a seedy dive down by the waterfront. Mother had just arrived in town, visiting an aunt and uncle, and had decided she liked Annapolis. She had taken a job as a waitress in the bar, saving money for college.

And that, according to the closely held family secret, was the real way that they met.

I gave it one last chance. I said, "The Rusty Dinghy. Mom told us all about it—you remember it, too, don't you?"

He nodded. "It's still there? It was a bar in Annapolis."

"It was the last time I was there. Is there anything in particular you remember about it?"

He launched into a description of the physical building, down to even the types of beer they'd served there during his years at the Academy. I heard a hint of desperation in his voice, as though he realized I was fishing for something in particular, but he didn't know what it was. As soon as I noticed it, I stood, leaned over the bed, and put my arms around him. "I can't believe it's you. Thank God you are alive. Dad, it's just—" My voice gave out on me then, but not for the reasons he suspected. I was not on the verge of tears because I'd discovered my long lost father. It was because I'd found out just how far the Russians would go to deceive me.

Ilanovich met me in the hallway, a guarded expression on his face. I walked up to him and threw my arms around him, catching him by surprise, then pulled back before he had a chance to feel the gun. "Thank you," I said. I turned to the hospital administrator. "Is he well enough to travel?"

Ilanovich answered for him. "We expected that you would want to take him home. You understand, there are difficulties with that. His health, among other things."

"Other things." I knew what he meant by that. This was more than just a simple family reunion. It was hard evidence of prolonged treachery on the part of Russia and Ukraine. The damage it would do to international relationships was incalculable. "Perhaps I can help with some of those 'other things.' My uncle and I are not without influence."

"We had hoped so." Ilanovich spread his hands in a gesture of helplessness. "It was not me, not my generation. As we grew more senior, we learned what had been done. Many of us wished to make this disclosure years ago, but we could not. Now it is a time for setting things right, yes? Your help would be appreciated in cleaning up the problems we have inherited."

We parted with mutual expressions of understanding and goodwill. That night, I scribbled out my situation summary to the *Jefferson* and put it in my jacket pocket to give to one of the radiomen we'd brought with us. In it were certain words that would be meaningless to almost everyone on the aircraft carrier.

Everyone but Lab Rat.

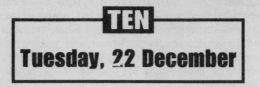

TEN

Tuesday, 22 December

0900 Local (+3 GMT)
USS Jefferson
Off the northern coast of Russia

Commander Lab Rat Busby:

The last message I'd gotten from our submarine hadn't been reassuring. The Akula and Victor still had her pinned down, and she had made no progress in repairing her engineering casualties. As a result, she had only a small fraction of her normal electrical power available to operate the ship, and had reduced her electrical load to a bare, life-sustaining minimum. The sonar, the air purifiers, and the heat—that was about it. The sub's skipper was convinced that the Akula had their range, and, reading between the lines, I could see he was worried. Real worried, as bad as I'd ever heard that cool Georgia Tech grad ever get.

Still, if anyone could pull it off, it was him. There are no certainties in the delicate game of USW, but there were few people who played it better.

That had been thirty minutes ago. Since then, nothing.

Under normal circumstances, I wouldn't have worried. After all, submarines usually maintain radio silence except for once or twice a day when they come to communications depth and query the satellite for the broadcast. So not being able to talk with him immediately, not following his evasion of the two attack submarines play by play, was nothing out of the ordinary. But couple that with an engineering casualty, and the increasing tensions ashore, and I didn't like it. Not a bit.

"But what's not to like?" Captain Smith asked me, leaning against my bulkhead in that calm, casual way he had. "Just playing the devil's advocate here, you understand. Remember, we're here for a friendship mission." He waved one hand vaguely in the air, intending to indicate the entire former Soviet Union. "Those MiGs—training opportunities. Nobody got hurt, did they? Airmanship, some good friendly competition—that's what this is all about."

"And you buy that?" I asked, immediately regretting the sharp note in my voice. Captain Smith was nobody's fool. He knew what was going on, had played this game during the Cold War, when the stakes were so much higher.

"Sorry, sir. I know what you're trying to do," I said. "But I think there's plenty to worry about right now. Those air games—pretty suspicious how everything has gone wrong during them. Wouldn't you say so?" I'd have been suspicious even without Tombstone's message the night before. I wondered if Captain Smith had noticed those bland phrases, the ones that seemed to contribute nothing to the message's content. Seen them, and thought of our earlier conversation on the secrets of admirals.

The captain said nothing, his eyes boring holes in me.

"And those two attack submarines," I pressed, "the Russian ones. Awful odd that the first major engineering casualty we have onboard our battle group submarine, they show up, don't you think? If I could figure out a way to blame them for it, I'd begin to suspect that they'd even caused the main coolant pump failures. But that would be stretching it a bit far, wouldn't it?"

Captain Smith nodded, still saying nothing.

"So I guess what I'm recommending is a heightened state of readiness," I finished. "There's no reason to suspect we're going to war with the Russians—not under the circumstances. After all, there's a reasonable explanation for everything that's happened."

Captain Smith finally stirred. "If you say so. I would say so, of course—in public." He shot me a sardonic, half-amused, half-worried look.

"But in private?" I asked.

He shook his head. "This is the way it always starts," he said softly. "You go at it too long, you start thinking about it as a game. But it's not, it never really was. Even this airdale stuff ashore—just another way to show the flag a bit, for both sides. If the Russians win, you think they're going to let us forget it? Remember, just as much as we're trying to scope out their capabilities, they're looking at us."

I stood up and carefully brushed at the front of my trousers, wishing there were some way to do something about the wrinkles. Not that it mattered, really—after as long as we'd been at sea, the cotton fabric seems to take on a life of its own. Still, it's always good to try to look one's best when going to see the admiral.

"You going somewhere?" Captain Smith asked.

I nodded. "You didn't come down here just to shoot the shit with the spooks. Call it a little intelligence at work, but I think Admiral Wayne sent you down here to get me. And, since there was no particular hurry or time frame expressed in the admiral's orders, you decided to take the opportunity to go on a little fishing mission of your own. Kind of see how the spooks feel about things, get a lay of the land before you drag me back down the corridor with my head up my ass." I saw by the expression on the captain's face that I wasn't far off the mark. "And maybe, if I'm way off base, set me straight before I go in to see the admiral. That about it?"

There was a grudging look of respect in the captain's eyes. "You figure things out pretty good for an intelligence officer."

I shoved open the heavy security door that led to my private office. "There's a reason they call us that."

We found the admiral in TFCC, slouched down in his brown leatherette elevated chair, staring dully at the giant-screen display before him. A cup of coffee that looked to already be cool was in one hand. From what I could tell, Admiral Wayne was seriously short on sleep. Conducting antisubmarine warfare is like watching grass grow—the pace is almost as fast and exciting, except when things are going really, really wrong. But the tension in a situation like this is nonstop—you know that the second you leave, something will happen. It's a fact of life.

"Sir, Commander Busby wanted to brief you on the latest intelligence," Captain Smith said quietly. He motioned me forward.

This was news to me. From Captain Smith's cryptic comments, I had had the impression that Batman wanted to talk to me, not vice versa. God knows I had nothing new or exciting to offer, no arcane insight into the tactical scenario. It was just what it looked like—an uncertain, unclear situation in which judgment calls would have to be made. And those would be made by Admiral Wayne, not me.

Nevertheless, the captain had gone out of his way to make sure I understood what was going on. It wouldn't do to fail to support him. I cleared my throat and stepped forward to the side of Batman's chair. "Admiral?"

Batman turned to stare at me, and I almost started at his expression. The lines in his face looked deeper, his eyes tired and worn. In the last eighteen months that he'd had command of the battle group, we'd been on the front lines almost continually. I'd seen him go from a jovial front runner with a booming voice to a quieter, leaner, and more deadly appearance. It was unsettling, as though conflict had burned away the polish and smooth political veneer that Washington had laid down, exposing the heart of the true man. For some reason, I had a flash of insight. This was what he'd looked like when he first started out, when he was still flying combat air patrol missions and bombing runs.

If the Russians and Ukrainians had counted on encountering something besides a fully qualified and deadly serious flag officer on this ship, which Batman's reputation ashore may have led them to believe, then they were wrong. Real wrong.

"Talk to me, Lab Rat," Batman said. Despite his appearance, there was no trace of tiredness in his voice. "You got any good news for me?"

I shook my head, wishing that I did. "No magic answers, Admiral. It's just what it looks like—problems." Briefly, I summarized the intelligence reports of the last several hours, emphasizing that all our summaries, assessments, and conclusions were mostly speculation. Finally, I said, "And as for our submarine, Admiral—the last report was thirty minutes ago. He doesn't appear to have suffered a fatal engineering casualty, at least according to the acoustic sensors we have in the area. Nothing on sonar to indicate that he's putting out a lot of noise or that he's had to light off any emergency gear."

"I think he's OK for now," Batman said slowly. He gestured at the large-screen display. "Sure, those two bastards hunting him are deadly. But this skipper—I know him from way back. If I had to guess, I'd say he's searching for somewhere to hole up for a while, maybe an underwater canyon of some sort. Somewhere that he can have a little protection from the sensors of our two bad asses out there, take some time to think through the situation. That's what they do, you know—submariners. The ballistic missile guys more than the fast attack, but they're all of the same breed. Quiet, cautious, and absolutely deadly once they've made their minds up. No, I'm not immediately worried about him—when he needs our help, you can be sure that he'll let us know, one way or the other."

I nodded, relieved in some undefinable sense I could not describe. As closely as I'd worked with submariners in the past, I knew that Batman had a better sense of how they fight their own silent wars beneath the waves. "Then we sit and wait?"

Batman smiled slightly. He pulled himself up to sit straighter in his chair. "I don't think so. I think we can give our friend a little help, maybe he's had something he hadn't planned on. TAO," he said, raising his voice slightly so that it carried to the flag tactical action officer, "how long does that S-3 have on station?"

"Another two hours, Admiral," the TAO replied immediately. "Plenty of gas, plenty of sonobuoys—hell, he's bored out there."

The years seemed to slip away from Batman as his face grew animated. He hopped off the pedestal his chair was perched on, and walked forward in the small compartment. He stood immediately behind the TAO, one hand resting lightly on the man's shoulder. "Then let's give them something to think about. Have the S-3 lay a pattern of DICASS buoys as close to on top of that Akula as he can. And I want them all pinging, constantly. I want him convinced we can nail his ass to the bottom of the ocean floor anytime we want to. And I'm willing to bet that we'll see him and his little playmate bug out real shortly thereafter."

"But our orders are to *avoid* USW operations," Captain Smith said, once again acting as devil's advocate.

"I know what my orders are," Batman said calmly. Judging from his reaction, the admiral was used to Smith voicing the objections no one else had the balls to. "I also know what my inherent right of self-defense encompasses. In my judgment, a unit under my command is in imminent danger. I'm justified in taking all reasonable and appropriate measures to protect here. Under the circumstances, that means letting the Russians know that we know they're there. No more safety-of-navigation ops bullshit. They've taken this to a new level with those MiGs."

"Admiral?" the TAO asked, his face stunned. "You want to give away our hand like that?"

"You bet I do!" Batman said. He rolled back to look at me, pointed one finger at me. "You tell your boys back there that I want to know the second there's any increase in radio traffic or communication with this submarine. Or any hint that the Russians are objecting to us making a lot of noise out here, you hear?"

I nodded. "I'll just head back to CVIC and—"

The sudden blare of the bitch box cut me off. "TFCC, CVIC. Sir, we have indications of MiG-31 launch—looks like four aircraft—sir, they're just taxiing now. As soon as they rotate and get to altitude, I'll know which way they are headed."

"Get our Alert Five aircraft airborne," Batman snapped. "And spin up four more Hornets and two Tomcats on the deck—I want them at Alert Five now. A tanker, too—and an E-2. I want gas and eyes in the air the second we need them."

"TFCC, CVIC. TAO, those MiGs are headed in our direction. They're just clearing ten thousand feet and already starting their turn, sir."

"Roger, copy all." The TAO's fingers were flying over the keyboard as he orchestrated all the firepower of the battle group. He stabbed a button on the bitch box, got the bridge, and said, "Launch the Alert Five aircraft. And get six more birds on alert, including a tanker and an E-2."

Seconds later, I heard the raucous blare of the 1MC announcing emergency flight quarters. Overhead, the Alert Five aircraft were already turning, their hard, screaming engines rattling the overhead fixtures.

"If CAG doesn't have them off the deck in six minutes, I'm going to have his ass," Batman muttered. From what I could hear over the bitch box, it sounded like CAG might break his own record for setting flight quarters.

Sure enough, four minutes after Batman had given the order, the first F/A-18 ripped off the catapult and into the air. I suspected that CAG and the air boss had stashed a couple of people up in the tower just in case of this very event.

In short order, all the fighters, along with the SAR helo, a tanker, and an E-2, were airborne. They clustered in the sky overhead, the Hornets taking a quick top-up off of gas from the tanker before vectoring out toward the inbound Russian fighters.

The TAO was fielding calls from the lead fighters now, and he turned to the admiral and asked the million-dollar question: "Do we shoot first?"

"Not yet," the admiral answered. "Tell them to continue to close the MiGs and keep their fire-control radars in search mode only. Let's see how serious they are about this.

And put another section of Hornets in Alert Five." By now, the ones he'd ordered into an alert status earlier were already fully fueled and armed, just waiting for their turn. Another aircraft shot down the deck and into the air, shown in deadly menacing shades of gray on the plat camera. The first of the on-station Hornets started howling for fuel. The afterburners chugged it down like it was beer.

"They're turning," the lead Tomcat reported. Seconds later, our tactical display confirmed what his eyes saw first. The MiGs were peeling off, heading back the way they'd come. By the time the second section of Hornets launched, there were no more MiGs to deal with. Overhead the E-2C Hawkeye kept an anxious eye on the entire arena but there were no more indications of MiG launches or other hostile activity from our Russian friends.

"Harassing action, just like last time," Captain Smith announced. "Seen it before—it's an old Soviet standard ploy to get us to expose our hands."

"But why now?" I asked.

Batman evidently overheard our conversation, and turned toward us and away from the screen. "You think it has something to do with the submarine?"

I nodded. "I don't know what they'll try, Admiral, but nothing else makes sense. Why did they launch on us? And why only four MiGs? That's not the Russian style, not the Russia I know. They deploy air assets in waves of overwhelming numbers—you know how they are, they always have to have numerical superiority. So why just four? That's not enough to do any damage to an aircraft carrier that's on the alert. And they have to know we're on alert—those submarines are talking to their masters, too."

The Admiral frowned. "You may be right," he said slowly.

"The other thing that's odd is that there's no indication that they were prepared to launch missiles, other than from the aircraft. A real Soviet-style attack would come from all quarters and from all platforms," Smith said. "That's why I think it was intended solely as harassment."

"I'll keep that in mind, sir, when I debrief the pilots. See if they saw anything odd about the weapons loadout, about the formation, anything that might suggest that this was intended to distract us from the submarine problem," I said.

Admiral Wayne nodded gravely. "You do that, Lab Rat. And I want to know immediately what you find out. In the meantime, I'm going to keep an eye on things in here." He turned back to the screen and studied the positions of the three submarines. They were moving with glacial slowness compared to the air contacts we'd watched fight it out just moments earlier. "I don't like this—I don't like this one little bit."

"Expand the range," Batman ordered. The TAO complied immediately.

A new chart sprang into being on the wall in front of us. I sucked in a hard breath, and realized that Batman had already suspected what we all now knew. To the south, still well inland, were four blood-red inverted V's. They were flying in sets of twos, the symbols so close together that sometimes they merged.

Behind them were three more sets of fighters, giving us a total of ten enemy aircraft inbound.

"MiG-31s by the looks of them," Batman muttered. "Shit. What the hell do they think they're doing?" He turned to me. "I'm open to ideas."

I shook my head, now fairly well at a loss. The admiral wasn't asking me what he should do about the incoming MiGs. The well-oiled machinery of the *Jefferson*'s combat watch team was already swinging into motion, vectoring the aircraft now airborne toward the new threat and launching additional Hornets and Tomcats.

What the admiral wanted from me was something much tougher. *Why?* was his real question. Why were the Russians after our submarine, and why this air attack? Why now?

The compartment filled with the hard, shuddering roar of a Tomcat on the catapult. It built up, vibrating deep in our bones, until the deceptively gentle whoosh and thud of the catapult indicated that it had launched. Seconds later, another Tomcat spooled up.

"They're not going to attack, Admiral," I said, thinking furiously. "You're right—not with that few aircraft. The Russians' intelligence network is almost as capable as ours, and they know they don't stand a chance with an Aegis cruiser in our battle group and with our own air support. Therefore, there's something else behind this."

"Nuclear weapons? Maybe they're going for the EMP again," Batman said, pulling the fire-retardant flash gear over his hands. "Like when we were going into the Black Sea that time."

I shook my head. "I don't think so. Too close to their own soil. The Russians have a real thing about ever risking exposure to radiation within their own population. Not after Chernobyl."

"Chernobyl is exactly my point." Batman pointed at the large-screen display. "And their history in submarine operations. The Russians have been none too careful to make sure that their crews weren't exposed to serious radiation hazards from their own nuclear reactors onboard. And that's the only way that I can think of that they'd be able to hurt us. Same argument," he continued, "against a chemical or biological attack. We're not that far out—too much danger of any biohazard drifting in and affecting their own population."

"Then what are they trying to do? Send a message of some sort?"

Batman nodded. "Probably. But like they say in the movies, 'If you want to send a message, use Western Union.'" He slid into the brown leatherette chair mounted in the center of TFCC. "My bet is they're not gonna wait around for a reply to it, either. Not with what I'm about to hit them with.

"Now, get over to SCIF and get me some warnings and indications. I want to know two seconds before those bastards light off any fire-control radar."

I darted next door into the SCIF and pulled on the rest of my General Quarters gear. I was the last one to arrive at my General Quarters station, and the watch officer dogged down the hatch after me.

So far, nothing. The sensitive electronic spy gear and

national asset receivers we had were silent. The MiGs were inbound without radar, without jamming, without any electronic indication that they were doing anything besides conducting routine training operations.

Except for the submarines. And except for the fact that they were inbound on our location.

I picked up the white phone and punched in the number for TFCC. Although they were just next door, we stayed closed up during General Quarters.

"Admiral, I think I might have it," I offered. "It's just an idea, but—well, given that we're running the flying competition on the mainland with our people and theirs, maybe they're going to claim that this is just an expansion of that. There was that paragraph, you know. The one about other opportunities for training as they arise? Well, I think that's going to be their explanation for both launches."

"So what happens when I light off a fire-control radar on the Aegis?" Batman asked when I was finished. "We lose this game of chicken?"

"And if we don't—" I glanced forward at our own tactical display, and saw the MiGs closing to within weapons range. "And if we don't, we're sitting ducks."

"Jesus, look at that," one of the electronic warfare technicians shouted. The screen in the forward part of our compartment was identical to that in TFCC, and I still had the admiral on the line.

"You see that, Lab Rat?" Batman demanded. "Talk about a game of chicken—Jesus, I hope these people know what they're doing. Unless I have a Russian flag officer on the horn in the next two seconds, I'm giving my aircrews weapons free."

I stared in horror and disbelief at the battle unfolding before me on the screen. The Russian submarines had increased their speed to flank, and were rapidly closing the location of our own. The MiGs were just at the edge of their firing envelope, although they were still radiating no hostile emissions. Our own Tomcats and Hornets were poised midway between the carrier and the MiGs, in combat spread, waiting and ready. They had their normal air-search radars lit off, but were not yet in targeting mode.

"Aegis has a firing solution, sir," my electronics technician announced. "Is the admiral going weapons free on them as well?"

I turned to face him. "I don't know."

"All units in the battle group, this is the Alpha Bravo." I heard Batman speaking simultaneously over the radio-circuit speaker and the telephone. The two seconds were up. He was going to go weapons free.

But before the admiral could get the words out, the MiGs did what they'd done before—turned away from the battle group and headed back toward Russia.

Captain Smith shot me a knowing look.

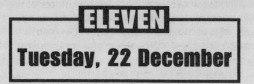

ELEVEN
Tuesday, 22 December

Midnight Local (+3 GMT)
Kursk, Ukraine

Vice Admiral Tombstone Magruder:

Vladimir and his friends came for me at midnight. They wore the dark black-and-gray patterned nighttime camouflage uniform, all rank and unit insignia removed, feet shod in dull black crepe-soled boots. Even without their collar devices, I could sort them out by ranks. One officer, Vladimir, and three enlisted men, the latter all battle-toughened veterans. The final man in the group was a civilian. He was smaller than the rest, with the pale, unhealthy look of a man who spends too much time inside drinking vodka. He was wearing the same outfit as the others, but his bearing told me he was something besides military—KGB, GRU, or whatever the modern equivalent for internal security was. Vladimir nodded a greeting, then motioned to the civilian.

There was an air of nervousness about the civilian—nervousness, yet determination. I saw the others following his lead, standing slightly back.

They moved into my room without invitation, taking up corners and crowding it by their very presence. The civilian walked over and stood before me, studying me for a few minutes. Finally, he held out his hand. "It is very nice to meet you finally."

Now that threw me for a loop. In my studies of the history of Russia's internal security measures, that was not a normal approach. "Have we met? Should I know you?"

He shook his head. "No, there's no reason you should." He considered me for a moment, as though assessing how far to go. "But I know you. And I knew your father. You weren't fooled today, were you?"

"About what?"

"With the man they said was your father. I told them it wouldn't work. But you know how they are—they think themselves so clever." He shrugged, an oddly casual gesture that one would make when talking to an old friend. "Even without Vladimir's warning, it would not have convinced you, I suspect. And they are convinced they succeeded. Too willing to believe their own brilliance, I suspect. A common military failing." He studied me for a moment longer. "But I know better. I know who you are, Admiral Magruder."

"Then you have me at a disadvantage, sir."

He laughed softly. "And one that won't be remedied anytime soon, I assure you."

His accent was slight, the words a bit stilted but spoken with near native proficiency. He had to have been educated abroad, or in one of the Russian camps that had been constructed during the Cold War to mimic American cities and towns. Either way, his accent spoke of connections further into the intricate web of Russian intelligence and counterintelligence than anyone I'd encountered so far. "You have no reason to trust me, Admiral Magruder," he continued. "I realize that. But if you are ever going to know the truth, if you are ever going to answer for once and for all those questions, then you must come with me. This is your only chance. I dare not take this one again."

"But why?" I burst out. "Why the elaborate charade today?"

"Why do you think?"

Now it was my turn to examine him, as though the answers to that very question would be written somewhere on his face. "I can think of no reason," I said finally.

But I could. Millions of them. If the Russians believed

they had convinced me my father was alive, he then became a bargaining chip. Perhaps it would weaken my resolve, make me hesitate to act when—

When what? Russian counterintelligence plans were often intricate works of art, each piece gently moved into place in perfect sequence to effect an overall result. These invitations to mock war games, the bad information we'd been fed about the previous missions, the charade with my supposed father—to what purpose? Even if I knew, I was not about to admit to this man, a man whose name I did not even know, what I suspected.

"Well? Have you made your decision?" he asked.

"About what? You haven't been particularly clear on that."

He sighed, a truly Russian sound. There are depths of meaning in those sighs, ones that hint of the deep, tragic passions that run all through the Russian psyche. "Your father is not alive. He was brought to Russia, and later to Ukraine. That much was true. But, unfortunately, he was seriously injured in the ejection from his aircraft. He lived for a while. It might have been longer had the Vietnamese given him better medical care. By the time he came to us, he was too weak—too far gone."

He was telling the truth. There was no doubt in my mind of that. How I knew, I could not tell you, but there was something in his voice, a depth of feeling and sympathy that made disbelief almost impossible.

His words arrowed straight into my gut, twisting and coiling like a vicious serpent. For so long we'd said that we believed he was dead, but somewhere deep down we'd never really given up hope. Never—not really. Now, to hear the final confirmation from Russian lips, what the U.S. authorities had told us for all those decades, was too painful. I believed this man in a way that I had not believed the countless United States government officials who had sworn my father died in Vietnam.

"I will take you to his grave this evening," the man continued quietly. He reached out and laid one hand gently on my forearm. "My sympathies, Admiral. It is very difficult to lose a member of your family, even during times of war. This is something we Russians understand well. One out of every ten Russians died during World War II, do you realize that? Do you know what an impact that has on a nation's character?" He shook his head gravely. "Millions— tens of millions—Russian families felt the same pain, knew this loss. I myself lost my father, and two uncles. But still, even for the fact that so many of us have lost, it is never easier for an individual."

"You said you would take me to him," I said. "How do I know you're telling me the truth?"

"You have a photograph," he said. "One that you obtained from the POW-MIA groups. It was I who gave the photo to Vladimir to send to you. I can give you every detail of it, where it was taken, who took the picture. I can even tell you who we used to impersonate your father."

"The man I met at the hospital?" I asked. *And just who had he really been? Another American brought to Russia? How could I walk away and leave him here?*

Because he broke the trust. When he agreed to impersonate my father, no matter what the threats, he betrayed the faith. I was not entirely comfortable with that analysis, but decided I would have to live with it.

He nodded. "And I can tell you something else, something you father told me. He knew that you would not believe, you see. During those days that I guarded him, I tried to convince him to talk, and later tried to make some sense of his ramblings; he knew that you would come. He always believed his government would come for him— he never lost faith in that—but more than anything in the world he believed that his son would grow up and insist on the truth."

"Tell me what you know," I said.

He began, and first recounted the story of how my father and mother met. The true story, not the one I'd heard today from the ersatz father. Even as he started to talk, I knew I was hearing the truth again. Then, finally, he said, "Your father told me about the words he scratched into the wall in Vietnam. 'Go west.' He said that, didn't he?"

I nodded finally, acknowledging the truth of what he was saying. "I did find that. I had hoped—but I was so young when he left. He couldn't have known—"

The man was silent for a while, and let me work through it for myself. Finally, I said, "Can you take me to him?"

"Of course. But it must be now, tonight. I had to wait until members of my unit—the right members—were on guard here. Another night, another watch section, and I will not be able to take you out unobserved." He pursed his lips for a moment, and looked faintly worried. "You realize, for a number of reasons, you will never be able to tell anyone about this. Never. Too much is at risk."

"My mother. She has to know." It was not a request.

He appeared to consider that for several moments, then nodded. "Your mother. But not your uncle—not ever. He could not let it pass, you understand. He would be forced to take action. And then, those small bits of information I am able to pass to your groups, the thin trickles of information, will dry up. Silence, only silence."

"And false hope is better?" I thought he was probably wrong about my uncle, but now was not the time to go into that.

"Which would you prefer?" He saw the answer written on my face, and nodded. "As will most of the families. They would prefer a confirmation, even if they can never share it with the rest of the world, over that uncertainty that gnaws at them. Come, we must go."

He made a motion with his hand, then turned and walked from the room without waiting to see if I would follow him. I hesitated for a moment, then gave up. If there was a chance of seeing my father's grave, his final resting place on this alien soil, then I owed him that much. Owed him that for the heritage of genes and family that had stood me in good stead, that had brought me to the Navy and to the fighters. I owed him.

I followed, and the four soldiers fell in behind me. We moved quickly through the silent visiting officers quarters and out the front entrance to a parked, covered truck. The tailgate was down, and the four soldiers assisted me in jumping into the back. One moved around to the driver's side and the civilian slid into the passenger side in front of him. They were separated from the aft compartment by a sliding glass window that the civilian opened immediately.

"It is thirty minutes away from here, more or less. We cannot move too quickly—it would arouse suspicion. There is some slight danger associated with being out anyway, but I thought it would be a risk you are willing to take. The consequences—well, if we're stopped, I will say that you wished to see the evening sky. They will not believe it, but it will give us enough time to think of something else. Agreed?"

"Agreed." The truck started up then, a loud, rumbling diesel engine. It jerked into motion, rattling and thumping along the pavement, the motion getting worse as we transitioned to a potholed and rutted dirt road.

It was too noisy inside the truck to talk, but I had enough to think about. While I'd brought my coat with me, the cold was quickly seeping in through it. One of the Russian soldiers observed that, and reached into a corner of the truck to pull out a thermos. He twisted off the top, then poured it full of dark, steaming liquid. I accepted it gratefully.

Tea, hot tea, heavily laced with sugar. I drank it and appreciated the warmth that coursed down to my stomach. "*Spacebo*," I said, using my limited Russian to thank him.

He nodded in acknowledgment, then passed the cup and the thermos around to the other men. They each drank sparingly.

Finally, with one final jolt, the truck pulled off the road. The engine idled for a moment, then fell silent. The soldiers stood, stretching the kinks out of their cold joints as I did, then moved to the rear of the truck and jumped to the ground. One turned to offer me assistance in disembarking, but I refused it.

The woods were a study in black and white, stark trees cutting a web across the moonlit sky. We couldn't be that far from the base, but there was no sign of the lights that surrounded its perimeter. There was utter silence, except for the faint keening of a chill, cutting breeze through those bare limbs. The trees themselves gave off faint groans and creaks as the wind blew through them.

"It is down this path," the civilian said. He started forward again, once more not looking back to see if I'd followed.

I had slipped on winter boots over my shoes, and they were far too thin for this weather. The cold ate through them, seeping from the ground and creeping up my legs. The cup of hot tea seemed like it had been hours ago.

I fought the cold off. It was not important, not tonight. The only thing that mattered was the truth.

We walked for maybe five minutes, then came to a small clearing. During the summer, there would probably be some light groundcover, and a few skeletal bushes surrounding the area confirmed that. Overhead, the trees closed in, creating a solid canopy.

The civilian knelt and brushed away the light coating of snow and winter debris that covered the ground. His fingers left deep, icy trenches in it. Within minutes, he had uncovered a dull steel marker.

He stood, then guided me over to look down at the spot. "There. That is the number." He shook his head, then said, "That's all they were given, the numbers. No names." He shot me a sideways glance. "You understand the reason for that, I am certain. It would be evidence of a particularly damaging kind."

I stared down at the marker. So little to be left of so great a man, one who'd loomed throughout my life as the ideal naval officer, the aviator who died in service of his country. Mom had kept it alive, occasionally reminding me. Her harshest rebuke would be simply "Your father would not have liked that." That one indication of his name alone had the power to stop me in my tracks.

"How do I know it is him?" I asked.

"You don't. Other than my assurances, there is no other proof I can give you. There is a roster, to be certain, but it is still held as a state secret. Even if I could gain access to it, it would be unreasonably dangerous to do so. I am sorry, but in this matter, you have only my word alone."

Was it enough? I knelt down to the marker, stripped off my glove, and ran my hands over the freezing metal. My fingers stuck lightly as the sweat on the ends of my fingers froze to it. I pulled them off, leaving something of myself at the gravesite.

It was as he said. I would never know for certain, but his words carried a chilling conviction, and instinctively I knew he was telling the truth. If twenty-five years in the Navy had taught me nothing else, it had at least taught me to generally be able to discern that.

"We haven't much time. I'm sorry about that, too," he said. He motioned to the other soldiers. "As I said, it is a function of which men are on guard. Much longer, and they will be missed."

I nodded, and stood. My knees creaked with the motion. This, then, was the end of that mystery.

For so long, my family's obsession over my father's fate had seemed to drive almost every decision. Underlying every thought, every plan, every action was the possibility that someday, no matter how remote, my father might return. Mother had probably suffered the worst for it, refusing to consider remarrying or even dating again.

Now, so many years later, I realized how strong our obsession had been.

I bent down again, brushed away the remainder of the snow, and scooped up a handful of the frozen dirt. I crushed it between my fingers, having my imprint in it, then carefully pulled out my handkerchief and wrapped the ground up. So little—but it might be all I ever had.

I looked up at him, dry-eyed with an overwhelming sense of closure. "Why? Why did you do all this? The man in the hospital, the faked photographs, all of it? Can you tell me that much?"

He shook his head. "Much of it would not make sense. Internal politics, jockeying for position. Amidst all of it, there are those of us who would do the right thing. Correct the errors of the past, make amends in what small ways that we can."

"Why?" I asked again.

"Isn't it enough that we do it?" he said. "It will have to be. Perhaps, sometime when Russia returns as a world power, you will remember that at least some Russians are not monsters. You will stop, remember this night, these stars, and there will be a chance that the man in your gun sights will do the same. We make what is wrong, right. And hope that it will not be necessary again."

We left the clearing, walked back to the truck and took up our previous positions. The noise of the truck seemed almost blasphemous in the still, quiet woods.

I wasn't sure I bought his explanation at all. The idea that there might be a group of Russians who simply wanted to do the right thing, to begin to heal those wounds so long ago inflicted—well, it went contrary to everything I'd grown up with. Russia was the Evil Empire.

Wasn't it?

I remembered the kinship I'd felt with Ilanovich in the air, two old aviators dogging it during a competition just to steal a few more minutes in the air. If our positions had been reversed, if I had known that he was seeking a final truth to his father's fate, would I have done something similar? Arranged to lure him to America where he could be told the truth?

And would there have been agencies in the United States that would have coached an imposter, hoping to gain a hold over a potential source in the Russian military? I thought I knew the answer to that one as well.

As we neared the base, the lights came into view again. They were blazing now, all of them, not the few spotted security lampposts I'd seen when we left. Even over the noise of the truck, I could hear a siren wailing in the distance.

There was angry, uneasy muttering among the men in the back. They were pointedly not looking at me. I rapped on the forward window. "What's happening?"

The civilian looked back at me, his face a mask of worry. "I do not know. But whatever it is, it increases the danger. Quickly now—we must have a story."

We finally agreed on a plan. They would drop me and one guard off at a relatively deserted point on the base. The others he would take back to quarters. The story would be that I was unable to sleep, had decided to go for a walk, and, per his orders, one of the guards had decided to accompany me. It wasn't great, but it was better than nothing.

As I left to follow my guard, the civilian caught me by the arm. "Tell no one. Especially not until you leave Russia. If they know that you do not believe that is your father, they will not let you live. They cannot. It would put everything at risk."

"They'd kill me?"

He nodded. "As they have undoubtedly killed the man who is supposed to be your father. They would never have let him go, you know. For the same reasons."

The base was alive with activity, but all the noise was drowned out by the sirens' raucous bleat. Finally, I heard cut through it one other sound I recognized—the deep throated roar of a combat aircraft preparing to roll out. There was a crowd in front of the visiting officers quarters, not a large one, but sufficient to worry. I glanced over at my guard, saw him take a deep breath and compose his face. Now would be the acid test of whether or not our alibi would work.

At least initially, it seemed to. The crowd parted and let us through, and my guard led the way down to my quarters.

Inside my room was another story. The admiral was already waiting for me there, along with two aides.

"Where have you been?" he demanded immediately. "It is not safe to be wandering around the base at this hour. I must insist on an explanation." The cold frost to his words made it clear that it was more than an explanation he wanted.

I mustered up our cover story, passed it off as convincingly as I could. The admiral listened, then turned to my guard and rapped out a few hard questions in Russian. I was relieved to see that the man neither looked nervous nor fumbled his answers. I started to believe that they would believe.

The admiral turned back to me. "You and your people

will return to your carrier at once. There are . . . difficulties with you remaining at this station."

"Difficulties? And what is the exact nature of these difficulties?" I demanded coldly, every inch an offended foreign naval officer on a diplomatic visit. "Aside from the weather, I am aware of no such difficulties."

The admiral fumbled for words for a moment, then said, "Evidently your colleagues onboard the USS *Jefferson* have kept some matters from you. Earlier this evening, your fighters attacked six of our aircraft on a routine maritime patrol of our northern shore."

"Attacked? What exactly happened?" It is always better to ask for more information than give immediate explanations when the situation is unclear. I could think of a large number of actions that would constitute an "attack" on the part of *Jefferson*, ranging from simply launching alert aircraft or lighting off fire-control radar, to maneuvering too close to another aircraft, to missiles off the rails. Until I knew more, I didn't want to speculate.

The admiral was not about to clear up the ambiguities for me. "Fortunately, there were no casualties," he continued smoothly. "But, under the circumstances, I've been instructed to terminate the contest. You understand, we must take precautions."

"Well, then, first thing in the morning we shall prepare to—" The admiral cut me off with a gesture. "Not then. Now."

Now, that stumped me. As a fellow aviator, the admiral surely knew that it was not a good idea to fly combat aircraft without adequate rest and preflight briefing. Yet here he was, apparently suggesting that I fly north, roust my boys and girls, and that we get in our aircraft and just get the hell out of Dodge. Well, we could do that if we had to—God knows I've flown tired and hungry more times than I care to think about. But given a chance, I choose safety over macho gestures now. "Tonight? Surely, Admiral, you're not suggesting that."

He nodded once, then rapped out a series of orders in Russian. "I've instructed your other aviators to be awoken and told to pack. They will be waiting for you. You will be provided all assistance in your preflight briefings and in any service requirements for your aircraft."

"But what about our maintenance crews?"

"Your COD transport is waiting on the airfield with your people. All in all, I think we have taken everything into account."

"Almost everything. What about my father?" I asked.

He sighed heavily. "You understand, he was not a well man. In the last few days, we'd had hopes—knowing that he would see you seemed to give him new life. But this afternoon, I am sorry to say that he passed away quietly in his sleep." His face made a pass at sympathy, but his eyes were hard and cold. "I am sorry."

His words chilled me. If I'd needed confirmation of what I'd already known to be true, this was it. I mentally assessed my own readiness to fly. Sure, I thought I was good to go, but it wasn't a good idea. Nevertheless, it appeared that we were being offered no choice in the matter. I drew myself up to my full height. "Then, if you would be so kind as to grant me some privacy, I shall make my preparations."

The admiral considered this a moment, then nodded abruptly. He made a gesture, and the aides marched out of my room. The admiral followed them, pausing at the doorway to say, "I would give very much to know exactly where you were this evening, Admiral Magruder."

1400 Local (+3 GMT)
USS Jefferson
Off the northern coast of Russia

Rear Admiral Batman Wayne:

There was a knock on my door, then the chief of staff barged into my cabin. He's got the privilege, one of the few who take advantage of it, of surprising me in my bedroom area when I'm only half-dressed.

"You're going to have to make the call on this one," he said, handing me the message. I finished poking my arms into the shirt and then took it from him. The chief of staff doesn't abuse his privileges lightly—if he thought it was important enough to interrupt one of my few chances to escape for a workout, it was. And it wasn't like he hadn't seen me in my skivvies a number of times before.

I scanned the message, then looked back up at him. "He sounds OK to me. So what's the problem?"

The chief of staff shook his head gravely. "You have to read between the lines as an engineer, Admiral," he said. He wasn't arguing, just bringing his peculiar talent as a surface warfare officer and superb engineer to put the whole thing in context for me. "You know how those sub skippers are. He'd rather go to the bottom than quit, I think."

I read the message again, then looked up at him. "It's that bad?"

The chief of staff nodded. "Worse, probably. I'm only speculating, mind you. And it's not like he's not telling us the truth, sir," he added, seeing the look on my face. "Everything he says is true. But he's a smart man, they don't let the dumb ones go into submarines. He knows you're not going to understand all the context."

I sat down on the bed and sighed. It looked like my workout was going to get pushed further away than I wanted, for the second day in a row.

The message had been brief but to the point. It was short, as most submarine messages are, transmitted through the ELF network. Someone in CVIC has broken the code already, giving me a plain text translation beneath the sequence of apparently random letters.

The sub's skipper said that they had gotten control of their engineering problems, had made the repairs required. The remaining damage was, to use his words, "within allowable limits for these mission perimeters."

Like a fat, dumb, and happy aviator, I'd taken that to mean there was no problem. Evidently, the chief of staff read it otherwise.

"So translate for me, damn it," I said, handing him back the message. "Tell me all these details you're reading between the lines."

"He's OK as long as we don't ask him to do anything fancy," the chief of staff said bluntly. "Remember, his mission was to accompany us and remain in a silent patrol observer role. For that, he's fine, which means he's not making a lot of noise." He hesitated for a moment, then added, "And I think that means that some of the damage is beyond repair. Quiet equipment—that's been damaged—is equipment that's off line, not in standby. So, say he has two out of four main coolant pumps left. He can do what we brought him here for—but if we need a few days of full-power reactor runs, he's got a problem. That's what I think."

"Shit. So what do I do? Send him home?" I asked. "That

will go over real well, won't it? Here the guy is, trying his damnedest to finish the deployment, and I pull the rug out from under him. Either way, his career is dead when he gets home."

"I think there are more problems, as well," the chief of staff continued, not answering my question but not exactly evading it either. "You know about SUBSAFE procedures, right?"

I nodded. "As much as I need to, I guess. Which parts do you have in mind?"

The SUBSAFE Program was a conglomeration of safety procedures that really began with the loss of the USS *Thresher* on the east coast. Since that time, procedures had been revamped to require a number of inspections on the repair of any critical component, submarine certification for repair of most components, and dramatic changes in emergency procedures in keeping the men on a submarine alive. Preserving the capacity to surface, or at least come shallow enough to let the men escape through the escape trunks, was a primary goal in any disaster onboard a submarine.

"I think he's probably running on the margin of acceptability for SUBSAFE," the chief of staff continued. "Look at paragraph three—he's talking about intending to maintain a constant depth, asking us not to order depth changes unless it's absolutely necessary to mission accomplishment. And we know, one of the casualties was to a high-pressure air compressor. You add it up—like I said, reading between the lines—and he might be just a teensy, eensy bit worried about his ability to do an emergency blow and get back on the roof if he has to."

I exploded. "He can't surface? What the hell is he doing—"

The chief of staff invoked one of his other rare privileges and interrupted me. "No, I imagine he can surface. He would have told us if he couldn't. And do some depth changes. Remember, those are all mission-essential capabilities. But what I'm saying is he hasn't got the reserve that he'd like. If he has to hit the roof, then he may not have the reserve capacity to submerge and come up again. And, sitting where we are, this far from home, that's a real problem."

I shut up to think. If what the chief of staff was saying was true, then our submarine escort was one hurting puppy. Space onboard a fast attack boat is limited, so they don't carry extensive repair facilities and spare parts.

The carrier, on the other hand, did. "Any chance we can give him some help with anything?"

A slight grin tugged at the corner of the chief of staff's mouth. "I think there might be. But remember, it's going to cause him to have to come up to the surface to take onboard some gear. In these waters, with the weather this bad, that's a problem. Not to mention the political problems when our Russian friends fly over and see the submarine that we swear we don't have surface alongside us. However, there might be a way."

Now it was my turn to interrupt. "You sly old bastard, you never present me with one of these insoluble problems unless you've got something on your mind. Spit it out before I have to beat it out of you."

"Well, I checked with the meteorologists. They say this storm should blow over today, and tomorrow we might have some unusually calm conditions. Still a little wave action, but not much at all. It's all blowing inland. So, say we were to be operating at night. Say we put the carrier between us and anybody who might be flying over or watching from land, and brought the sub up to the surface on our seaward side. You get him in close enough, he's under the overhang of the flight deck and won't be any easy target for overhead observers. Plus, you do it at night. I'm willing to bet the odds are better than even that we could pull it off."

"That close to the carrier." I shook my head. "That skipper isn't going to be loving life, you know that."

"I know it. But if he pulls it off, one attaboy makes up for a lot of oh shits, particularly if he pulls his boat together and can continue on station until we finish this mess off. Judging from his messages and the times I've met him, I think he'll go for it. What do you think?"

I thought about it for a few moments before replying. If

you look up the word *risk* in the dictionary, you'll see the insignia of the U.S. Navy printed as a definition. We don't get the job done by being timid, and that man in command eight hundred feet below my keel had earned the right to take this chance. "Set it up. You write the message. Tell him we understand what he's saying without pulling the sheets down too far. We'll let him maintain the illusion that everything is OK for now."

"There's just one other thing," the chief of staff said. "Those Russian boats following her—she'll know for sure that our boat is surfacing. And she may have an opinion about that."

"If we can't protect our own submarine while she's tied up damn near on our flight deck, then we're the ones who're in trouble."

The chief of staff left, and I dug through my dirty clothes for the pair of running shorts I'd used the day before. I had a hell of a lot more stress to work off than I'd had just ten minutes earlier.

Then again, if it didn't work, I'd have a hell of a lot more time on my hands to work out, when the Navy got rid of me.

I had just finished three miles on the treadmill when Lab Rat tracked me down. The chief of staff moves fast when he wants to. Sometimes I see the intermediate steps, sometimes I don't know what he's been up to until I see the final results. Whatever the case, my senior intelligence officer looked pretty damned unhappy. I, on the other hand, was floating along with that sense of well-being that you get when the endorphins start kicking in, when all you've had to worry about for the last thirty minutes was your pulse rate and whether the belt under your feet was still moving.

Lab Rat settled into a waiting posture, that determined look on his face that I recognized. Lab Rat's got a finely honed sense of priorities, and I could tell from the way he was standing that he thought his news was (1) important enough to come find me, and (2) could wait until I finished running. But not until I'd finished the entire workout, and certainly not until I'd showered, shaved, changed back into my uniform, and been once again swept away by the massive amounts of paper in my in-box. No, this was definitely a "get him after he finishes running but before he showers" sort of emergency.

I nodded in acknowledgment in his direction, then waved him off. Lab Rat got the message—he could wait till I finished five miles.

Twenty minutes later, he was still standing in the same spot, looking neither bored nor annoyed. Just that same look of keen intelligence, showing that ability he's got to integrate all sorts of facts into one single comprehensive picture that's of use to an admiral in command of a carrier battle group.

He walked up while I was doing another mile as part of my cooldown routine, moving closer and in front of the treadmill.

"Talk," I said. With Lab Rat, you don't really have to worry about hurting his feelings, the guy's focused on his job, and all he wants to know is when to begin.

"It's not a good idea to have the submarine surface," he began, stepping closer, with his voice pitched low so that it would reach my ears only. "The chief of staff told me to come talk to you about it, because we don't entirely agree on the conclusions."

"What's up?" I asked, keeping my questions short as my breathing returned to normal.

"One of the biggest advantages of an attack submarine is her ability to remain undetected and hidden. We bring her to the surface and she's at risk for more than getting spotted by an aircraft. That Russian boat, the *Victor*—there's every chance she carries a team of Spetznaz onboard her. If they get close enough, with our submarine all opened up for taking on repair equipment, they could try to board her while the Akula does some serious damage to her if they can't."

"Pirate her? Come on, Lab Rat, surely you can't be serious?" Floating along on my post-run high, I chuckled lightly.

Lab Rat nodded. "That's exactly what I mean. Admiral,

it's at least a possibility, however remote it might seem. Look at the facts. Russia is desperate for hard currency, and one of her major exports is diesel submarines. Nuclear submarines she hasn't been as successful with, first because hers are dangerous to own and operate, and only second because of world treaties against nuclear proliferation. But suppose Russia was manufacturing a small nuclear submarine for export, one that had U.S. technology for sound quieting and weapons control onboard it. Not to mention reactor safety standards. What do you think that would do for the Russians?"

The treadmill spun down to a slow amble, and I started thinking out loud. "The Russians would surely love to get their hands on one of our Los Angeles—class fast-attack boats," I said, just doing stream of consciousness without trying to bring any analytical capabilities to bear on it at this point. "It would make a world of difference in their own programs and, you're right, the export programs as well. But right alongside us?" I shook my head. "Commander, that would be the height of foolishness. We'd have to kick their asses over that, no way around it. Besides, the submarine has some defenses itself, doesn't she?"

"Only some small-caliber handguns and shotguns," Lab Rat said. "I'm not claiming it's probable—just a possibility we haven't really allowed for yet. And I'm not suggesting that we don't do this, Admiral. The chief of staff explained his reasoning quite cogently. However, we ought to make some preliminary preparations just in case."

"Like what."

"Destroy all old classified material onboard the submarine, sir. Crypto codes, that sort of thing. Personally, I'd like the entire crew standing by for self-defense and emergency destruct, but I don't think that will be possible."

I sat down on the edge of the treadmill, started stretching to keep my muscles from tightening up. If there is anything I hate, it's going to the trouble of trying to fight off the fat and then feeling stiff the next day.

"Taken in conjunction with the other danger signs,

Admiral, we have to prepare for this," Lab Rat said. His tone of voice came as close to insisting as I'd ever heard it.

Sure, we'd had the MiGs making their runs on us, but so far we weren't at war, although I had to admit that I'd come damned close to starting one. I examined my intelligence officer closely, wondering what other secrets he was keeping.

Like I should talk, after keeping the deployment of our own submarine secret from him and my staff.

The look on his face told me there was more to the story than he was letting on. "Commander, come on. Out with it."

Lab Rat took a deep breath. "Before Admiral Magruder left, he made certain . . . arrangements . . . with me. Arrangements for a code in his daily intentions message, in his status reports. He asked me not to tell you, but gave me the discretion to do so if I felt it was necessary in my judgment to fulfill our mission. His last message used the code word to indicate he was in danger. I suggest that whatever it is might extend to the battle group as well."

Now that was a stunner. I was supposed to keep secrets from him, not the other way around. Another flash of anger. This was *my* intelligence officer, damn it, Tombstone. Not yours—not anymore. And what the hell business did he have making plans about anything operational behind my back? There were going to be some serious words exchanged when he got back, not between a one star and a three star, but between lead and the man who used to fly wingman on him.

"And?" I loaded the one word with as much of a threat as I could.

"The admiral's in trouble. He had time to get off one message to me before he left Ukraine, but not much at that. The Russians are kicking them out of the country."

"Kicking them out?"

Lab Rat nodded. "It's not being put that way, of course. And I don't understand all the ramifications. Admiral Magruder barely had time to get the message off to me, and it was obvious he was in a hurry. But yes, there are problems ashore. And why would this surface now, with U.S.-Russia relationships breaking new ground in free trade? Why all these mistakes in the war games scenarios? Why the MiGs? To me, Admiral, it all adds up to something going on. Just what, I don't know, but it's why I'm worried about the submarine." Lab Rat was speaking rapidly now, as though if he could get the words out fast enough it would make up for not telling me before. Both he and I knew it wouldn't.

"So what are you suggesting?" I said finally, leaving behind the question of what I would say to Tombstone and how I would deal with Lab Rat later. The mission had priority over my own annoyance at this point.

Lab Rat, like the chief of staff, is a nasty, devious man. He started explaining, and I forgot to keep stretching. By the time he was finished, my muscles were as stiff as wood.

THIRTEEN

Tuesday, 22 December

1500 Local (+3 GMT)
Kursk, Ukraine

Vice Admiral Tombstone Magruder:

We weren't under arrest, but neither were we ever left alone. During the entire transit back to our war gaming base in Russia, there were always two, usually more, armed guards within an arm's reach of me. They had a hard, lean look, and I decided immediately that they must be Spetznaz, elite Russian special forces. They were men on a par with our SEALs, and given the right equipment, they probably could have done just as good a job.

We left Kursk almost immediately, and I was just given enough time to shuffle my belongings into a duffel bag before I was hustled to a transport aircraft. The engines were already warmed up and turning as we boarded, and we were given immediate clearance for takeoff. We climbed, banked, then turned north.

It's my custom on long flights to take the opportunity to catch some sleep. It's a skill you learn early as a Navy pilot because time to sleep and meals are all too rare some days. I fidgeted until I found a relatively comfortable position, then shut my eyes and tried to doze.

Of course, there was little way I could under the circumstances. The conditions of our departure, as well as the welfare and well-being of my people back in Russia, was of serious concern to me. I silently damned the impulse that had led me down south, the one that involved paying homage to a man I had never known but who was my blood. Where do our loyalties lie, in a situation such as this? To the dead, or almost dead? Or to the living, the men and women who depend on us to keep them alive? Who had trusted me, who had followed me to this godforsaken frozen land. Had I let them down at the expense of a ghost?

And to what end? I was no further along in getting hard proof of my father's death in Russia than I ever was, although admittedly I was convinced myself on a personal level. He had died here, and I had touched and seen the grave that held his body, although I would never be able to fully describe it to another person. Even my mother . . . I let that thought hang for a moment, trying to decide what and how I would tell her about these events.

And what of Russia herself? The war games that had begun as covert intelligence-finding opportunities on both sides had quickly turned into something more ugly. There was no way a few years of outwardly friendly cooperation on international matters would ever really erase the decades of Cold War scars that existed between our two nations. To have thought they could was the ultimate in political naïveté.

And had Commander Busby intercepted my message? No doubt he had—Lab Rat was good about things like that. Still, would he understand the phrases I cobbled together so hastily, and be prepared to take appropriate action? I hoped so, not so much for my own sake as for that of my men.

Finally, despite the turmoil filling my mind, I did drift off. I awoke when we began a long, slow bank that brought us in on an approach profile to the field. The terrain below me was familiar, recognizable from our departure just days before.

I was not surprised to see Gator, Skeeter, and Sheila, and the rest of the remaining flight crew standing along the side of the runway waiting for my return. There was every evidence that our aircraft had already been serviced and

were ready for immediate takeoff. As I watched, the COD
taxied over to them and they started loading out. I checked
the wings of the Tomcats. Good, they'd loaded the remaining live fire weapons onto the wings. Safer than carrying
them back in the COD.

I walked up to the group and exchanged a hasty salute.

"Admiral, I can explain," Skeeter began. I saw Gator
elbow him sharply in the ribs. Skeeter grunted, shot the RIO
an angry look, then turned back to me. "I mean, it was all
my—" Again the jab to the ribs.

Gator has always commanded my respect in a way that
few non-pilots do. He knows when people should be talking
and when they shouldn't. Right now, surrounded by Russian
security guards, Skeeter needed to keep his mouth shut. I
nodded a quiet acknowledgment to Gator.

"Let's get our checklist started, shall we?" I asked. It
wasn't really a request, and they understood that. Sheila
jerked Skeeter aside and herded him over toward their
aircraft. I could see the hand gestures, the heads bent close
together, and knew a hasty explanation and admonishment
was taking place.

Gator fell in behind me. "Good move," I said.

"Thanks. Skeeter's OK, he's just—"

"A lot like Bird Dog," I finished for him.

Gator fished a message out of his pocket and passed it
over to me. "You need to see this one. Came in a couple of
hours ago from the carrier. There's some odd stuff in
it—figured it might mean something to you."

I scanned the text, not surprised to find a coded message
from Lab Rat. But what he was proposing—well, it wasn't
something I would have tried to pull off. It was a good thing
he let me know, though. The MiG forays at the carrier, the
problems the submarine was having—all could quickly go
critical.

The checklist went quickly, and before I knew it we were
up the boarding ladder and settling into our aircraft. I
plugged my ZIP drive into its slot. Since our own support
personnel had gone ahead, Russian technicians performed
the duties of checking our restraining ejection harnesses,

pulling the pins from the ejection seats, and getting us settled in. They spoke passable English, albeit with a rough accent.

From their movements around the aircraft, I surmised they'd spent a fair amount of time studying our own people during our short stay here. That was confirmed as we taxied off the apron and toward the runway. The plane captains directing our motions could have been American, for all you could tell from their hand signals. Another data point. Had we learned as much about them as they had about us?

I rolled out first, followed ten seconds later by Skeeter and Sheila. We followed the vector given to us to depart the airfield, as we had done in the previous days, then turned north toward the coast and open water.

"We're gonna have company, Admiral," Gator said. Somehow, I'd figured we would. "Looks like MiGs—yeah, MiGs," he said, checking the electronic warfare detection gear to confirm his guess. "That's their radar."

"We're going home, that's all," I said. I clicked on to tactical. "Skeeter—I don't want any problems with our escort, you hear?"

It wasn't his RIO I was worried about. She'd already proved her levelheadedness too many times to count. No, that little message was for Skeeter alone. "All they're going to do is escort us to the coast, maybe to the twelve-mile limit," I said, hoping they didn't know I was guessing. "But keep your heads up—we're not going to be the aggressors, but neither will we take the first shot. That clear?"

"Admiral, I—"

"We've got it, Admiral." Sheila's cool voice broke in. "Message sent and received."

I laughed. "Skeeter, son, you just stay welded to my wing. If there's any heavy thinking that needs to be done, you let Sheila do it."

Two sharp clicks on his microphone key—Skeeter's or Sheila's, I wasn't sure which—acknowledged my transmission.

There were six MiGs, grouped in sets of two. They took station on either side of us, with a final pair trailing and slightly higher. A good formation, one that gave them a fairly clean shot no matter what we decided to do. A little too close for comfort—except for the trailing pair, the MiGS were only three hundred feet off our wings.

I had the carrier's TACAN loud and clear by now, and I adjusted my course slightly to vector in on it. Once we were settled in, I clicked on the ICS. "Eyes peeled," I said. "That goes for you, too."

"Of course, Admiral," Gator replied, his voice calm and unruffled. "Anything in particular I should be aware of?"

I hesitated for a moment, wondering just how much to tell him. It was instinctive, this need for secrecy and caution, a lesson I had learned the hard way during the Cold War. Yet there was something to be said for briefing my backseater in full, to a degree that not even Batman knew. If anything happened, it was going to happen fast, and I needed his immediate reaction without explanation. Skeeter and Sheila, too, for that matter, but they'd follow my lead.

"Our approach on the carrier—it may be a little bit different than you're normally used to," I began, thinking my way through it. "I'm not sure exactly why, but—oh, hell. There's something on the seaward side of the aircraft carrier that we don't want them to see. So, if whatever it is is still there when we get to the carrier, we'll have to make up some excuses to delay trapping. *Jefferson* will help us out on this, I know. We may tank, we may take a couple of practice looks at the deck, but whatever it is, we have to keep the MiGs away from the ship."

"Yes, Admiral, I understand." Again, there was no trace of curiosity in his voice. That worried me a little. But then he said, "If you can't tell me, I understand. But it would help."

"I'm not entirely sure why it is myself," I said, faintly relieved. "But it's got something to do with our submarine."

"Our submarine?" Finally, a break in the professional monotone of Gator's voice. So he was surprised—that wasn't anything like what I was going to face when I hit the deck of the carrier and Batman found out about my little collusion with Lab Rat. "Yes, our submarine. There's been one trailing the battle group the entire time. It was supposed to be a covert mission, but I take it something's gone wrong."

"Huh." And that was it, no further comment.

We were almost there now. The carrier had been painting on the radar for several minutes, and I thought I could see it out on the horizon, a small irregular bump on the otherwise flat horizon. There was an E-2 Hawkeye up for command and control, as well as a KA-6 tanker. I let out my breath as a friendly voice spoke reassuringly in my headset.

"Roger, Admiral, I hold you at sixteen miles, inbound on radial one-eight-zero. State souls and fuel status, sir."

"Two, and," I glanced down at the fuel indicator, "eight thousand pounds."

"Roger, sir, copy eight thousand pounds. Recommend we top you off before your first pass at the ship, Admiral." The E-2 pilot's voice betrayed no emotion, but he and I both knew that at eight thousand pounds I ought to be taking a look at the deck first before I tanked. If I got on on the first pass, there would be no need for it. Still, Batman's message had warned me to be ready to respond instantly to any unusual approach guidance, and I quickly complied. "Roger, Hawkeye, copy all. Give me a vector to the tanker, if you would."

"Roger, Admiral, turn left and come to the new heading two-niner-zero."

The same query and directions were repeated to Skeeter, and I heard Sheila answer the call. Evidently she'd decided to take her hotheaded young pilot out of the loop of talking with the rest of the world.

We turned smoothly, moving as one, Skeeter never varying a millimeter out of position. I swear, that man drives me to distraction some days, but truth be known, he's an excellent pilot. One of the very best, and if we'd been in the same Top Gun class, at the same age, he might have been the only one who could have beaten me.

Might have been. Even now, I wasn't willing to admit that anyone could have pulled it off back then. But still . . .

I knew the MiGs were listening in on our frequency.

There was only a second's hesitation before they, too, joined the smooth turn east. "Give me their positions relative to us," I said over the ICS.

"They're out of position a bit, Admiral," by backseater replied. "The one trailing us has descended by three hundred feet, and is only four hundred feet above our altitude at this time. The two on the wings look like they're not as comfortable with night formation flying. They've moved out a little bit, increasing separation to three-quarters of a mile. And . . . that's funny," he said, a worried note in his voice. "Admiral, I thought they would return to the briefed distance when we finished the turn, but they're still opening. Not opening, they're—Admiral, they're peeling out of formation. One set's going high, the other low."

"Combat formation," I snapped immediately over tactical. "Skeeter, you take high. Get that guy off my tail first. Break right, break right."

Almost before I'd gotten the words out of my mouth, I saw Skeeter's Tomcat peel off my wing. I followed, cutting hard to the right and underneath him, losing him, losing altitude as I did so.

The MiGs reacted instantly. The Hawkeye was howling warnings now, too. He broke off mid-sentence as he evidently saw on his radar scope that we were doing. He fell back into the mode for which the aircraft was designed, giving us long-range warnings. Had there been other fighters airborne, he would have been watching who was Winchester, vectoring other aircraft in to engage additional targets as necessary.

As it was, with only two of us, he wasn't much use.

I kicked the Tomcat over, tightening the turn until it felt like we were pivoting on the right wingtip. Both wings were fully swept back now, the automatic mechanism compensating for our angle of attack and speed. Behind me, my RIO called out distances and bearings, keeping me mentally in the picture as I fought for position.

"I'm on him—fox two, fox two." It was Skeeter now, calling out in savage glee as he toggled off a Sidewinder at the tail MiG. I grunted, clicked my mike twice in response, straining against the G forces that were pulling the blood away from my brain and trying to pool it in my extremities. I tightened my muscles again, forcing it upward, fighting off the gray that was creeping in around the edges of my vision. I could hear my RIO behind me performing the same maneuver.

"Break left, break left," Gator called out. "Too much debris to—"

I didn't wait for the rest of the sentence, and instead reversed my turn immediately. Getting too close to an exploding MiG was the last thing I needed right now.

Shards of fuselage and aircraft peppered my Tomcat. Directly overhead, the canopy cracked and starred into a fragmentation pattern. The safety fibers embedded in it kept it intact, but its ability to withstand the strain of high G maneuvers was now seriously in doubt.

"Any other damage?" my RIO called out.

"Negative. Give me a vector to the unengaged MiG."

As it stood, we had five MiGs still in the air—four, I amended, as I heard Skeeter cry out again the deadly fox two warning. "Two on one, by God," Skeeter cried. "Hell, those aren't even fair odds, not for them."

Still, taking on two MiGs with an aircraft in less than optimal condition was not something I thought of as good odds. The MiGs were faster, more maneuverable, but the Tomcat made up for that in sheer power and endurance.

"Give me a vector to the pair," I repeated, then I found it myself. They were off my starboard quarter, closing fast, automatically falling into combat spread. It was the most effective fighting position for two aircraft ever invented, and one that we had perfected and taught them ourselves.

My pair of MiGs had evidently misjudged exactly how fast I could come out of the turn. That, or they hadn't anticipated my sudden cut back to the left. Either way, they were out of position, too high and off angle for an infrared missile, and in each other's field of fire for a radar lock. I took advantage of that, jammed the throttles full forward, and grabbed for altitude like a bat out of hell. I split up right between the two of them, their rate of closure dangerously high, and my rate of climb too slow.

The MiGs peeled back out of my flight path like a banana. There was a moment of confusion, as they tried to sort out who was following me up and who would linger down below.

The Tomcat was picking up airspeed now, her heavy engines pounding against the air behind us. The full-throated scream of the afterburners roared through the Tomcat's interior, and I glanced upward to check my shattered canopy. It appeared to be holding, but I suspected we were dangerously close to the envelope of what it would withstand.

In the moments when we passed between the two MiGs, I didn't think we would make it. The Tomcat was bringing every inch of power to bear in those massive engines, hurtling us straight up with virtually zero speed over ground as every erg of energy was diverted to increasing our altitude. Finally, I felt the response, saw indeed that we were going to clear the MiGs, and I knew that I'd just tipped the balance in my Tomcat's favor. One MiG spiraled up after me, his rate of climb considerably slower than mine. The other cut tight circles down below, waiting for the moment when I would inevitably be forced to trade altitude for airspeed. The Tomcat has an effective combat threshold considerably above that of a MiG, and I was counting on those few extra thousand feet to give me the break I needed.

The distance between us and the trailing MiG grew wider. I heard the brief beep of a radar trying to lock on.

I glanced at the altimeter. Good, just where I wanted it to be. I cut the Tomcat hard, wrenching her into a violent turn, then darted east back toward Skeeter. There was not much I could do to help him at this point, not if he were in trouble, but it was a good idea to stay within fighting range of each other.

The MiG below me took the easy, angular vector away from his direct climb and followed. By moving into the vertical, I had just decreased the amount of energy he would have to expend to catch up with us, while simultaneously complicating my own problems. Below me, the lower MiG paced us, waiting for his chance.

As the MiG reached a range of ten thousand yards, I turned back into him. The G stress was worse this time, cutting almost half my field of vision despite a hard push on the M-1 maneuver. I felt the first lazy, soft drifting of my thoughts, redoubled my efforts to stay conscious, and finally eased my rate of turn.

We descended on the MiG, now in head-to-head closure rate in excess of twelve hundred knots. I was still in full afterburner, the Tomcat gulping down fuel at a tremendous rate. It was risky, but not as dangerous as having two fully capable MiG-31s after my ass.

The trick to fighting a MiG, I've always found, was to keep the battle in the vertical. There is no way they can match a Tomcat for sheer climbing power and endurance, and you have to take advantage of that. It you let a MiG force you into a horizontal knife fight, you're going to lose. No matter how good a pilot you are, how good shape your Tomcat is in, the damn things are just so light and maneuverable that it's like swatting at flies. You have to keep a MiG climbing, keep him fighting for altitude and airspeed until you have a chance to take your shot.

This MiG must have been paying attention. I was descending on him, and he had broken out into level flight now, twisting and turning to prevent a radar lock. He couldn't know just how good our avionics were, and how little a chance he had of avoiding that, but I gave him points for trying. Finally, he made a fatal error of descending slightly, exposing for a few moments that warm, rich source of energy that a Sidewinder loves so well—his tailpipe. "Fox one," I called, as I toggled off a Sidewinder. I followed up with a Sparrow, after checking to make sure that we were still well clear of Skeeter and Sheila. Then the MiG made the last mistake he'd ever make. He panicked.

He headed for his wingman, descending rapidly now and racing for the surface of the ocean. There was at least a chance that the Sparrow would get confused by the sea-clutter radar return off the surface of the water, but that played right into the strongest capabilities of the Sidewinder. Hot jet engine, fiery exhaust, warm metal silhouetted against the cold, black ocean—add to that a starlit night, with no sun to generate a dangerously attractive alternative source of heat.

As luck had it, neither the Sidewinder nor the Sparrow minded descending at all. Eight seconds after I'd toggled them off, they found their prey.

I could hear my backseater swearing, and easily deduced the cause. Gator had made the mistake of glancing out the canopy just at the moment of missile impact, and the explosion had robbed him of his night vision. Fortunately for him, I knew enough to look away from the fire spewing out of the tail end of the missiles, and had had my eyes shut at the moment they'd caught up with the MiG.

"Where is he? Where is he?" he demanded.

"Get your head back in the scope until your vision clears," I snapped, silently damning every RIO that had ever lived who had been so incautious as to poke his or her head up like a gopher coming out of a hole at just precisely the wrong moment. "You've got the radar—use it."

I saw the second MiG before he had a chance to vector me in on him. He was almost at my altitude now, arrowing straight in, curving around behind me. Maybe he counted on me being slightly blinded by the explosion, maybe not, but whatever his intentions, it put him in almost perfect firing position.

There was no way I had time to climb, not with having expended so much energy in turning and firing on the first MiG. I took the only other option available to a Tomcat who needs to get back in the game.

I tipped the Tomcat's nose over and headed for the deck. The altimeter clicked past eight thousand feet, and the Tomcat was quickly picking up speed. I let it spin out for another two thousand feet, jinking and weaving across the sky to make myself a more difficult target. This MiG was a little bit more cautious—or maybe he was just a fast learner. He followed, but kept sufficient separation between us to avoid getting lured into the vertical battle.

I could almost hear him thinking, read his mind as he tried to compute the vectors. The MiG knew as well as I did that we weren't going to fight in the horizontal, that the only reason I was screaming down toward the surface of the ocean was to build up enough speed to start my net ascent. I would be hoping to lure him into a yo-yo maneuver, heading first up, then back down, drawing him in on me until I could maneuver into position behind him. The MiG knew that's what I was thinking—and he evidently decided not to play. As my Tomcat passed to five thousand feet, he pulled out of the descent and broke out in a wide turn that quickly steepened into a sharp arc. If he'd timed it right, it would bring him right back in on me in perfect firing position just as the Tomcat came thundering past him on its next upward pass. I watched his progress through the canopy, shifting in my seat to see past the star-crazed section of the windscreen. There he was, tailpipe hot and bright against the field of stars, looking like a giant stingray must look as it passes over creatures deeper in the ocean.

The only way to deal with a MiG that's trying to avoid the vertical game is to force him into it. I pulled out of the descent, but instead of pulling back into a climb, I broke hard right, kicked the afterburners back in, and pivoted virtually in midair, until I was directly underneath him.

A beautiful target, although not the best firing position in the world. Still, the Sparrow howled out its radar lock, almost demanding to be released. I toggled one off, waited for a moment, then rolled the Tomcat away again and broke away from the immediate vicinity.

Seconds later, another explosion told me that however good the MiG pilot's training had been, however much intelligence they'd gleaned from one recent knife fights in the sky, it hadn't been good enough. That's the problem with fighter combat—good enough isn't.

"Where are they?" I demanded, searching the sky over-head for the familiar shape of a Tomcat. I hadn't heard another missile call out of Skeeter since he'd taken out the lead pair, nor had my backseater given me any indication what was going on in the other battle. "I can't find him—what happened?"

"He's at eleven o'clock, high," he said. "In trouble, too, from the looks of it. Tombstone, he needs us over there buster. Something's wrong."

"Skeeter," I said over tactical, hoping to get some idea of what he had planned. "I'm here, buddy—what do you need?"

There was no answer for a moment, then my backseater said, "Tombstone—I think we've got company." Another MiG was closing in on us.

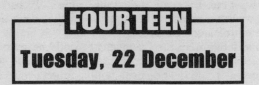

1534 Local (+3 GMT)
Inbound on USS Jefferson
Off the northern coast of Russia

Lieutenant Skeeter Harmon:

With a MiG on my ass, I didn't have much time to worry about Tombstone. I didn't have time to listen to Sheila wailing from the backseat either. I'll be damned if I know how I put up with that day in and day out. Talk about your candy-assed, weak-kneed RIO. That was Sheila.

It didn't help that she was right this time. She starts muttering about the MiGs the second we left the tarmac and she kept at me on the way out like it was a pop quiz or something. We'd already done a couple practice engagements with them—what, she wasn't paying attention or something? She ought to know by now that I knew how to handle a MiG. Or a couple of them.

Oh yeah? And just how the hell had I gotten myself in this fix?

My mama wouldn't have liked the words I was saying, but they were coming at a steady stream now. Quiet, only half said out loud, but swearing nonetheless.

It had started off pretty straightforward, but if I'd been the admiral, it would have started sooner. The second those bastards started edging away from me, I would have taken the first set out. But we'd waited, like I guess we had to do. Finally, when the admiral heard the other shoe drop, at least he turned me loose on mine.

The first two were easy, since they didn't know who they were up against. I got the Tomcat twisted around and in firing position before they even really realized we'd disappeared from the center of their tight little cattle herding formation. By the time the wing guard set of MiGs was back in on us, I was ready for them. The first one took a long shot at me, but I was ready for that, too. The flares, the chaff, a few other fancy countermeasures, and that MiG didn't have a chance. I rolled out of my evasive maneuver and headed straight into the pack. That was when Sheila really started howling.

OK, OK, there's something to what she was saying. If you're going to fight close in, then you have to count on the MiG being able to outmaneuver you. Still, we trained against that, and we'd done all right with it in the last war game. So why wasn't it working now?

"You fool," Sheila said, ever the backseat driver. "Don't you figure that maybe they let you get a little overconfident during the planned evolution? Maybe played dumb, suckered you in some? You take on a couple of MiGs under GCI control, and you think you're hot shit. Damn it, Skeeter, you get some altitude on this aircraft or I'm punching out on you. Maybe I'll get lucky and somebody'll shoot up my chute on the way down."

I ran the geometry in my mind real quick, and suddenly realized just how big a mistake I'd made. Two MiGs, one Tomcat, all in level flight and approaching each other with a rate of closure that you wouldn't believe. No, not a good place, not for this Skeeter.

I hauled the Tomcat up, but by then it was almost too late. We slid over them, gaining altitude as the Tomcat's engines clobbered the air, but we were still too slow. Too slow and too low—a deadly combination when you're fighting against a little guy like that MiG.

I kicked it into full afterburner, saw the altimeter starting to creep up faster now. It was moving at almost the same speed that my fuel status was spooling out—couldn't keep this up forever, but then I didn't need forever. I just needed a few minutes, a little bit of luck, and for that damn backseater to shut up for a while and let me do my job.

I pulled out of the climb just as the MiGs were starting to join on it, when they were at their most vulnerable. You don't have to stall during ACM in order to be too deadly slow. So when I hauled back around, I was expecting to see two MiGs climbing like they were flies caught in amber, relatively good targets for a nice Sparrow shot.

Except I was short on Sparrows. I'd already let off three at the trailing MiGs, had only one left, and was down to Sidewinders and Phoenix other than that. Phoenix wouldn't do much good. We were too close. That big, slow missile would be like throwing a telephone pole at them, no problem to evade even at the edge of the envelope like they were now. Still, it was better than nothing, and might force them into a reaction that would put them in a vulnerable position.

Nose-to-nose like we were, Sidewinders weren't the weapon of choice, either. Sidewinders love those tailpipes, but they'll settle for engines. Nose on, though, is a bad shot, and I wasn't completely sure just how far Tombstone was away. That would be the worst result possible, of course, if the nifty little Sidewinder blew right past the two MiGs and headed for my lead.

I waited for the growl, then toggled off a Sparrow at the lead aircraft. Then, just 'cause I wasn't going to need them anymore, I added a Phoenix to the mix.

As I predicted, the Phoenix wasn't much of a problem for them. You could almost outrun it. But the Sparrow was still a good shot, and as I pulled away, I looked back over my shoulder, expecting to see a happy fireball, my third of the hour.

No such luck. Sparrow is usually a pretty reliable missile, but this one must have had a fusing problem or something. For whatever reason, it sailed on right past its designated MiG, fat, dumb, and happy. No fireball, and no good angle for the Sidewinders. In fact, I'd been counting pretty heavily on only having one MiG to deal with after that last shot. I was just starting to cut back in, figuring I'd grab some altitude and deal with the remaining one at my leisure, when all at once I've got two of them coming nose on at me again, both balls to the walls. And both very, very pissed from the looks of it.

Sheila's yelping was starting to bother me. I yelled back, heard Tombstone's fox calls over the radio, then saw one of the MiGs pull out and turn away. So we had two left now, and it was one-on-one for the remainder of the engagement. Nice odds, and I liked them a lot better than what I'd had just a few seconds ago. Still, it was kind of insulting in a way, too. I mean, did this MiG that was still headed for me think I was such a pussycat that he could take me by himself?

Well, I'd already taken care of his two trailing MiGs in the earlier formation, and one little old MiG by itself wasn't about to bother me. I'd slipped out of afterburner for the engagement and still had a fair amount of airspeed. Time to get this battle going my way, and get into position so I could use my remaining Sidewinders.

"No guns," Sheila said. "No, no guns. Oh please, don't do that. Bird Dog would, you know. He—"

Her voiced choked off as I put the Tomcat into a steep climb, the G forces catching her by surprise. With an older chick like Sheila—hell, she must be almost thirty—it doesn't take a lot to knock her out of the loop for a minute. The Tomcat thrummed gently under my hands like a sweet classic car, every inch of her sweet fuselage alive and ready for battle. I felt like I was floating, part of the metal framework myself. You get an aircraft like that, there's nothing in the world that can beat you. Except there was still this little problem with the MiG, the one that was hanging off my ass and trying to catch me.

Well, they'd caught me once not watching, and that wouldn't happen again. Higher and higher we went, until at around thirty-two thousand feet I pulled out of the climb, looped over, and looked back down for my adversary.

He wasn't there. He was waiting for me down at the

bottom, looping around and ascending slightly, staying nose-on to me. I wonder if he'd been counting. Did he know I was down to Sidewinders and Phoenix, or was that just a lucky guess?

It didn't matter, I could deal with it. He popped off another missile, and I thumbed the countermeasures. I could see it ascending toward me, like a small, white straw, reflecting the light from the stars and the moon. It wavered for a moment as it crept up toward me, picked up speed, and then settled in at me on a deadly straight arrow. I jinked, danced the Tomcat around the sky, then tipped the nose over and left the missile behind in a cloud of flares and chaff.

The MiG rose up to meet me finally, taking the bait, at least for a little while. This was exactly what I wanted, yo-yoing up and down, trading altitude and speed back and forth until I was firmly settled in on his ass. I watched him move, saw his wings slide forward to reconfigure for more lift, and waited for the moment. Now. I yanked back hard and pulled out of the dive, turning at the same time so I would end up directly behind him.

Except he wasn't there again. He'd pulled out of his climb, circled around, and now was diving back in toward my six. I pulled back around, turned to follow him, figuring we'd start off on a racehorse-type track slantwise in the sky until I could force him into a stronger vertical game. But he turned inside of me again, still high and fast, and bore back down on me with deadly precision.

"Fox one, fox one," I heard Tombstone cry. And where the hell was he? Dealing with the one MiG that had peeled out of my pack? Had to be. And a good thing it was, too. By now, this one MiG was proving a lot harder to handle than I'd thought he'd be.

"Lead, we could use some help back here," I said finally. It hurt like hell to say it, but by now the geometry of this whole mess was crystal clear in my mind. I was out of position, and the one MiG I'd had left to deal with was closing in for the killing shot.

"On my way, two," I heard Tombstone say. "Just a few seconds, Skeeter. Be ready to break when I tell you."

By now, I was bobbing over the sky like a crazy man, trying to keep the MiG from getting a good solution on me, while at the same time staying out of gun range. No matter what I did, he stayed glued there, falling behind sometimes when I climbed, but still within range. Waiting for that right moment.

I saw Tombstone's Tomcat, finally. It was streaking across the sky above me, curling in toward me now and descending. Tombstone was probably going to try to fall in behind my MiG, order me into a quick break, then take a quick Sidewinder shot at it. You hate being in close to another pilot when you do it. There's always the chance of fratricide, blue on blue. The only thing worse than missing a MiG is nailing a friend when you do it.

I was sweating bullets. If I'd been listening to Sheila, if I'd made the MiGs play my own game instead of assuming that I'd taken out one with a Sparrow shot, I wouldn't be in this fix. I could've taken care of both of them by myself, sent them off to hell with the two brothers they'd had behind me, and then be headed back to the boat. But now there was nothing I could do, and every time I turned, it was only on the desperate hope that I could keep confusing his firing solution long enough for Tombstone to vector in and save my ass.

"Break right, break right. Now, Skeeter." Tombstone sounded even closer now, as he yelled the commands over tactical.

I broke. No need to warn Sheila; she'd heard the same transmission.

The MiG was breaking with me, still turning so tight I could hardly believe it. You forget how big the Tomcat is, how unwieldy in the air it is against certain other aircraft, but there's nothing like a MiG to make you a true believer again.

Was there enough distance? I pulled off the tightest turn I possibly could, approaching stall as my airspeed dropped. We were at fifteen thousand feet now, enough altitude that I'd have the chance to pull out if we edged out of envelope, but not a lot of safety factor.

"Reverse your turn. Now, Skeeter." More orders from Tombstone, but he wasn't the one watching the airspeed indicator drop down to dangerous levels.

I reversed my turn, and felt the Tomcat go sluggish and heavy in the air. Slow, way too slow. I pitched the nose down, starting the dive that I hoped would give me the speed I needed to stay airborne. But you don't have many options when you're in that situation, and damned little maneuverability. All I could hope for was that the Sidewinder was going to do its job.

The MiG peeled off, spewing countermeasures out from its undercarriage, dancing around in the horizontal until it evaded the Sidewinder.

The Tomcat was feeling better now, slipping through the air with more authority, and I felt some control return to her. I breathed a sigh of relief, slowly eased back around, and stayed in level flight until I was back up to combat speed.

Tombstone had somehow managed to lure him into a vertical, although I don't know how. I thought the MiG driver was smarter than that, but evidently he'd slipped up somehow. I turned back into the fight, watched the horizontal tail chase edge-up into the vertical, then made my call.

"On the next down loop, Tombstone, break out hard to the left. I'm coming in after you."

"I can get him." Tombstone's words were hard and clipped, and I could hear him straining against the G forces of the climb. "Just stay back, Skeeter. This next circuit—"

I cut him off. "I'm right in on him, Tombstone. Do it smart, buddy. ACM is a team sport, remember?"

Two long seconds, then two sharp clicks on Tombstone's mike acknowledged my last.

Five seconds later, Tombstone reached the top of his circuit, seemed to hang in midair for a second, then started the downward loop. The MiG turned inside, and began descending even closer in. I was inbound at the same time, trying to gauge the altitude, watching for the moment that I knew Tombstone would feel as well, exactly the right second, when he—

There. Tombstone broke hard, and the MiG tried to

follow, exposing for a few seconds those precious, precious tailpipes. "Fox one. Tombstone, head for the deck!"

The Tomcat was already plummeting out of the sky, headed for the black ocean below us. He was at twelve thousand feet, picking up speed now, approaching the ocean far too fast.

The Sidewinder streaked toward the MiG, who at the last second seemed to realize that he was in deep, deep shit. The MiG jerked violently, shuddered as the pilot tried to bring it out of the descent. It seemed like he might pull it off for a moment, then his luck ran out.

The MiG exploded into an ugly yellow ball of orange and yellow, gas and black smoke boiling out from it. I whooped a war cry, and heard Sheila chime in. Maybe she wasn't such a bad guy, after all. But where was Tombstone? I scanned the ocean, looking for that white-gray fuselage against the water. Finally, I spotted him. "You OK, man?" I said over tactical.

"I'm OK," his voice came back, steadier now that he was no longer fighting the G forces. "Thanks, Skeeter."

"How 'bout we head back to the boat, sir," I asked, the adrenaline still throbbing through my system. "Me, I'm so hungry I could even eat a couple of sliders." The sliders, the greasy flat hamburgers that seemed to be the mainstay of the late-night galley watch section, gave me my year's worth of grease and fat in one sitting.

"I like the sound of that. Wait for me there—I'll climb back up and you can join." True to his word, Tombstone's Tomcat picked up altitude quickly, and soon I was smack-dab off his wing where I was supposed to be.

"What was that all about, sir?" I asked finally. "Why did they wait until we got out this far and then jump us?"

"I don't know for sure, Skeeter, but I've got some ideas on it. We'll talk about it when we're back on deck, OK?" It was clear from his tone of voice that the admiral was in no mood to answer questions. And now that we were out of the frenzy of the battle, we were no longer equals. No more shoving him around, telling him to break off and let me make the shot like I'd done with the last MiG.

Not that that should have mattered, anyway. The MiG
was mine to start with. Three kills—now, that was something. Hell, I might even have two sliders.

"Tomcat flight, this is Home Plate. Be advised that we are
red deck at this time. Repeat, red deck. Tanker support is on
its way, guys." The operations specialist continued, and
reeled off a vector to our airborne gas station. I clicked back
over to Tombstone's circuit, and asked, "What's going on?"

The answer was slow in coming, and when it finally got
there, it wasn't much help. "*Jefferson*'s got a few more
important things on her mind just now. So button up, let's
get some gas, and we'll wait her out."

Great. Those sliders were getting farther away with every
minute that passed.

FIFTEEN

Tuesday, 22 December

1600 Local (+3 GMT)
USS Jefferson
Off the northern coast of Russia

Commander Lab Rat Busby:

I knew that Batman would rather have been down on the flight deck, standing on one of the catwalks that run just below it and supervising the whole evolution personally. Nevertheless, he was here, on the bridge. A gaggle of surface warfare officers and boatswain's mates were where he wanted to be, with another cluster on the elevator that had been lowered to the level of the hangar bay.

I would have rather been down closer to the action as well. After all, it was my plan.

And my career on the line if it failed.

But if the admiral felt that command leadership required him to be here on the bridge, calmly seated in his chair and watching the evolution from the top of a ten-story building, then the least I could do was keep him company. He had as much riding on the whole thing as I did.

The submarine had come shallow two hours earlier and poked her UHF antenna up above the surface. We had coordinated the entire evolution in short bursts of conversation, and so far it had gone well. We had slowed to two knots, bare steerageway. The submarine approached us from astern, since she was a little bit more maneuverable than we were. From there, it had gone like any standard underway replenishment operation, with the submarine maneuvering into position, then making her dash forward to come alongside us.

We couldn't stop, not completely. To do so would leave both ships at the mercy of the oceans, and the force of the water would eventually push us around to stay beam-on to the swells. Not too terribly troublesome for a carrier, but a real disaster for a round-hulled boat like a submarine. As it was, we had planned to have her come onto our leeward side to shelter her a bit from the seas and the wind.

A sharp crack split the air, one we could hear even from the bridge. The first shot line, the small cord tethered to a weight that was fired over to the carrier from the submarine. Attached to it were a heavier line, then another one, each one more substantial than the last. These would form the basis of the rig we would use to transfer a spare air compressor to the submarine, along with assorted other provisions and equipment.

It had been quite a chore, convincing the submarine's skipper that this was what he wanted to do. He hadn't initially, citing first the possibility of detection and later the dangers inherent in underway replenishment between a carrier and a submarine. The admiral had had to threaten to send them back to the States before the sub's skipper had capitulated.

So far, everything had run like we'd practiced this every day of the year. The high line was rigged, and the first transfer of loaded pallets was beginning.

With Tombstone and Skeeter safely back within the Aegis cruiser's air-protection envelope, at least one potential problem had been eliminated. But one of our biggest problems still remained—the Russian submarines lurking somewhere below the surface of the ocean. Our last detection had been twelve hours ago, and at that time she'd been ten miles to the north. Too close for comfort, but perhaps far enough away that our submarine could sneak out of area and move alongside us without being detected. Just before we'd commenced the entire, tedious approach maneuver, Batman had launched tankers and S-3 Viking ASW aircraft. I thought about having them take along box lunches, just in case something went wrong.

Not only were the S-3s the best aircraft equipped to keep the Russian submarine out of area, and detect it if it tried to make a run on us, but they were also excellent aircraft for sea-air rescue. We also had helicopters in Alert Five, both SH60 ASW ones and straight SAR ones. God forbid that one of the submarine sailors should fall overboard, or one of our people either. But if it happened, we were prepared to deal with it.

The submariners had immediately laid down a long barrier of sonobuoys to the north, then laid a second line just for good measure. The two Vikings patrolled out up ahead of us, while two more monitored our northern flank and astern. I had no great faith in their ability to detect a nuclear submarine acoustically, not if said submarine were really determined to make a silent approach. But if it were there, at least we had a shot at catching it.

The walkie-talkie Batman clutched crackled to life. "Ready to transfer the first pallet, Admiral."

Batman lifted it to his mouth. "Go ahead. And notify me when it's complete."

"Aye, aye, Admiral."

We were standing on the bridge railing, outside of the bridge proper and exposed to the elements. The submarine was perhaps sixty feet off our port side. Two thick lines ran between the two ships, onto which were attached the pallets and parcels we were transferring to the submarine.

To an outsider, the bridge would have seemed like a noisy, frantic space. There were four radio speakers mounted on the overhead, another two on each bridge wing. Into those were piped the various tactical circuits, including those that we were required to monitor continuously. Adding to the din were the commands from the conning officer, standing on the bridge wing with us, the OOD who was on the bridge itself, and the repetition and acknowledgment of other orders and directions. In addition to Batman, the officer of the deck and the safety officer held walkie-talkies as well.

When the trouble started, it was with the most innocent of reports.

"Home Plate, this is Hunter 701. Buoy seventeen pattern Bravo Six Niner is hot." The voice of the Viking TACCO was excited. "Classify this contact as a possible Russian nuclear submarine, Victor Class."

Batman stomped back into the bridge. "Get the Alert Five helos airborne. I want the bastard pinned down to the ocean floor until we decide what to do with him." He lifted the walkie-talkie. "Prepare for emergency breakaway. I say again, prepare for emergency breakaway. Do not execute until my signal. All stations acknowledge."

A chorus of aye, ayes came back across the circuit, and Batman turned to me. "So what are our chances now?"

I spoke up immediately. "Good, Admiral. There's no indication that the Russian sub has detected our submarine yet. He knows he's there; he's been tracking him for days. But he doesn't know he's alongside us now, nor does he have any idea of how critical the engineering problems might be. I say we continue as is." I pointed out toward the side of the carrier. "They're almost done, Admiral. If they can get that air compressor onboard and installed, it's going to solve a lot of problems."

Batman grunted. I watched him mull over the facts, accustomed by now to the way that he thinks this out. It would do no good to start arguing my position at this point. He had all the facts he thought he needed, and the admiral had no problem making decisions. Despite all his time in Washington and politically advantageous billets, Batman at heart was a fighter.

The SH-60 helicopters were launching off the stern of the carrier. In reality, they shouldn't have been conducting flight ops. Not with the submarine alongside. It violated one of the prime tenets of naval aviation. The winds weren't particularly good for them, but fortunately the helicopters aren't as picky about wind across the deck as fixed-wing aircraft are. Nevertheless, trying to conduct flight operations in the middle of a transfer of cargo between two ships was a prescription for disaster.

The first helo peeled away from the carrier just three minutes after Batman had given the order. Another followed as soon as it was safe. They formed up—and is there anything more odd-looking than helicopters flying formation?—and headed out to the horizon, toward the S-3s.

Still, Batman had not yet decided to kill it. Who knew how the rest of the story would play out once we reached the States—the attack on Tombstone and Skeeter by the Russian MiGs? It might all be disguised as something very foreign from what had actually happened, if it suited certain political purposes. But sinking a submarine—there would be few ways to avoid full-scale media coverage of that.

"Hot on buoy seven as well," the S-3 TACCO reported over the circuit. "Home Plate, it looks like he's making a beeline for you."

"Helo assets inbound your location right now," the carrier replied. With a top speed of around a hundred and twenty knots, it would take the helicopters about ten minutes to get in position.

"Home Plate, interrogative our weapons status?" the S-3 TACCO asked.

"Yellow and tight at this time, Hunter 701," was the answer. The aircraft was allowed to fire its weapons if attacked—that right always lies with the commander of any aircraft or surface ship—but for now he was not given permission to attack hostile contacts.

"Home Plate, he's coming shallow. He's at launch depth. Request advise." The concern in the TACCO's voice was evident now. The submarine had probably heard the S-3 above it, or it heard the noise of the sonobuoys dropping into the water. By now the water around it was virtually peppered with the small acoustic sensors and transmitters. It would know they were there—and know it needed to escape.

Or attack.

"What's the latest on their weapons capability, Lab Rat?" the admiral said quietly. "Any indication they're carrying the Tomahawkski?"

The Tomahawkski was the Russian version of the Tomahawk cruise missile. But so far as I knew, this particular class of ship was still equipped primarily with torpedoes.

"There are rumors that they've got Tomahawkski on board," I said. "I doubt it, though, Admiral. But I could be wrong."

Batman grimaced. "That's the problem with intel. There was always too many possibilities, and never any hard facts."

For a moment I felt called upon to defend my chosen profession within the Navy, but I refrained. The problem was, he was right. Intelligence deals with estimates, possibilities, indications and warnings. There are rarely hard facts, absolute indications that a particular platform is fitted with a certain weapon, or that the enemy intends to execute a particular plan. We do the best we can, but the war fighters on the front line are constantly frustrated by what they feel are intelligence evasions. The short answer is—we simply don't know.

"If he's got Tomahawkski, he could be a real danger to the carrier," Batman continued. Unspoken was the second part of that sentence—that if the Victor were carrying antisurface missiles, Batman would need to act preemptively, to take the submarine out before it could launch. Neither of us wanted to depend on antimissile defense systems against one.

The fact that the submarine had changed depths, to one at which he could launch land-attack missiles, was ominous. Why would he forsake the relative safety of deep water unless he intended to launch?

"Admiral, last cargo transfer completed, sir." The voice of the officer in charge of the replenishment detachment sounded relieved. "Should we proceed with emergency breakaway, or normal separation procedures?"

"Emergency breakaway," Batman said promptly. "Tell him over the sound-powered line to get buttoned up and get back down below. And I want him vectoring out in front of us. With so much airpower on top of that Russian submarine, I don't want to take any chances."

"Missile launch, missile launch," a voice broke in over the tactical circuit. Probably the pilot of the S-3, rather than the TACCO. "Home Plate, I say again—vampires inbound."

That decided it for Batman. He snatched up a radio microphone for the tactical circuit and said, "Hunter 701, you are weapons free on all Russian subsurface contacts. I repeat, weapons free."

The bloody speed leader of the missile materialized on the tactical screen, streaking up from the submarine contact symbol. You could see the intended target easily, tracing out the direction of the speed leader. It was headed directly for *Jefferson*.

The Aegis skipper saw it, too. "Got it, *Jefferson*." As he spoke, the screen showed the designation of the missile as a contact by the cruiser and a weapons assignment. Seconds later, a Standard missile shot out from the cruiser symbol.

"*Jefferson*, roger your last," the S-3 broke in. "We have a firing solution. Fire one." A pause. "Fire two." Evidently the pilot had been prepared for just this moment.

The submarine-launched missile continued its track inbound. Five inches of screen separated its symbol from that of the *Jefferson*, and the distance shrank measurably while we were watching.

Four inches: A second, then a third missile arrowed out from the cruiser, the speed leaders intersecting that of the inbound missile.

Three inches: The OOD onboard *Jefferson* activated the collision alarm. "All hands brace for shock" came over the 1MC. I saw the TAO reach down for his seat belt and buckle himself into his chair. I sat down on the deck, my back to a bulkhead.

Two inches: The first missile the cruiser had fired was

clearly a miss, although a close one. The two symbols passed so close to each other that they merged for a moment of time. I thought for a second she'd gotten it, but then the blotch of symbology broke apart into the incoming missile and the Standard missile. The second and third missiles still had a chance.

One inch: The second missile veered away from its projected course and headed out toward open ocean. Something in the guidance system, maybe a propulsion problem—we'd probably never know. "CIWS tracking," the TAO announced, repeating the report he'd heard over his headset. The Close-In Weapons System—our last-ditch defense against incoming missiles. Not much of a defense, either. At the ranges at which it was effective, the shrapnel from the missile would do devastating damage to the flight deck, the superstructure, and the aircraft spotted on the deck.

The missile looked so close that I thought I'd be able to touch it. Surely the lookouts could see it by now. Or maybe not—even traveling that fast, it was still at least twenty miles out, a telephone pole arcing through the sky toward us.

Suddenly, a cheer rang out. "They got it—*they got it!*" On the screen, the last Standard missile had merged with the incoming vampire, barely closer to it than any of the other antiair shots had been.

But close enough. The plat camera aimed back at the stern of the carrier showed a black-and-white picture of an oily, billowing mass of smoke and fire.

With the missile destroyed, we now had to face taking out the platform that had launched it. The TAO reached out and turned up the volume on the USW C&R. The S-3 TACCO's voiced boomed out, giving us a running commentary on his own attack. "Two fish away. Acoustic indications—they're lit off, entering search pattern." The torpedoes were programmed to commence a standard search pattern once they hit the salt water. "Searching . . . Searching . . . Contact. Torpedo one entering attack profile." The sonar dome inside the nose of the torpedo would have gone to the high-frequency, search-sector *ping* once it detected a target of interest. It was homing in on that now, guided partly by the acoustic sounds emanating from the submarine, as well as the reflection of its own sonar transmissions off the hull.

"Active countermeasures—Home Plate, I have active countermeasures in the water. Submarine is evading—he just knuckled and headed deep."

I stared off at the horizon, which was bland and featureless. There was nothing that would indicate to the naked eye that a deadly battle was taking place beneath its surface. Only cold, slate gray water and a few clouds. The aircraft and helicopters themselves were indistinguishable.

"Second torpedo acquiring. Commencing approach run."

"I've got him on the sonar dome," the first helicopter pilot reported. "Holding good contact. I think the bastard's going deep, trying to get below the thermocline and try to evade. Going active now."

"Launch three. Launch four." The Viking pilot was taking no chances, peppering the water with warheads.

"He got him. Home Plate, this Hunter 701," the pilot said, sheer glee plain in his voice. "I have explosive noise, breaking up. Should be—yes, there it is. Home Plate, oil slick and debris in the water. Classify one Russian submarine as destroyed."

"Admiral, flight deck supervisor. The submarine is clear of us, sir, and requests permission to submerge. She sends her thanks."

Batman nodded. "Tell her captain that he owes four guys on a Viking a steak dinner. They just rid that sub's neighborhood of a few pesky rodents." The strident gonging of the General Quarters alarm cut off his last word.

There are some advantages to being an admiral. One of them that during General Quarters, even with the entire crew of the carrier scurrying to their battle stations, you can still get through. The stream of sailors hurtling through the passageways at breakneck speeds parted slightly as Batman approached, even though we were going counter to the ordered flow of traffic. I stayed close on his heels as we made for TFCC.

We pounded to the conference room and into the small compartment located at the back of it. A sailor thrust flash gear and a gas mask at me as I got to the compartment.

The large scale display told the entire picture. Two waves of MiGs, fourteen per wave, were just leaving the coastline of Russia. This wasn't any escort force. Coupled with the submarines lurking to our north, it meant only one thing. As the gonging of the General Quarters alarm stopped, I heard the first sounds of the Tomcats turning their engines overhead. The structural steel and tarmac that separated us from the most potent weapons ever built in this century could only diminish, not block out, the thunderous sounds of those powerful engines.

Then another sound chimed in, the lighter, almost insect-like scream of the Hornet engines turning. Powerful in their own way, the perfect adversary against the MiG, yet lacking the legs and sheer firepower of their larger brothers. Either Tomcats or Hornets alone had disadvantages, but together they were deadly.

Russians have their own ways of making war, and this attack was no exception. Even before we'd left home port, we had worked up how we would fight an air war if necessary. The decades of the Cold War had taught us how the Russians liked to fight. They come in waves—heavy, massive waves of aircraft, throwing sheer tonnage of steel and weapons against a carrier battle group. They seek out the carrier, the vital soft heart of the fighting force. Without it, the battle group retains some capacity for self-defense, particularly when there's an Aegis cruiser along. But even though that battle group might be able to stave off missiles, it couldn't fulfill the primary mission of an aircraft carrier and battle group: to wreak devastation and damage on the soil of another nation.

Our Aegis cruiser was turning now, taking up her assigned station at flank speed. Her skipper was on the circuit, reporting all stations ready for battle. His ship would already have set General Quarters, being so much smaller than the carrier. Three minutes, four tops. It wouldn't have taken much longer. For the aircraft carrier it took longer.

Nevertheless, even before General Quarters was fully set, *Jefferson* was already poised to wage war. I heard the notification come from the officer of the deck—Pri-Fly had requested a green deck, and the OOD had granted it. Seconds later, the scream of engines overhead built to a higher level, then the noise that can be best described as a roller coaster, the catapult driven by steam yanking the aircraft forward and accelerating it in a space of seconds to the speed necessary to stay airborne. One cat shot. A few minutes later, another. The flight deck had lit its rhythm, and was shoving aircraft into the skies faster than I could keep count. But the MiGs were faster. Even as our last fighter left the deck, the first missiles were inbound. They traced their way across the screen, bloody red symbols deadly stark against the blue background.

The Aegis was on them. The second the first one crossed our missile engagement zone, the cruiser fired. I watched on the closed-circuit television, dividing my time between that and the tactical display, as missiles rippled off the deck of the Aegis. She was equipped with a vertical launch system, which made engaging that many targets at once theoretically possible. Theoretically—no nation had yet put it to a test. Until now.

Our own aircraft were vectoring around behind the Aegis, leaving the missile engagement zone via a safe corridor marked out for their use. The Aegis would shoot nothing within that area, and nothing outside of her missile engagement zone. The Tomcats and Hornets were to get out of the area quickly, circle back around, and engage the fighters outside the MEZ.

In the midst of the chatter from the Hornet pilots verifying the existence of the tanker, the Tomcat pilots divvying up the incoming MiGs, the lone S-3 Viking pilot we'd left to the north patrolling the last detection of the submarine chimed in. He had not much to say, just wanted to remind us that he was out there. Alone. Without any antiair missiles. Batman promptly recalled him, bringing him into the starboard marshal pattern to get him out of the Aegis's MEZ, and told him we'd get him back onboard when we could. The S-3 declined, saying he just needed some gas and would prefer to remain airborne in case another submarine entered the area.

The fighters were dominating the circuit now, shouting out those brief incomprehensible phrases that mean everything to the men in the air and nothing to the ones in the ship. The E-2 Hawkeye was frantically slipping in and out of the link, troubleshooting some avionics problem that kept her from being fully operational. It was her role to control the dispersion of the fighters, warn them of incoming threats, and generally maintain an overall tactical view of the air battle. It wasn't working, and until she could get her link fully operational, her data only garbled the incoming contacts from the aircraft themselves. The TAO wisely slipped her out of the data link until she could get her problems solved.

It was over faster than I'd have ever thought possible. Six MiGs down, no American losses. The surviving MiGs turned back toward Russia, lucky to escape with their skins.

Thirty minutes later, we'd gotten *Jefferson* headed back into the wind, with good wind across the deck. Tombstone and Skeeter slid into the starboard marshal, waiting for their turn to get onboard.

"I'll be wanting to talk to Tombstone," Batman said quietly. "This little business you and he had going on with the codes—what do you think about that, Commander? A fair thing to do to me?"

I considered that for a moment. "I don't think so, Admiral. But I don't know what was on Admiral Magruder's mind at the time he laid it out for me."

Batman was silent for a moment, then he said, "It better not happen again. You hear me? Now, let's get the hell out of here and go home." Without waiting for an answer, he turned and stalked off.

I had a feeling that one of the first people that Tombstone Magruder would encounter when he reentered the ship would be Admiral Wayne. And from the look on his face, the conversation was not going to be pleasant. I decided to stay up on the bridge for a while longer, give them a chance to clear the area. When the elephants dance, it's a foolish man that walks in the middle of them.

SIXTEEN
Wednesday, 23 December

1610 Local (+3 GMT)
USS **Jefferson**
Off the northern coast of Russia

Rear Admiral Everett Batman Wayne:

On my way up to the flight deck to nail Tombstone, I stopped in at my cabin to cool off. Captain Collin Reddy, skipper of *Jefferson*, was waiting there for me.

Reddy was a good man, one of the few S-3B TACCOs I was certain was headed for flag rank. It's not an easy job he has, playing airfield to an admiral and a CAG, and I extend every courtesy I can to him.

"Saved me a trip," I said. "We're done here. Let's get the hell out of Dodge before the MiGs come back."

When Captain Reddy didn't roger up immediately, I groaned. Problems, more problems—just what the hell was so complicated about heading home? "OK, give it to me," I said.

"We can't make best speed, Admiral," Reddy said bluntly. That's one of the things I like about him. He doesn't try to blow sunshine up my ass. "It's the ice. We're in clear water here, but I've got visual reports from the S-3 that it's starting to close in a little further north."

We'd rounded Scandinavia on our way in and then

headed a bit south, so I knew what he meant. "How bad?"
I asked.

"I don't know for certain. Normally, I'd ask that we get
one of the Russian icebreakers out in front just to be safe.
But under the circumstances, I figure they're probably not
willing to oblige."

"I wish someone could tell me what the hell exactly the
circumstances are," I said. "I'll be damned if I know what's
going on up here."

Reddy shrugged. "For what it's worth, this is one of those
times I'm glad I'm not in your shoes. As for *Jefferson,* I'd
like to stay below ten knots until we clear the danger area.
A little slower after sunset, even. We should be able to
resume normal transit speeds in about thirty-six hours."

"That long? What does it do for our maneuverability?"

"Restricts it some if we find thicker ice." He hesitated for
a moment, then continued. "I recommend we contact the
Norwegians. Ask them to stand by to assist."

"Good thinking." That was the kind of planning that
would earn him those stars. "They're not going to want to
come into Russian waters, but I'm pretty sure they'll be
willing to meet us at the line of demarcation. I'll have my
chief of staff take care of it."

Reddy stood. "Then, with your permission, I'll get this
boat headed north."

I clapped him on the shoulder. "I'll be on the flight deck
if you need me."

On my way out, I stopped by COS's office and filled him
in. He was flipping through his procedures gouge as I left.

I trotted down the passageway and hung a left, headed for
the ladder that would take me up to Air Ops and the flight
deck. I'd just set my foot on the first rung when the General
Quarters alarm sounded again.

I started swearing as I wheeled around and headed back
for TFCC. I passed Reddy in the passageway. He shouted,
"It's the sub. She's in trouble," and continued running
forward for CDC.

Sailors were swarming now and I was running against the
tide. I made it into TFCC in record time and ran forward to

the TAO console. He heard me coming and looked up. "It's the sub, sir. She had some problems just as she started down and she's back on the surface. The Akula is still submerged but closing fast."

"What's the problem?"

"The reactor coolant pumps. The last one on line tripped off and the skipper's not going to be able to submerge until he gets it on line."

Submerging even with only one pump was risky. I'd been foolish to let him move away from us before he had at least two of them back on line. "Where is he now?"

"Fifty miles astern of us, sir. Headed this way at five knots on emergency diesel propulsion." The TAO, a submariner by trade, looked distinctly worried. "She's like a freight train with that thing running. They won't need a visual or outside targeting data to find her."

"How many S-3s do we have in the air?"

"Just one, Hunter 701." He circled the cursor around the symbol. "And he's at bingo fuel."

"Figures." I buzzed CDC and got Reddy on the phone. "We need to set Flight Quarters and get gas in the air along with some more USW assets."

"Working on it now, sir. We're coming right as I speak."

I glanced up at the ship's heading indicator and saw he was right. Like I said, Reddy's a good man. "How much longer?"

"Eight minutes, maybe a little less. We're crewing up helos and S-3s right now, along with a tanker."

"What about fighters?" I asked.

"I've got them on deck after the S-3s."

"Move them up. Two of them at least." I could not have pointed to any one factor that made me give the order. There were no launch indications coming in from SCIF, no other data to suggest that we were about to have MiGs inbound again. But they'd been so ready to send them out before, had done so twice already with absolutely no provocation. I wasn't taking any chances this time.

"Aye, aye, Admiral," Reddy said after a moment. He was waiting for an explanation, but I didn't have time for one right then. I hung up the phone and reached for the microphone to tactical and got the cruiser on the circuit.

"Same MEZ and safe passage sectors as before," I told the TAO. I could hear the activity in the background behind him. "No indications—just be ready to launch on a moment's notice."

"We're ready now," the cruiser TAO answered. "Just give us a target."

"I hope you don't have one. Be ready anyway." I signed off and turned back to my own watch team. They were puzzled but ready.

COS poked his head into TFCC. "Admiral, the Norwegians are pleased to help out. They're dispatching one of their deployed icebreakers. She'll rendezvous with us at the line of demarcation, about fifty miles ahead."

"Do they have any reports on the ice?" I asked.

"It's setting in now, sir. But nothing their ship can't handle."

"How about *Jefferson*?"

Silence then. "They said it might be tricky, sir. They're talking with Captain Reddy now, working out a plan."

"We can get through, can't we?"

"If we steam straight for them right now, sir, we can."

The wrong answer. There was no way I could head for the icebreaker, not with my submarine under siege from two very potent Russian boats. I glanced up at the relative wind indicator. We'd come around to a decent course for launching aircraft. Just at that moment, I heard the rumble overhead increase into a full Tomcat howl. The plat camera showed two fighters on the cat with the USW assets lined up behind.

"Tell them to stand by, then," I said. "Try to get a feeling about whether or not they're going to be willing to come in after us if we get in a tough spot."

I saw doubt on COS's face. Privately, I agreed it would be unlikely, but I wasn't going to say so in front of the troops. The Norwegians had to live in this part of the world with the Russians, and they weren't likely to want to charge into the middle of a confrontation between the U.S. and Russia. "We'll take whatever they can give us."

"Roger that, sir." COS headed off to make sure everyone was playing from the same game book.

"Sir? Is there anything I should know?" the TAO asked.

I knew why he was asking. I'd known about the sub; maybe there was something else I was keeping from them. The TAO had the balls to put me on the spot about it.

"No, nothing. Just call it a bad feeling, that's all," I answered. I watched the screen as the fighters arced out from the carrier, followed in short order by their slower USW brethren, with the helos bringing up the rear. The fighters would be first on station over the sub.

"Admiral, all aircraft launched and four Hornets in Alert Five," the TAO said. "The air boss is ready to recover the fighters in the stack."

Tombstone. There was no time now for what I needed to say to him, not with the sub in trouble and air on the way to the rescue. Maybe later. Might be better that way anyway— give us both a chance to cool off, avoid saying words that we could never take back.

"Very well," I said. "And Admiral Magruder should be first on deck, shouldn't he?"

The TAO pointed at the screen. "He would have been."

I started swearing as I saw what the double nuts bird was doing.

SEVENTEEN
Wednesday, 23 December

1630 Local (+3 GMT)
en route to USS Jefferson
Off the northern coast of Russia

Vice Admiral Tombstone Magruder:

As I saw it, there wasn't much choice. I'd been monitoring the problems with the sub on tactical and saw the carrier start its turn into the wind. The word came out that we'd stay in the marshal pattern while the fresh fighters and USW birds were launched. But I could tell from the seas that it was going to take some time to get into favorable winds, and the ice creeping out from the shoreline and down from the north was going to be a problem in sustained operations.

So there we were, flying fat, dumb and happy with a hefty fuel reserve—what else were we supposed to do?

"Skeeter," I said over our private coordination circuit, "you ready?" Two clicks acknowledged my transmission. "Let's go, then. Combat spread, you take high." Another two clicks, and I saw Skeeter up above me peel out of marshal and head east. I was just a split second behind him.

Skeeter climbed and settled in at the correct altitude, taking his cues from me. I descended to seven thousand feet, with Skeeter maintaining the correct separation slightly behind me.

The submarine was tough to pick out at first. The sea up here was dark, oily black. Gator vectored me in on her LINK position. I finally found a streak of black in the white-caps and blowing spray. "Got her," I announced.

"Me, too," Skeeter said. "Looks like her playmates are still submerged."

"I'm going down to take a look, maybe reassure her that we're in the area. Stay at this altitude unless I tell you otherwise." Two clicks again.

I descended in a tight spiral centered on the stricken sub. There were people in her sail, three of them that I could make out. No obvious signs of damage, no smoke. They stared up at me. I was at five hundred feet, low enough that they could make out my tail insignia. I wanted to make sure that they knew who we were.

The men in the sail were armed with shotguns. Even from this distance, they looked cold and miserable.

Then I saw why. Barely below the surface, only three hundred yards away, I could see an area of darker water. A feather trailed aft from a periscope poking up from the sea. As I watched, the Russian submarine's sleek sail broke the surface of the water, followed by the bow at a slight up angle and then the stern. An odd conical pod stuck up from the tail assembly.

The Victor, then. But where was the Akula? And just what did they have planned for our sub?

The Victor was edging in, her own sail now filling with people. Two of them were struggling with equipment. They propped it up on the edge of the sail, evidently into a slot built to accommodate it, then stepped back.

Machine guns. Probably fifty cal from the looks of them, or the Russians equivalent. Not much use against anything except a lightly armored craft.

Like a submarine.

Or a Tomcat.

The USW aircraft weren't going to be much use, not unless they had loaded a gun into the slot on the SH-60. I doubted that they had—using the fifty cal required leaving the side door open, and the windchill factor in this climate would be deadly.

The Victor continued to close until she was barely one hundred feet away from the U.S. boat, a deadly close range for ungainly submarines surfaced in open sea. Then I saw the canisters dangling over the Russian sail. Self-inflating rafts, their mechanism activated by salt water.

The Victor's crew lowered one into the water. After a few seconds, it started expanding into a brilliant yellow rescue boat. It wasn't designed as an assault craft—merely as a lifeboat—and its rubberized hull couldn't withstand a blast from a shotgun. It would fill quickly and sink within a minute, consigning its crew to the frigid water.

Surely the U.S. sub skipper knew that. But he wouldn't—he *couldn't*—let the Victor's lifeboat approach.

Or would he?

He would. I saw the hesitation in his movements, the arm upraised to hold fire. Did he think that the Russians might simply want to talk to them? Could he possibly believe that after the cat-and-mouse game they'd played for the last week?

Or did he feel what I'd felt with Ilanovich, a kinship of fellow warriors that transcended national boundaries? Could he blast the lifeboat, knowing that that action would condemn men just like him to certain death? Would he hold on to any sliver of hope that there might be an innocent reason for their entirely insane deployment of the life rafts?

The life raft was pitching in the seas, sliding up the side of one swell sideways and coming down bow-first on the other side. Russian sailors were piling into it now, none of them obviously armed. There could have been sidearms, though, and I was certain that there were. Then they cast off from the Victor, and sailors manning paddles steadied the boat in the seas and headed for the U.S. sub.

"We've got company." For a moment, I had the illusion that the sub skipper was talking, then I realized it was Skeeter. "Four MiGs inbound, Tombstone. I think you better grab some altitude before they close on us."

"On my way." I slammed the throttles forward and nosed

the Tomcat up into a steep climb. With MiGs inbound, I wasn't going to be able to stay at sea level and baby-sit a sub skipper who was about to make a serious mistake.

Gator, Sheila, and the ship all started yelling at the same time. Launch indications, this time for submarine-based antiship missiles. Long-range ones, more than capable of reaching the carrier thrashing about in the icy water.

The Akula. Judging from the roiling water I saw ten miles to the north, she was the culprit.

"Tombstone." Batman's voice was deadly. "Get the hell out of there. You're inside the missile engagement zone, clobbering the Aegis picture. Get down to sea level, stay out of the way. There's not time for you to clear the area—now *move*."

"Tombstone, we can't just—" Skeeter started.

"You heard the admiral," I snapped. "Now head for the deck." Unless we wanted to risk being the unintended recipient of a Standard missile, we needed to be well outside of her targeting area. "Gator, find out where the safe-passage corridor is and get me in it."

"Already on it," Gator said. "Turn right to heading three two zero. We're two minutes out."

"Skeeter know?" I asked even as I was standing the Tomcat on wingtip to comply, all the while descending as well.

"Better. Sheila does."

I pulled us up at barely one hundred feet above the sea, too close under almost any conditions except these. But cold air is thick, easy to fly in. It gave us a margin of safety that we wouldn't have had in warmer climates.

"They're coming after us," Gator warned. "Range, fifteen miles and closing. Descending through ten thousand feet now."

"Tomcat zero zero, maintain present altitude and heading," a new voice said. "It's going to be close, sir, and I need your cooperation. Keep your wingman on your right."

The Aegis then, asserting her rights over this wedge of airspace. I acknowledged the orders and hoped to hell they'd hurry. There's no more helpless feeling than being wings level at sea level with enemy fighters inbound.

The airspace around me felt clobbered with danger. The missiles inbound on the carrier, the MiGs, even my own cruiser launching missiles in my general direction. This wasn't the way it was supposed to be, not for a fighter pilot.

It is if the fighter pilot doesn't obey orders.

Yeah, but the submarine—we were the closest thing to a cavalry around.

You think maybe they know how to manage this war without your help?

No.

I quit second-guessing myself. There was a reason I'd peeled out of the marshal stack, a sound tactical one. If they'd been thinking onboard the carrier, they'd have sent me themselves.

The submarine. What was one fighter compared to that?

"Skeeter, stay here," I ordered. "No matter what."

"I don't leave my lead, Admiral."

"Don't argue with me."

"You've got two choices, Tombstone. You talk to me, clue me in on what we're doing and give me a better chance to survive it all. Or you roll out on your own. Either way, you look to the right, you're going to see me. Like I said—I don't leave my lead." Skeeter's voice made it clear that he had no intention of obeying any orders I gave him that involved leaving him behind.

"We've got to get back to the sub," I said, capitulating to the inevitable. "There's something going on there."

"Roger. The Aegis knows how to break a Mode IV IFF. She does her job, we do ours."

I hoped to hell it would work. I slid the throttles forward, increasing power more gently this time, buying myself time to think, and the Aegis time to react. I thought about explaining it to her, then decided against it. Like Skeeter said, the Aegis could break Mode IV and would be able to distinguish our radar paint from that of the Russians.

"Fire one," the Aegis TAO said. Four more missiles

rippled off her rails in short order, the first aimed at the incoming cruise missile and the others at the MiGs.

"You have the missile?" I asked Gator, building the plan in my mind as we ascended.

"Yeah—still behind us. Come right to zero one zero, altitude two thousand feet. That'll put us at a slight angle to it."

"OK, then." I'd just nosed through angels two thousand, headed upward. Two thousand was fine with me, since the MiGs—and the Aegis missiles after them—were still well above that. But for how long?

I edged back down slightly to maintain altitude, and started scanning the airspace around me, twisting around in my ejection seat and trying to get a visual on the missile. Gator was feeding the plan to Sheila at the same time.

"I got it," Skeeter announced. "Tallyho."

"Take the shot if you get it," I said, still searching the sky where Gator said the missile was.

"Fox one," Skeeter announced, launching an AMRAAM at the missile. Then again, "Fox one," as he fired a second AMRAAM.

Then I saw it, the AMRAAM's intended target. It would be massive up close, but from this distance was merely a small gash of white against the sky.

"Where to, lead?" Skeeter asked. "One of those two will get it."

His missiles were streaking across the sky, bright splashes of yellow fire gouting from their tails, much more visible from this angle than their intended target was.

"Stay on the missile," I ordered. "Make sure you've got it—we can't take a chance. I'm going after the submarine."

Skeeter started to protest, but I ignored him. Too many lives were at stake to simply assume that the AMRAAMs would find their marks. I slid off to the right and turned back around to locate the submarine.

By the time I got there, the skipper had evidently realized how critical his situation was. Skimming the ocean at only three hundred feet above the deadly sea, I could see that he had a megaphone in his hands. Both his crew and the lifeboat Russians looked up as my Tomcat screamed by overhead. One Russian lifted a three-foot tube to his shoulder.

Stingers. If he could sight in on me and get it off while I was within two miles, he was no less deadly for being low-tech. Each tube was a one-shot antiair missile, and I couldn't tell whether they had more than one onboard the raft.

There was only one way to find out, and I wasn't going to wait on the submarine any longer. I pushed on past them maybe three miles, and orbited for a moment while I thought through the plan.

"You fly, I'll spot," Gator suggested.

"I'm trying to think of anything we could do to increase our chances against that Stinger. You saw it, I take it?" I said.

"I did." A sigh then. "There's no way through this except straight through it—we both know that. You handle the evasive maneuvering, keep them from getting a lock. I'll watch and see what else they're pulling. You're going in with guns, right?"

"The only weapon I've got for this," I said.

"The sooner we get it over with, the sooner we're back on the boat."

I turned back in on the sub and life raft. A puff of black smoke wafted out of the sail. The life raft was now only thirty yards from the sub, fighting the swells and the weather.

"Here we go." I dropped down to barely one hundred feet above the waves and started a series of hard zigzags that I hoped would defeat their targeting solutions. My finger rested on the weapons control switch for a moment, then I selected Guns.

I fired a short test burst—the life raft was far too close to the sub for my liking and I wanted to make sure of the line of fire. The rounds, every tenth one a tracer, bit into the ocean, stitching a ragged line ahead of me.

"Get the hell up! Altitude, altitude," Gator shouted. "Tombstone, MiG inbound!"

I wrenched the Tomcat around to the left and shoved the throttles forward into afterburner. The sky streaked by my windshield, dull and foreboding. "Where is he?" I asked, scanning the sky around me. No contrails, no glint of sun on metal gave away his position.

"Three o'clock, high." I looked in the direction Gator indicated and found him. He was maybe at ten thousand feet, descending rapidly, nose onto us. I turned into him, still in afterburner, then glanced down at my fuel status. This engagement was going to have to be short and deadly.

"He's got a lock, he's got a lock," Gator chanted, his voice cutting through his ESM receiver beeping. "Break right, Tombstone!" I broke and heard the thump as canisters of chaff and flares spit out of our underbelly.

"Looking good," Gator said. "I think it's—yes, it's going for it!"

I wasn't going to wait around for the fireball. With fuel getting critical and the MiG fast approaching to within knife-fighting range, there wasn't time. As soon as I got tone, I shot two Sparrows and headed back for the submarine. The Russians had managed to make another ten yards of progress toward the sub. Just as I was starting to descend on them, a shotgun blast boiled the water immediately in front of the raft. Then another, even closer this time as the submariner found his range.

"He's got us," Gator said. "The Stinger's—hold on, he's going to shoot."

"Just inside minimums." I fired a quick burst from the gun.

Or tried to. An angry buzz came from the gun—but no rounds. Something jammed it, whether a misfeed or a faulty round or just the brutal weather I couldn't tell. It didn't matter—trying to keep firing it would only run the risk of blowing off our own wing.

"Tombstone, we got to get out of here. Let the sub handle it," Gator warned. "You've got nothing that'll hit a surface target that size if you don't have guns."

"I've still got an aircraft." I shoved the throttles into afterburner. The force slammed me back into my seat. The speck of the lifeboat grew larger quickly until I could make out the individual expressions on the man's faces. The sub skipper stared up at us, his face cold and angry as he shouted orders to his crew.

"Now!" Gator screamed.

I broke right so hard that my wingtip almost grazed the surface of the ocean. The water was so close it seemed to fill the cockpit. Fighting the temptation to pull up, I pulled the turn tighter until we seemed to pivot on one point. The life raft swung out of my view.

But not out of Gator's. He must have been contorted like a pretzel as he watched the action behind us. "*Yes!*"

I eased out of the turn, coming full circle to face the submarine alone in the ocean. The life raft was overturned nearby. One head bobbed briefly in the water, bracketed by flailing arms, then sank out of view.

The crew in the sail of the Victor scrambled back down into the safety of their submarine. They must have been standing by to dive, because within a minute the sub slipped back down beneath the surface.

"You fellows need some help out here?" a voice drawled over tactical. "Jet wash ain't gonna help much after they dive."

Rabies Grill. I recognized the voice. "Sure, come on in now that we've got them running scared for you."

"Running's just fine. Makes them noisier than hell. Maybe these passengers I'm carrying can find them."

I pulled the Tomcat up, relieved to be farther from the ocean. "All yours, Rabies. What are you going to do about the U.S. boat?"

"Gonna tell him to stay surfaced. These here torpedoes are set on deep. They won't even look at anything above one hundred feet."

I was breathing easier now that we were climbing back through five thousand feet. Off to my right, two stubby-nosed S-3s were inbound. Behind them, a couple of helos were scampering to catch up like kids running after an older brother.

"Funny thing," Rabies continued. "Almost flew through a

nasty patch of smoke and metal back there a ways. Looks like you got you a MiG while you were trying to horn in on our business."

"You got a union now?" I asked.

"You betcha."

I left the USW aircraft to finish off the Akula and the Victor. From what I heard over tactical, it didn't take them long before they had firing solutions on both boats. Seventy sailors on each submarine would be joining their lifeboat brothers in an icy grave before I reached the ship.

The ship. There'd be more music to face back onboard *Jefferson.*

Running on fumes only, we took a quick plug and chug from the tanker and headed back to *Jefferson.* I caught the three wire. I hoped it was an omen.

The moment I walked into Batman's office, I could see that it was coming. It was there in the set of his jaw, the hard, cold look in Batman's eyes. I debated pretending not to notice, then gave it up as a lost cause. You don't treat your old wingman like that, even when you're sporting two more stars on your collar than he is.

The ocean floor around us was littered with the remains of MiGs and MiG pilots. The remains of the Victor and Akula were mixed into the brew, and I hadn't even started to worry about the furor that that was going to cause back in the States.

But at least we'd won. And in the end, that's all that matters.

"It's got to stop, Tombstone." Batman fixed me with a hard glare. "We shouldn't even have to have this conversation, you know." He stood up from his desk and walked around to confront me. "But it has to stop."

Gone were all traces of the smooth, politically astute pilot that I'd grown up with in the Navy. This was sheer, hard warrior. And a pissed-off one at that.

I turned away from him slightly, and walked across the room to sit down on his ugly couch. Not so long ago it had been mine, just as this whole carrier and air wing had been.

Short of the presidency, there was no more powerful position in the world, I thought.

"Well?" Batman's tone indicated he would not take my silence as an answer. He wanted victory, every last bloody shred of it.

I would give him part of it, as much as I could. But there were still things I couldn't tell him. "I assume you are talking about Lab Rat?"

Batman nodded. "You would never have tolerated this from someone else when you were in command of *Jefferson*. You know you wouldn't."

I nodded in agreement. "No, I wouldn't have. And I probably would have spoken to a senior admiral in exactly the same tones that you're using with me. Nor would I have been any more understanding than you're going to be when I tell you that there are some things I simply cannot discuss with you. So, for what it's worth, I'm sorry the plan had to be executed in this manner. You should have been in the loop—if it had been my choice, you would have been."

Batman got very still. His face reflected a whole range of emotions, running from anger through suspicion and down to pity. "So that's the end of it. You're not going to tell me the rest of it." He appeared to consider that, then shook his head. "I don't buy it."

"I don't care what you buy, Admiral. That's the way it will have to be." I hated speaking to him that way, I found cold solace in the justification that not disclosing the rest of what had happened in Russia and Ukraine might keep the elite network of MIA informants in place. Perhaps that would eventually ease the pain for other families, as it had eased it for me. There were facts that couldn't be disclosed, contacts that were put at risk if even their existence was admitted. If that were the price—an angry friend who believed I no longer trusted him—then it was one I would have to pay.

I stood up from the couch, now at least at peace in my own mind with what I had to do. "I am sorry. Sorrier than you'll ever know. And, for what it's worth, I wish it could have been otherwise." I turned and walked toward the hatch.

"Tombstone?" Batman called after me. There was an almost pleading quality to his voice as he said my name. "This isn't the end, is it?"

I turned back to him and considered him for a moment. "Of course not. For some things, perhaps. But not for anything that needs to still be alive. Those things that are ended are those that need to be ended."

"It's about your father, isn't it?"

I kept silent. As was often the case, Batman had made one of those intuitive leaps that marked his brilliant way of conducting his affairs.

"Well, then." Compassion, sympathy, and something much, much deeper. He was not happy, but he had found a way to live with what I'd told him must be. And for that, I was grateful.

"Where are you going?" Batman asked.

I shrugged. "Right now, I'm going up to the flight deck. Get a little taste of Tomcat fever for a few minutes. In the long run—well, who knows. There will always be wars, and for the foreseeable future, there will always be a need for carriers. So wherever the Navy needs me, that's where I'll be."

Batman walked over to the hatch to stand next to me. He clamped one hand down on my shoulder and dug his fingers in. "Want company?"

Glossary

0–3 level: The third deck above the main deck located at the waterline. Designations for decks above the main deck (also known as the damage control deck) begin with zero (e.g., 0–3). The zero is pronounced as "oh" in conversation. Decks below the main deck do not have the initial zero, and are numbered down from the main deck (e.g., deck 11 is below deck 3; deck 0–7 is above deck 0–3).

1MC: The general announcing system on a ship or submarine. Every ship has many different interior communications systems, most of them linking parts of the ship for a specific purpose. Most operate off sound-powered phones. The circuit designators consist of a number followed by two letters that indicate the specific purpose of the circuit. 2AS, for instance, might be an antisubmarine warfare circuit that connects the sonar supervisor, the USW watch officer, and the sailor at the torpedo launched.

C–2 Greyhound: Also known as the COD, Carrier Onboard Delivery. The COD carries cargo and passengers from shore to ship. It is capable of carrier landings. Sometimes assigned directly to the air wing, it also operates in coordination with CVBG from a shore squadron.

air boss: A senior commander or captain assigned to the aircraft carrier, in charge of flight operations. The "Boss" is assisted by the Mini-Boss in Pri-Fly, located in the tower onboard the carrier. The air boss is always in the tower during flight operations, overseeing the launch and recovery cycles, declaring a green deck, and monitoring the safe approach of aircraft to the carrier.

air wing: Composed of the aircraft squadrons assigned to the battle group. The individual squadron commanding officers report to the air wing commander, who reports to the admiral.

airdale: Slang for an officer or enlisted person in the aviation fields. Includes pilots, NFOs, aviation intelligence officers, maintenance officers, and the enlisted technicians who support aviation. The antithesis of an airdale is a "shoe."

Akula: Late-model Russian-built attack nuclear submarine (SSN). Fast, deadly, and deep diving.

ALR-67: Detects, analyzes and evaluates electromagnetic signals, emits a warning signal if the parameters are compatible with an immediate threat to the aircraft (e.g., seeker head on an antiair missile). Can also detect an enemy radar in either a search or a targeting mode.

altitude: Is safety. With enough airspace under the wings, a pilot can solve any problem.

AMRAAM: Advanced Medium Range Antiair Missile.

angels: Thousands of feet over ground. Angels twenty is 20,000 feet. *Cherubs* indicates hundreds of feet (e.g., cherubs five = five hundred feet).

ASW: Antisubmarine Warfare, recently renamed Undersea Warfare. For some reason.

avionics: Black boxes and systems that comprise an aircraft's combat systems.

AW: Aviation antisubmarine warfare technician, the enlisted specialist flying in an S-3, P-3, or helo USW aircraft. As this book goes to press, there is discussion of renaming the specialty.

AWACS: An aircraft entirely too good for the Air Force, the Advanced Warning Aviation Control System. Long-range command and control and electronic intercept bird with superb capabilities.

AWG-9: Pronounced "awg nine," the primary search- and fire-control radar on a Tomcat.

backseater: also known as the GIB, the guy in back. Non-pilot aviator available in several flavors: BN (bombadier/navigator), RIO (radar intercept operator), and TACCO

(Tactical Control Officer), among others. Usually wear glasses and are smart.

Bear: Russian maritime patrol aircraft, the equivalent in rough terms of a U.S. P-3. Variants have primary missions in command and control, submarine hunting, and electronic intercepts. Big, slow, good targets.

bitch box: One interior communications system on a ship. So named because it's normally used to bitch at another watch station.

blue on blue: Fratricide. U.S. forces are normally indicated in blue on tactical displays, and this term refers to an attack on a friendly by another friendly.

blue water Navy: Outside the unrefueled range of the airwing. When a carrier enters blue water ops, aircraft must get on board, (e.g., land) and cannot divert to land if the pilot gets the shakes.

boomer: Slang for a ballistic missile submarine.

BOQ: Bachelor Officers Quarters—a Motel Six for single officers or those traveling without family. The Air Force also has VOQ, Visiting Officers Quarters.

buster: As fast as you can (i.e., bust yer ass getting here).

CAG: Carrier Air Group Commander, normally a senior Navy captain aviator. Technically, an obsolete term, since the air wing rather than an air group is now deployed on the carrier. However, everyone thought CAW sounded stupid, so CAG was retained as slang for the Carrier Air Wing Commander.

CAP: Combat Air Patrol, a mission executed by fighters to protect the carrier and battle group from enemy air and missiles.

Carrier Battle Group: A combination of ships, air wing, and submarines assigned under the command of a one-star admiral.

Carrier Battle Group 14: The battle group normally embarked on *Jefferson*.

CBG: *See* Carrier Battle Group.

CDC: Combat Direction Center—modernly, replaced CIC, or Combat Information Center, as the heart of a ship.

All sensor information is fed into CDC and the battle is coordinated by a tactical action officer on watch there.

CG: Abbreviation for a cruiser.

Chief: The backbone of the Navy. E-7, -8, and -9 enlisted pay grades, known as chief, senior chief, and master chief. The transition from petty officer ranks to the chief's mess is a major event in a sailor's career. Onboard ship, the chiefs have separate eating and berthing facilities. Chiefs wear khakis, as opposed to dungarees for the less senior enlisted ratings.

Chief of Staff: Not to be confused with a chief, the COS in a battle group staff is normally a senior Navy captain who acts as the admiral's XO and deputy.

CIA: Christians in Action. The civilian agency charged with intelligence operations outside the continental United States.

CIWS: Close-in Weapons System, pronounced "see-whiz." Gatling gun with built-in radar that tracks and fires on inbound missiles. If you have to use it, you're dead.

COD: *See* C-2 Greyhound.

collar count: Traditional method of determining the winner of a disagreement. A survey is taken of the opponent's collar devices. The senior person wins. Always.

commodore: Formerly the junior-most admiral rank, now used to designate a senior Navy captain in charge of a bunch of like units. A destroyer commodore commands several destroyers, a sea control commodore the S-3 squadrons on that coast. Contrast with CAG, who owns a number of dissimilar units (e.g., a couple of Tomcat squadrons, some Hornets, and some E-2s and helos).

compartment: Navy talk for a room on a ship.

Condition Two. One step down from General Quarters, which is Condition One. Condition Five is tied up at the pier in a friendly country.

CONUS: CONtinental United States. Normally used to refer to the mainland only.

crypto: Short for some variation of cryptological, the magic set of codes that makes a circuit impossible for anyone else to understand.

Glossary

CV, CVN: Abbreviation for an aircraft carrier, conve~~n~~tional and nuclear.

CVIC: Carrier Intelligence Center. Located down the passageway (the hall) from the flag spaces.

data link, the LINK: The secure circuit that links all units in a battle group or in an area. Targets and contacts are transmitted over the LINK to all ships. The data is processed by the ship designated as Net Control, and common contacts are correlated. The system also transmits data from each ship and aircraft's weapons systems (e.g., a missile firing). All services use the LINK.

desk jockey: Nonflyer, one who drives a computer instead of an aircraft.

DDG: Guided missile destroyer.

DESRON: Destroyer commander.

DICASS: An active sonobuoy.

dick stepping: Something to be avoided. While anatomically impossible in today's gender-integrated services, in an amazing display of good sense, it has been decided that women do this as well.

Doppler: Acoustic phenomena caused by relative motion between a sound source and a receiver that results in an apparent change in frequency of the sound. The classic example is a train going past and the decrease in pitch of its whistle. When a submarine changes its course or speed in relation to a sonobuoy, the event shows up as a change in the frequency of the sound source.

Double nuts: Zero zero on the tail of an aircraft.

E-2 Hawkeye: Command and control and surveillance aircraft. Turboprop rather than jet, and unarmed. Smaller version of an AWACS, in practical terms, but carrier-based.

ELF: Extremely Low Frequency, a method of communicating with submarines at sea. Signals are transmitted via a miles-long antenna and are the only way of reaching a deep-submerged submarine.

Envelope: What you're supposed to fly inside of if you want to take all the fun out of naval aviation.

EWs: Electronic warfare technicians, the enlisted sailors

. man the gear that detects, analyzes, and displays
:ctromagnetic signals. Highly classified stuff.

F/A-18 Hornets: The inadequate, fuel-hungry intended replacement for the aging but still kick-your-ass potent Tomcat. Flown by Marines and Navy.

Familygram: Short message from submarine sailor's family to a deployed sailor. Often the only contact with the outside world that a submarine sailor on deployment has.

FF/FFG: Abbreviation for a fast frigate (no, there aren't slow frigates) and a guided missile fast frigate.

flag officer: In the Navy and Coast Guard, an admiral. In the other services, a general.

flat passageway: The portion of the aircraft carrier that houses the admiral's staff working spaces. Includes the flag mess and the admiral's cabin. Normally separated from the rest of the ship by heavy plastic curtains, and designated by blue tile on the deck instead of white.

Flight Quarters: A condition set onboard a ship preparing to launch or recover aircraft. All unnecessary persons are required to stay inside the skin of the ship and remain clear of the flight deck area.

flight suit: The highest form of navy couture. The perfect choice of apparel for any occasion—indeed, the only uniform an aviator ought to be required to own.

FOD: Stands for Foreign Object Damage, but the term is used to indicate any loose gear that could cause damage to an aircraft. During flight operations, aircraft generate a tremendous amount of air flowing across the deck. Loose objects—including ·people and nuts and bolts—can be sucked into the intake and discharged through the outlet from the jet engine. FOD damages the jet's impellers and doesn't do much for the people sucked in, either. FOD walkdown is conducted at least once a day onboard an aircraft carrier. Everyone not otherwise engaged stands shoulder to shoulder on the flight deck and slowly walks from one end to the other, searching for FOD.

fox: Tactical shorthand for a missile firing. Fox one is for a medium-range missile guided by radar, such as an AMRAAM or Sparrow; fox two is for an IR-guided missile

such as a Sidewinder; the fox three is for a long-
Phoenix missile.

GCI: Ground Control Intercept, a procedure used in t.
Soviet air forces. Primary control for vectoring the aircraf.
in on enemy targets and other fighters is vested in a guy on
the ground, rather than in the cockpit where it belongs.

gib: *See* backseater.

GMT: Greenwich Mean Time.

green shirts: *See* shirts.

handler: Officer located on the flight-deck level responsible for ensuring that aircraft are correctly positioned,
"spotted," on the flight deck. Coordinates the movements of
aircraft with yellow gear (small tractors that tow aircraft and
other related gear) from maintenance areas to catapults and
from the flight deck to the hangar bar via the elevators.
Speaks frequently with the air boss. *See also* bitch box.

HARMS: Anti-radiation missiles that home in on radar
sites.

Home Plate: Tactical call sign for *Jefferson.*

hot: In reference to a sonobuoy, holding enemy contact.

huffer: Yellow gear located on the flight deck that
generates compressed air to start jet engines. Most Navy
aircraft do not need a huffer to start engines, but it can be
used in emergencies or for maintenance.

hunter: Call sign for the S-3 squadron embarked on the
Jefferson.

ICS: Interior Communications System. The private link
between a pilot and a RIO, or the telephone system internal
to a ship.

inchopped: Navy talk for a ship entering a defined area
of water (e.g., "inchopped the Med"). Leaving a body of
water is called outchopping.

IR: Infrared, a method of missile homing.

isothermal: A layer of water that has a constant temperature with increasing depth. Located below the thermocline,
where increase in depth correlates to decrease in temperature. In the isothermal layer, the primary factor affecting the
speed of sound in water is the increase in pressure with
depth.

⌐: Jet Blast Deflector. Panels that pop up from the deck to block the exhaust emitted by aircraft.

USS _Jefferson_: The star nuclear aircraft carrier in the U.S. Navy.

leading petty officer: The senior petty officer in a work center, division, or department, responsible to the leading chief petty officer for the performance of the rest of the group.

LINK: _See_ data link.

lofargram: Low Frequency Analysing and Recording display. Consists of lines arrayed by frequency on the horizontal axis and time on the vertical axis. Displays sound signals in the water in a graphic fashion for analysis by ASW technicians.

long green table: A formal inquiry board. It's better to be judged by three than carried by six.

machinist's mate: Enlisted technician who runs and repairs most engineering equipment onboard a ship. Abbreviated as MM (e.g., MM1 sailor is a petty officer first class machinist's mate).

MDI: Mess Deck Intelligence. The heartbeat of the rumor mill onboard a ship and the definitive source for all information.

MEZ: Missile Engagement Zone. Any hostile contacts that make it into the MEZ are engaged only with missiles. Friendly aircraft must stay clear in order to avoid a blue on blue engagement (i.e., fratricide).

MiG: A production line of aircraft manufactured by Mikoyan in 'Russia. MiG fighters are owned by many nations around the world.

Murphy, law of: The factor most often not considered sufficiently in military planning. If something can go wrong, it will. Naval corollary: Shit happens.

national assets: surveillance and reconnaissance resources of the most sensitive nature (e.g., satellites).

NATOPS: The bible for operating a particular aircraft. _See_ envelope.

NFO: Naval Flight Officer.

nobrainer: Contrary to what copy editors believe, this is one word. Used to signify an evolution or decision should require absolutely no significant intellectual capabilities beyond that of a paramecium.

Nomex: Fire-resistant fabric used to make "shirts." *See* shirts.

NSA: National Security Agency. Primarily responsible for evaluating electronic intercepts and sensitive intelligence.

OOD: Officer of the Day, in charge of the safe handling and maneuvering of the ship. Supervises the conning officer and other underway watchstanders. Ashore, the OOD may be responsible for a shore station after normal working hours.

operations specialist: Formerly radar operators, back in the old days. Enlisted technician who operates combat detection, tracking, and engagement systems, except for sonar. Abbreviated OS.

OTH: Over the horizon, usually used to refer to shooting something you can't see. Targeting data may be provided to the shooter by an aircraft, satellite, or ground forces in the area.

P-3s: Shore-based antisubmarine warfare and surface surveillance long-range aircraft. The closest you can get to being in the Air Force while still being in the Navy.

Phoenix: Long-range antiair missile carried by U.S. fighters.

Pipeline: Navy term used to describe a series of training commands, schools, or necessary education for a particular speciality. The fighter pipeline, for example, includes Basic Flight then fighter training at the RAG (Replacement Air Group), a training squadron.

punching out: Ejecting from an aircraft.

purple shirts: *See* shirts.

PXO: Prospective Executive Officer—the officer ordered into a command as the relief for the current XO. In most squadrons, the XO eventually "fleets up" to become the commanding officer of the squadron, an excellent system that maintains continuity within an operational command—and a system the surface Navy does not use.

rack: A bed. A rack-monster is a sailor who sports pillow ...ns and spends entirely too much time asleep while his or ...er shipmates are working.

red shirts: *See* shirts.

RHIP: Rank Hath Its Privileges. *See* collar count.

RIO: Radar Intercept Officer. *See* NFO.

RTB: Return to base.

S-3: Command and control aircraft sold to the Navy as an antisubmarine aircraft. Good at that, too. Within the last several years, redesignated as "sea control" aircraft, with individual squadrons referred to as torpedo-bombers. Ah, the search for a mission goes on. But still a damned fine aircraft.

SAM: Surface-to-Air Missile (e.g., the Standard missile fired by most cruisers). Also indicates a land-based site.

SAR: Sea-Air Rescue.

SCIF: Specifically Compartmented Information. Onboard a carrier, used to designate the highly classified compartment immediately next to TFCC.

Seawolf: Newest version of Navy fast-attack submarine.

SERE: Survival, Evasion, Rescue, Escape; required school in pipeline for aviators.

shirts: Color-coded Nomex pullovers used by flight deck and aviation personnel for rapid identification of a sailor's job. Green: maintenance technicians. Brown: plane captains. White: safety and medical. Red: ordnance. Purple: fuel. Yellow: flight deck supervisors and handlers.

shoe: A black shoe, slang for a surface sailor or officer. Modernly, hard to say since the day that brown shoes were authorized for wear by black shoes. No one knows why. Wing envy is the best guess.

Sidewinder: Short-range IR-guided antiair missile carried by U.S. fighters.

Sierra: A subsurface contact.

sonobuoys: Acoustic listening devices dropped in the water by ASW or USW aircraft.

Sparrow: Medium-range radar-guided antiair missile carried by U.S. fighters.

Spetznaz: The Russian version of SEALs, although the term encompasses a number of different specialties.

spooks: Slang for intelligence officers and enlisted sailors working in highly classified areas.

SUBLANT: Administrative command of all Atlantic submarine forces. On the west coast, SUBPAC.

sweet: When used in reference to a sonobuoy, indicates that the buoy is functioning properly, although not necessarily holding any contacts. When used in reference to bug juice served on the mess decks, it's redundant.

TACCO: Tactical Control Officer: The NFO in an S-3.

tactical circuit: A term used in these books that encompasses a wide range of actual circuits used onboard a carrier. There are a variety of C&R circuits (coordination and reporting), and occasionally for simplicity sake and to avoid classified material, I just use the world *tactical*.

tanked, tanker: Navy aircraft have the ability to refuel from a tanker, either Air Force or Navy, while airborne. One of the most terrifying routine evolutions a pilot performs.

TAO: Tactical Action Officer. A watch officer with complete authority to fight the ship, including authority to release weapons without consulting the captain of the ship.

TFCC: Tactical Flay Command Carrier. A compartment in flag spaces from which the CVBG controls the battle. Located immediately forward of the carrier's CDC.

Tombstone: Nickname given to Magruder.

Top Gun: Advanced fighter training command.

Undersea Warfare Commander: In a CVBG, normally the DESRON embarked on the carrier. Formerly called the ASW commander.

VDL: Video Downlink. Transmission of targeting data from an aircraft to a submarine with OTH capabilities.

VF-95: Fighter squadron assigned to Air Wing 14, normally embarked on USS *Jefferson*. The first two letters of a squadron designation reflect the type of aircraft flown. VF = fighters. VFA = Hornets. VS = S-3, etc.

Victor: Aging Russian fast-attack submarine, still a potent threat.

VS-29: S-3 squadron assigned to Air Wing 14, embarked

on USS *Jefferson*. The VS-29 Vikings were the first S-3 squadron to transition to the S-3B, known as the B bird. Best squadron around.

VX-1: Test pilot squadron that develops envelopes after Pax River evaluates aerodynamic characteristics of new aircraft. *See* envelope.

white shirt: *See* shirts.

wilco: Short for Will Comply. Used only by the aviator in command of the mission.

Winchester: In aviation, means *out of weapons*. A Winchester aircraft must normally RTB.

XO: Executive Officer, the second in command.

yellow shirt: *See* shirts.